# THE ROAD TO CHAPULTEPEC PARK

## A NOVEL BY DAN MARIANI

*"By Indirections Find Directions Out": from the Soliloquies in* Hamlet

ISBN: 1539835391
ISBN 13: 9781539835394
Library of Congress Control Number: 2016918341
CreateSpace Independent Publishing Platform
North Charleston, South Carolina

# CHAPTER 1

# THE PRISON

A frigid gloom hung over the prison dorm. Stray bullets lay wedged in the thin walls. The men were plagued by constant surface wounds from the sharp-edged craters of splinters these embedded ammunition created.

With the night as cold as the many preceding it, they had gone about their usual business of building a fire in the middle of the room. There, they huddled in small groups to keep warm and rubbed their hands and fingers together vigorously. If they kept rubbing them, their blood would keep flowing and they might avoid the fate of one of their fellow inmates who suffered frostbite earlier that night.

It had not gone well on the ice-fishing detail for Aaron. He found himself in dire straits while hauling in a leaping, very aggressive Lake Sturgeon. Both his hand and wrist got entangled in the long, thick wiry fishing line. The more he tried to disentangle the line, the more his fingers and hand became snared in the ball of line. When he tried to work his left hand free, his palm was badly gashed by the fish's serrated tail which caused large open wounds on his hand and fingers. Bleeding profusely, his hand froze into a huge sanguine knot leaving his hand hanging limply at his side. In the end, the medic had to amputate the whole hand, due to protracted frostbite from the cold and damage to his blood vessels, crudely performing the operation with a makeshift saw that was used to cut frozen meat.

That the bad memory of the incident involving one of their own still lingered throughout the camp was only natural.

The New Year, 2023, had brought in more than its share of tragedies. By the time the midnight hour struck, the United States had officially lost its name and nationhood. The power America had once wielded and the global recognition that societies and institutions like the U.N. once possessed abruptly ended. Not that the U.N. was a sacred institution, it functioned more like a powerful lobby but it, like all other institutions in the *Cold Zone*, was a mere vestige of what it had once been. Its once mighty influence had been reduced to nothing; the American Red Cross held more sway. But the Red Cross role had also been reduced, now far removed to the Hawaiian Islands, its influence barely noticeable on suffering former U.S. citizens.

The U.N. had also had been moved – it was now housed in a run-down building in Switzerland, in the village of Zermatt. The United Nations could not be reached by air and the pedestrian zone around the town kept motorized vehicles from reaching it. The large Alp ranges, including the majestic Matterhorn that encircled it, further isolated this international organization. Given that the Swiss had steadfastly held to their position of neutrality throughout the period of *turbulence,* it seemed a logical location for what was now a defunct and toothless organization.

Fulfilling its final mission, the Red Cross had served its purpose when greater world order reigned. It had provided creature comforts to the bitter end, and had helped support the rule of law. Now that so little hope remained, those who had survived lived on the margins of hypothermia.

Constructed by the Japanese, this particular prison camp was one of many that had been built throughout the countryside of what was formerly known as the United States. Weather-related destruction had led to the nation being spoken of in the past tense. Intense cold had swept out of the arctic, like a blitzkrieg, passing through Canada, blasting the far reaches of the continental U.S. This had made all lands north of Miami's latitude hopelessly uninhabitable. If you could secure a passage, south into Mexico past Monterrey was one of the best--truth be told, only safe and sustainable places to live.

The south end of the Floridian peninsula had devolved into a war zone. The several million who crammed into the tail end of Florida struggled for supplies, fresh water, and protection from predators. The polar bear population had swelled out of the North. They travelled like marching army ants (*Marabunta*) waging war with humans competing for nourishment. Polar bears were accustomed to being at the top of the food chain in the arctic world. With food scarce in their domain, they had acquired a new taste—for humans. They foraged in huge packs, like wolves, and the cries of the vanquished could be heard from miles around. The snow driven paths that were once roadways were now blotted with bright, red blood. There was no time for morning make-up or electronic trading; it was survival of the fittest (*or in some cases luckiest*).

Havana, once a wellspring of political upheaval, was today considered a safe port that is if you could find passage, but it was not without its own pitfalls. With Castro long dead, drug cartels had taken over governance of the country. Homicide and corruption were commonplace and people feared for their lives. The Belize key, *Ambergris Caye* was a safe haven, but it was also overpopulated and overrun and many of the Creoles from the mainland of Belize had settled there. Generally speaking, many Americans were unable to leave the mainland because the southern countries and ports were so overcrowded with refugees. The ones who survived and stayed foraged like scavengers and many were picked up by the camps.

The economics of survival in the aftermath of the *Big Freeze* was ghastly. Food was in short supply and commerce took place chaotically. Money had been replaced by an old method of doing business, the barter system. And, if you had nothing to barter with, well, you were just plain out of luck. Some parents, resorting to insanely desperate measures, had sold their children, using them as collateral, so they could escape the *Cold Zone*. Neither law nor any measure of justice existed to protect the freedoms of humanity and the rights of children. Nothing mattered but the present moment. How you navigated that moment meant everything; it was the difference between longevity and the fate of being lost in the gyration of panic and turmoil that engulfed the land.

3

Tonight, small explosions of gunfire ricocheting in the distance assaulted the prisoners' ears. But the everyday occurrence of such racket around the confines of the prison walls had rendered them almost oblivious to it.

It was estimated that about two thousand such camps existed in the former Continental United States. Since most of the previously lush land had now been transformed into compacted hard Tundra, its best use was as holding area for prisoners or society's disenfranchised. For those old enough to *remember,* the desolation depicted in the Star Trek movie *Wrath of Khan* comes to mind. To find a copy of the film would be nearly impossible, let alone to play it, leaving once treasures behind in the memories of a select few. The land had been terra-formed by constant, raging winds, highlighted by huge mountains of frost and a ceaseless cold. Because of the ice and unrelenting cold, very little food could be grown and stored without hardship. In fact, greenhouses, usually situated on the same lots where the prisoners lived, produced much of the sustenance. The massive spheroid structures dotted the landscape and were temperature and humidity-controlled. Porous Plexiglas allowed for sunlight to be collected and distributed through a network of dampers and ducts. Serving as solar traps, these gatherers warmed the interior surroundings to desirable temperatures conducive to germination. Highly-guarded and highly-desired, these hothouses were the root of much conflict in the *Cold Zone.* The availability of fresh water also caused much strife. Fresh water could be melted from ice, but at a high cost. You could melt it in the hothouses, but this limited resources for food production. You could melt it over a fire, but this took highly coveted energy to make. There were limited heating methods. The oil and gas supplies had long been depleted in the *Cold Zone.* To make matters worse, much of the drinking supply had been contaminated by toxins. Camps seeking to gain control of territory systematically poisoned each other's water reserves. They plotted against one another and raided each other's camps. They stole prisoners and attempted to destroy the infrastructure of enemies' prisons.

The culture of most camps ranked far worse than that depicted of the young British lads in *Lord of the Flies.* These were grown men bent upon chaos and destruction, struggling to live on meager supplies in a challenging

4

environment. To describe them as ruthless and uncooperative would be an understatement—each camp operated on the Greek model of a *city state*. Although each camp prided itself on being self-sufficient, they constantly warred with other camps to obtain incremental resources and greater real estate. Holding land was otherwise worthless except for the aggrandizement of camp supplies and the prisoners who performed most of the work.

Aaron, now handless, was one of the rare few who still harbored hope in this dystopia. Despite many hardships, he remained steadfast in his belief in the basic goodness of humanity. Early on before the outset of the *Big Freeze,* he had lost his family in a landslide near *The Old Man of the Mountain,* a famous landmark, in New Hampshire. They had been hiking along a well-known crevasse when a sudden torrent of debris raced down on them from Mt. Webster. Aaron had urged his two sons and daughter to run as fast as they could to avoid the avalanche, but they weren't fast enough. His wife had been knocked into the narrow breach along with the kids. Despite Aaron's best efforts, he could not rescue any of them. The crevasse was hundreds of feet deep and offered no footholds to ascent and escape. There was no way of reaching them. He later determined the fall had killed them when his incessant shouts remained unanswered. All that could be heard was the sound of his voice ricocheting off the sides of the deep chasm. Aaron suffered with survivor's remorse for many months after the accident, even attempting suicide by slitting his left wrist. It was only after the onset of the *Big Freeze* that he realized his family had been *spared* from the devastation, sparking his renewed hope in a greater purpose for his survival.

The only survivor from the avalanche had been his pet Maltese, Sam, whom Aaron had kept secret in his long trench coat when he was unceremoniously picked up by a Japanese patrol. Sam was bleached white in color and hypoallergenic. He was Aaron's lifeline and only connection to his lost family. Because of his natural camouflage and the fact that he did not shed fur, Aaron was able to smuggle the dog into the camp. Due to a stroke of scientific ingenuity, Sam had also been born mute, a canine trait that geneticists had been trying to achieve with most dogs before the Big Freeze. (A barking dog had been considered gauche in the later stages of societal evolution). In addition, Sam possessed other traits that distinguished him as a breed. Sam was engineered by biomedical scientists to withstand hunger and tolerate extreme cold. Maltese were part of a short production run experimenting with breeds that could survive in the permafrost. Aaron found this ironic given that the breed originated in Malta, where a warm climate was chthonic, and where Maltese were considered to be "floppy" and weak "lap-dogs" marketed to the gentrified. But here Sam was a reminder of great scientific achievements before the Freeze— progress now cut off like the blood flow to a frostbitten hand. He was also very intelligent and even though he did not possess the advantage of a bark, he leveraged body language to communicate. His eyes were very expressive and a window into a complicated and calculating being. Unbeknown to his creators he could also read minds and sense things beyond human comprehension; even Aaron was not privy to this.

Despite the odds, Aaron was determined that one day he would escape from the clutches of the Japanese. The crux of his problem boiled down to this: Although he might escape this camp, another one could easily pick him up. At all times, patrols remained on the lookout to add numbers to their stockade; they accomplished this by sweeping methodically across the countryside. Once taken captive the prisoners performed all of the grunt work to support the camp, and for their physical efforts they were treated like slaves living on a meager diet of foul fish and leftover scraps of greenhouse vegetables. The soups they served were despicable, some of the men thought the remains of humans were pureed to make the stock.

Comprised mostly of displaced Americans or foreign thieves or cutthroats, the prisoners' primary duty consisted of building high ice towers around the camps for protection from invasion. There was no rescue from the camps. Those who tried to flee were summarily executed. Those rare few who escaped immediate capture survived only a short time in the wild. Although he had no way of knowing it, Aaron was one of the luckier ones as he was a prisoner at one of the southernmost camps. Situated in San Antonio, 282 miles away from the designated safe zone above Monterrey, he was south enough to avoid the harshest areas of climate around Chicago and

Boston. It was said that survival in those areas was slim at best. Gangs of marauders pillaged the land and the camps in those areas were the most ruthless.

When he'd first been apprehended near Boston, he was shipped by Maglev
rail to this camp; high-speed trains were the last "hurrah" of American ingenuity still in use, although they had been first developed and introduced by
the Japanese. A German citizen, by the name of Hermann Kemper had been
able to patent ingenious commercial designs of what later would be called
magnetic levitation trains. This innovation gave the rails the ability to accommodate speeds up to 400 mph!

The men Aaron bunked with on the train, mostly loggers, died in large
numbers during their transport. To stay warm, they had built small fires in
the rail cars. It did nothing to prevent the cold air from seeping in through
the thin wood matrix that composed the outer shell of the cars. That exposed the captives to extremely low temperatures which spurred hypothermia, bronchitis then pneumonia and a variety of other cardiac ailments that
took root because of their weakened states. Those who did not make it were
thrown off the cars and left as carrion for the mélange of predators shadowing the trains. During the day the men viewed fields of ragged clothing, all
which remained of men who had travelled on these tracks before them.

Knowing the near impossibility of success did not sway Aaron in his
thinking that one day he could eventually escape. A former hunter and out-
doorsman he had confidence in his survival skills in the wild. He was also a
trained Climatologist and tenured at M.I.T. before the turbulence. No one in
the camp knew about his academic background; he kept it a secret. He didn't
know if it would benefit him to tell his captors how much he knew about the
cold that now plagued them. Other men who had been interrogated before
did not survive the ordeal.

Before the *Big Freeze*, Aaron had a very engaging and rewarding academic
life traveling between his home in New Hampshire and the M.I.T. campus in
Boston. He was a well-known climate researcher who passionately claimed
that the planet was undergoing unusual climate change and was warming up
faster than normal. He developed a plethora of climate models that showed
this to be exactly the case. Yet he had many detractors, mostly from the

corporate world and even surprisingly the government. They worried about the economic impacts of climate change specifically the cost of slowing down the escalating greenhouse effect.

Counter-intuitively, he also predicted that this general warming of the planet would bring on an onset of pole-like conditions in the lower latitudes of the Northern hemisphere where four seasons were customary. Even the well-researched ice core studies he presented that validated periodic shifts in the earth's climate fell on deaf ears. No one believed him; he was cast as a quack and marginalized. There was data, though; showing carbon dioxide levels had reached historic proportions, over 400 ppm which was significantly higher than the start of the industrial revolution when this information was first recorded. This data was from the government's own database recorded by the NOAA at the Mauna Loa Observatory in Hawaii. Carbon dioxide was a known greenhouse accelerator but even that they ignored.

Later, after the changes, the scientific community had been chastised for not predicting the climate change. By that time, the public had forgotten about Aaron's original research.

Acting on his own, Aaron had stockpiled provisions in his New Hampshire home and attempted to hunker down during the unprecedented polar vortex-like storms. The climate change came swiftly and suddenly. Millions were unprepared and died from exposure and lack of provisions. It soon became apparent to Aaron's family that they couldn't stay in New Hampshire and that they needed to move to lower latitude. It was then that the accident occurred that changed Aaron's life forever.

It was the images coming out of Florida on his satellite TV that finally moved them to act. The loss of control of the situation by the U.S. Government and the mass pilgrimage of millions of people to the southern border of Florida had been catastrophic. People with no place to go, attempted to use the Florida Keys as a staging area, to find refuge on a boat leaving for warmer areas in the Southern Hemisphere. Instead, the pileup had resulted in a vast killing field through the Keys with the stench of death evident from miles away. Near the coastlines thousands of bodies decomposed in the surf killing sea-life and creating a tidal wave of body parts that soon washed ashore onto the once pearly pristine sands, with some bodies even migrating to Cuba's coastlines. The rotten smell of death and sulfur filled the air and there were not enough burial spots for people to gather up and entomb all the corpses. Instead there were large bonfires on the beach that worked as crematoriums, black soot and clouds of smoke draped the skylines.

All of this carnage was not lost on Aaron as he contemplated his escape. The thought of traversing 282 miles of wasteland hardly appealed to him. Added to that, he would likely encounter at least a dozen international camps on the way over to Mexico, not to mention a Native American outpost of survivalists. All of them would be unfriendly except the Native American camp. The Russian and German camps were described like the desolate, ruthless gulag encampments that were strewn across the Soviet Union. The French camp was likened to a leper colony. It would be tough going. The trick would be to chart a course away from most of the camps and travel on lesser known and unmarked routes.

Aaron's one ray of hope was a story imparted to him by one of his train comrades before the man died. He spoke of an area reserved in Mexico City's central park, Chapultepec Park, designated as a safe haven strictly reserved for Americans. It was located in the *Warm Zone* and had been a destination for a number of displaced Americans. They were housed and fed by the Mexican government and were allowed to stay for a period of time before attempting to relocate and continue with their lives. Space was at a premium there but his friend told him that the installation was well-managed and medical care was provided to all. Aaron's friend had been re-apprehended in the United States when he attempted to return to help a family member escape prison to go to Chapultepec Park. Even though his friend had never reached Chapultepec Park he was assured it was a *friendly* camp.

There, if everything his comrade told him was true, Aaron reasoned, Sam would get care too. And with any luck, they could weather the climate changes peacefully.

Today, however, the immediate thorny problem remained getting enough food at the breakfast line to live another day to execute his plan.

Around two acres square, the prison grounds were relatively small but an impregnable wall of snow and ice had been built around them to make entry and escape almost impossible. Portholes were constructed through which the guards aimed high-powered, telescopic rifles that could kill people and even formidable wildlife for up to one or two miles away. The men worked in heavy Tyvek coveralls that were engineered for extreme cold. The mesh they were fabricated from contained a re-engineered GORE-TEX a synthetic waterproofing agent combined with a proprietary fiber that neutralized the effects of condensation. Condensation could be lethal in an environment that could be a low as − 76 degrees. Life and death were measured in seconds in this climate, with many men succumbing to pulmonary-cardiac events. To add perspective, the lowest temperature ever recorded on Mt. Everest was -76 degrees, where many men perished from hypothermia and frost-bite when trying to scale the summit. -76 was also the temperature that freeze-dried all bacterial life. People had to be very careful in this environment. One careless action could cost a life.

"Hey you, get out of my way," one of the men ordered as he rushed by. The breakfast flag, a blue and black banner, signifying this camp was run by the Japanese, had been raised.

Years earlier, the San Antonio River had been converted into a huge incubator for freshwater fish. As one of the first states to experience an onslaught of heat, Texas dairy farming and meat production had become an extinct occupation.

As Texas Bighorn faltered in the hot weather and the searing temperatures reduced the livestock; the state researched new ways to produce food. Fish "farming" offshore became more popular. Edible marine life became a primary source of food until eventually the seawater heated up to uncontrollable levels and oxygen levels plummeted, killing many of the edible species. These changes all occurred before the *Big Freeze* which eventually triggered mass migrations of both people and animals, and was many times more destructive. *But who was counting?*

Now the camp got larger fish from a nearby lake and a smaller amount from the abandoned Riverbed operation. The work was grueling as they had to constantly re-fracture the ice to position their nets. Also, the thickness of the ice they had to break through to get to fresh, moving water was daunting. There were many mouths to feed and sometimes there wasn't nearly enough sustenance to satisfy the hunger. It was the prisoners who suffered most when there were shortages.

Fish products were the camp's staple food and today's choices were no different. The menu lacked surprises. About the only thing that varied was the way it was served: it could be a sloppy gruel, or a thin and stock-like soup, or be dispensed sushi style in bloody, unappetizing chunks.

"Brother serve yourself," another man said as Aaron approached the front of the line. He had hoped there would be some bread with the soup so he could dip it into the soup and feed Sam small chunks of it. Before walking to the dining area, Aaron had placed Sam under his bed and covered him with a stolen burlap sack. The dog somehow knew to lay still. Call it "doggy" intuition but he knew it would be dangerous to call attention to his presence.

"Thanks I'll do just that," Aaron replied. "Any chance of having a little extra? We have someone who's sick and can't be here."

"Rat's ass to that," the burly cook said. "If you can't work, you can't eat. We don't make the rules then break them."

Still not deterred, Aaron whispered: *"I can bring you some chewing tobacco tomorrow. I have some left. It'll be as close as you're going to get to a cigarette."*

The cook winked at him and scooped out another tiny portion of soup. It was a small victory but better than nothing. There were a few solid parts in the additional soup he could feed Sam. He could mush it into smaller pieces that the dog's small throat could accommodate.

The walk back was tricky—the slippery surface of the ice rendered the footing treacherous. It was better suited for ice-skating than human traffic. Neither ice melt nor gravelly dirt was available to diminish the slick surface. If Aaron was serious about trudging to Monterrey he would have to acquire a better pair of walking shoes or preferably a pair of rugged hiking boots more suitable for the journey. Finding crampons would also be a bonus. His current pair of Timberland's was worn out and full of holes—he had used some scavenged duct tape to repair some of the openings visible along the sole but that would not be enough to withstand a long journey. He risked incapacitating frostbite and swollen, bruised toes that would hamper his progress. He was a goner if he was disabled in the wilderness, being able to walk was a necessity.

*As he walked with his comrades, Aaron mused that this was where the cook could help.* The food worker had access to the supply depot where spare boots were kept as well as other supplies. Aaron thought that perhaps he could bribe the cook to procure him a pair of boots. These boots usually came from recently deceased workers who were being held in a makeshift morgue at the edge of the camp. They were held there before they were filleted into cooking fuel. If the cook could also get him a pair of crampons from the patrol depot, that would serve his purpose even further. Crampons for his boots would be critical when traversing rocky terrains—the large amounts of ice and risk of falling necessitated them. The problem would be finding his size—only two or three of the Japanese were large enough to have a shoe size close to his. There was a greater chance that one of the prisoners who died would match his size.

The men marched back to their quarters, a thinly walled shack with a center fire pit and not much else. The intense cold made it difficult for the prisoners to separate their mittens – if they were fortunate enough to have a pair—from their skin. Perspiration caused ice blisters that were a never-ending nuisance and source of irritation--as was the latrine located just outside their dorm made of cheap plywood that was hastily tacked together to form a john of sorts. Inside it, the inmates had burrowed a six-foot deep trench hardly 12 inches wide which served as a final resting place for their bladder and bowel movements. The poorly contrived latrine reeked horribly and many men could barely tolerate a visit without retching. On one occasion a man had his buttocks frozen to the opening of the toilet and he had to be pried loose using a hammer and chisel.

In spite of everything, tonight the men had a special treat in store for them. One of the shack's prisoners, while out on a fishing run, had uncovered an old transistor radio that he was able to pry from under a fallen tree trunk. He had hidden it away in his bunk. One of the other captives had struck a deal in the supply area for a 9V battery to make it operational. Scuttlebutt had it that some ham operators were still broadcasting along the fringe of the *Warm and Cold Zones*—so there was some cause for hope. Even though they were situated in the Cold Zone they were close enough to catch some airwaves from other parts of the region.

"Alpha, Omega, Catchbasin 1," one of the men barked out the call name he and his comrades had selected, "anyone hear us? Please respond." Dead silence. "Alpha, Omega, Catchbasin 1," he tried several times. There was a brief flicker of hope when they thought they heard something, but they realized it was a vibration reverberating off the wall of the shack from a plane passing overhead that found its way into the headpiece. They decided to quit broadcasting and would resume again tomorrow.

While this was happening, one of the least-liked prison guards was heading in their direction. He had a pompous grin on his face and a huge night stick. He wielded a large Strion LED light that he was pointing at their cabin; he was waving it like a large laser beam across all the exit routes of the cabin. He looked like a dog catcher looking forward to putting a noose around a stray wild animal's neck. He bent down gazing at something; his binoculars swaying slowly around the contours of his bulbous waist; his night cap crowning a face that was more suited for a creepy circus clown 'than a prison guard.

Thinking that someone may have tipped off the guard, the men quickly stashed the radio away. To cull favors at the camp it was not unusual for prisoners to snitch on one another. Life at the camp dictated a constant state of wariness. On occasion, finks would be found dead in their bunks if their peers found them blameworthy. They were usually strangled but in several cases they were also castrated and their testicles nailed to a door. *"Justice for All"* had evolved into a brutal game of survival by force in the *Cold Zone*. Despots had control and dictators abounded. In the *Warm Zone,* a rule of law presided, but that rarely guaranteed a trial by jury.

The guard turned towards their shack and then veered off listening to minute changes in the howling wind. He was trying to discern something. Small even by Asian's standards, he stood less than five feet tall.

His overstuffed leg warmers made him look like a miniature prairie buffalo stomping on sagebrush in the plains. Looks, in this case, were very deceiving. His unusual alertness and extensive training to detect any small variation in the camp's routine made him formidable.

High, swirling winds blew steadily against the large ice caps that encompassed the camp. Bobbing snow drifted down from above, moving through the air in undulating waves like miniature Monarchs in a butterfly house. The hypnotic zigzagging motion of the flakes mesmerized the men.

Aaron wandered back to his youth when the controversy about global warming first started. Back then, people had been assured there would be no major impacts on the planet; the ocean was big enough to absorb the surplus production of land mass heat, as long as we reduced our carbon output. The ozone layer could be restored by banning CCFs, which did happen for a time. But the lack of ozone in the stratosphere in the short term also caused heat retention raising temperatures – a fact not lost on Aaron.

As a youngster, Aaron loved math and studied it eagerly. He was especially enamored with fractions, their derivations and roots, and was admired by his peers for his ability to compute uneven fractions several decimal points out doing it all in his head. His intelligence was not the result of being an autistic savant but the product of genetic favoritism. The number *pi* especially fascinated him and he could repeat back its value to twenty-seven decimal places. He was recognized as a local prodigy and expected to be successful in math and the sciences. His teachers praised him and predicted great things from him.

He was not a nerd though; he was also was an accomplished soccer and baseball player. His love of numbers translated into a complete encyclopedic knowledge of baseball statistics, he could tell you about Willie Mays' last-at-bat when he played for the NY Mets; how many homers Hank Aaron hit every year he played; the number of strikes Don Larsen threw in his perfect game. He even remembered all the numbers of his favorite all-star players in several sports. He remembered every Boston Celtics player that ever played basketball and could recite their full names and position starting with the original team chartered in 1946 of the Basketball Association of America.

His passion for numbers later served as the foundation for his evolution into a M.I.T. professor who specialized in climate change. Probability calculations with all their inner workings and propensity for variables held his attention. He loved to formulate scenarios, adjudge their risk for happening, and present his ideas to peers in the academic community. He was a gifted speaker and his dissertations became well-known in his chosen field of *Climate Change Science.*

His mother encouraged him but his father a blue-collar worker, did not like his flights of fancy, and tried to influence Aaron towards more practical fields like oil and rare metal engineering, finance, and the study of law. His father unwittingly drove Aaron further away from the mundane and into the margins where real discoveries were being made.

Aaron's notoriety attracted the attention of many corporations and private think tanks that were working on clandestine big data projects. Due to his many academic appointments and government contacts he was privy to industrial subterfuge and espionage that occurred behind-the-scenes. He was often bribed and asked to reveal proprietary information, but to his credit he kept to his moral principles and avoided disclosure.

Later on, he was put on retainer by the U.S. Government and worked with some of the country's top scientists and collaborated with the NSA and the Pentagon. Aaron was highly reliable in his assessments. He was correct better than 80% of the time which earned him a reputation as a solid academic prognosticator. Most of his predictions were extrapolated from data he accumulated from his research, but he also had premonitions which guided him. For instance, he knew in advance about the fate his family, even dreamed of falling into a dark crevasse while the light above slowly faded to black. This was the only premonition he chose to forget. Usually, out of body experiences predated these events—he would work very hard to get back into his body after some of the more lucid dreams. He would wake up in the middle of the night, sweating profusely; disoriented but feeling like a large malleable bubble on the verge of bursting, drifting between reality and unreality, lost in that plane known to Tibetan spiritualists. His intellectual pursuits in large part were powered by the mystic transformations that occurred in his dreams. He shared this with no one.

The Jap soon left without causing the prisoners any problems. With quietude reigning over the camp, the hut's occupants turned their attention to keeping warm by the fire and trying to salvage some satisfaction from the notion that they might soon make contact with someone from outside the claustrophobic sphere of labor camps.

The big Swede who had assumed command over the shack insisted that they keep a more careful watch over their hut. So they posted more guards around their dorm to watch for any unexpected visitors. Two men were assigned the first watch, a "down and out" Southerner who used to live in Myrtle Beach and a jovial fellow who went by the befitting name of "Jingles". In his prior life, Jingles was a security professional who locked down the restaurants along the Atlantic City boardwalk at closing time. As was his trademark, he always had a large ring of keys dangling on the side of his pants belt which earned him his still unshakeable nickname. In his heyday, he loved to walk the long deserted boardwalk singing old tunes, often out of key. These serenades included old folk songs from the 60's like "Mr. Tambourine Man" or "If I Had a Hammer" that he learned from listening to bushy-faced guitarists prowling Washington Square Park. He often traveled to NYC and wandered around the Park having no better place to go on his time off.

"Jingles" quickly became a favorite among the camp detainees; he brought a unique sense of levity and optimism to the place. A long silvery beard adorned his face and a lone buffalo nickel hung from a piercing in his left ear. He fancied himself a frontiersman like "Buffalo Bill" Cody. Although many thought he shared a likeness to General George Armstrong Custer.

The Southerner "Patches" who hailed from Richmond, VA—actually had more of a connection to the Wild West than Jingles. One of his distant relatives was a Calvary officer who fought on a campaign with Jeb Stuart during the Civil War. Well-educated, Patches was a sharp contrast to Jingles—he studied Engineering at the University of Virginia, and carried himself like an aristocrat which irritated some of the men. But Patches scored points with the men with his fearless demeanor and willingness to take risks on behalf of the group. He could be counted on when there was trouble looming. His name Patches was a nickname his friends gave him—his mother although they could very well afford new slacks, used to sew patches all over his pants. Patches was embarrassed by not only the number of patches on his pants but by the array of different colors his mother sewed on them which made matters worse. His childhood friends mercilessly teased him and to this day those memories of that time haunt him. The nickname never went away.

Before dispatching Jingles and Patches to their watch guard duties, the Big Swede warned them: "Be vigilant and report back anything that seems out of place." Jingles and Patches were a good pairing for guard duty---Patches would be serious and more guarded while Jingles would provide comic relief and be lighthearted.

The night passed slowly, the evening stars glistened in their appointed places in the sky—there were some stray meteorites flashing across the rim of the horizon providing the men with an unusual light show. Sam was burrowed in Aaron's lap, dimly aware of what was transpiring in the sky, but acutely aware of all the night sounds—his muteness offset by his supersensitive hearing. All seemed peaceful in the camp, but that would change.

# CHAPTER 2

# THE JOURNEY

The Soviets dug in beyond the enemy perimeter. Their advance scouts having informed them earlier in the day that they were approaching the Japanese outpost. A desperate need for prisoners to help them rebuild their camp drove them to this action. Their camp, located about 50 miles west of San Antonio was located in an open valley shielded and surrounded by low mesas. The considerable damage to their compound wrought by a group of Germans left them with a deficit of 14 prisoners as well as 8 less soldiers who were killed in action. They also had several wounded in their ranks; it was a *surprise attack*—as all conflicts were in this day and age.

For weeks they had been bringing back information from two observation posts they had set up beyond the roads the Japs typically travelled. They knew numbers, assessed strengths and weaknesses of the fortification and knew the habits of the workers. They particularly counted armed guards and identified breach points in the stockade. All this surveillance had helped give them the courage they would need to overcome stiff odds and the advantage of surprise which were needed to offset unrelenting cold that complicated any assault. Firearms jammed easily and frostbite could set in at a moment's notice curtailing their troops' effectiveness.

The Russian foot soldiers had spanned themselves 360 degrees around the camp. They planned to set off a diversion on the front side of the encampment while storming with overwhelming numbers the rear side of the camp, a military tactic called strategic envelopment. They had calculated a pre-dawn raid would catch most of the guards unawares sleeping at their posts. They had observed in the past weeks the guards getting very lax about their duties; through their high-powered binoculars they had seen some of the guards were even playing card games during their shifts and wandering far off the compound to relieve themselves, without their weapons.

The Soviets came heavily armed for the assault—they had picked up some RPGs and mortars from a prior raid. These were aimed to provide maximum damage to the wall they would be attacking, hopefully creating a large breach they could all pass through.

The forward line of Russian attackers stood poised, crouched on their bellies. Their fingers dug into the snow, as they inched forward. Knapsacks, loaded with meager provisions, rustled on their backs, with each herky-jerky forward motion. All they could see before them was a colossal heap of ice and snow that impeded their progress.

Word came down that they needed to stop the advance, a lone Japanese patrolman was heading in their direction making his way towards an old oak tree, that was covered with icicles—its boughs heavy with permafrost and its trunk ribbed by cords of ice. The tree, in its present state, weighed over seventy-five tons, and the ice acted like cement, keeping it intact even through the most violent storms.

The wayward guard had come out to urinate at the base of the tree; the liquid vapors crystallized before they hit the ground. One Soviet soldier was so close he could smell foul urine as it was released. Perhaps the guard was diseased and was trying to hide that fact from his superiors, knowing that they would release him from the camp if he was found out or they would unceremoniously shoot him, lacking the ability to earn his keep.

Men confined to these outposts did not have it easy. Aside from malnutrition, other ailments such as chronic infections, vitamin deficiencies, heart disease, immunosuppressive disorders and overexposure ran rampant. That they could withstand the daily affront of the harsh environment was further proof of their toughness.

As the Jap turned around, he found himself entwined in strangle wires. He tried to twist loose the wires from his neck but that caused deep lacerations on his fingers as he did so. The harder he tried to free himself the tauter they became. The wires soon made their way through the main arteries in his neck and his limp body signaled his end. Two Soviet soldiers pushed his body into a ditch covering up the bright red blood with fresh snow so that they and the body remained concealed. They could count on the body being discovered, but that would be in a day or two when a Polar Bear or some other scavenger visited and made a feast of it.

With the guard out of the way, the Soviets continued the slow advance to their target, the secondary guardhouse that punctuated the area between the supply depot and the front gate. There was an ice parapet above them on a rampart where two Japanese guards patrolled the area; but as luck would have it they had their hands shoved deeply into their pockets and their hoods so tightly snug over their heads that their vision was impaired.

One of the Soviet snipers raised the RPG he was carrying and aimed it at the gap between the two men. On a command from their leader he fired the grenade launcher hitting the wall of ice supporting the watch tower. This collapsed the ice bridge and sent the two guards tumbling through the air. The opening was large enough to let 50 of the Soviets in, charging and cursing and firing as they went. They stormed in like many soldier ants on a mission. If they were not praying they were invoking their gods each in their own way.

They soon opened the back gate where the balance of the Soviet soldiers was waiting to pounce, overrunning the camp.

Many of the Japanese were still in their beds, when they awoke they were being fired upon, scrambling to put on their winter gear and grabbing their weapons at the same time. Most of them were sitting ducks and chaotic bedlam reigned throughout the camp. Bed sheets were smattered with blood and pillow feathers were flying across the room as if it was snowing inside the walls, as the ordinance rained down upon them. .Along with this, a cacophony of sounds filled the camp, inchoate and primal, like surging tides hitting a primeval sand swept beach. Only the extreme cold seemed to diffuse the screams and cast a surreal penumbra on the event.

Sam, forever watchful, heard the oncoming onslaught and whimpered, alerting Aaron who was stirring in his sleep. Only when the battle was upon them did the men react. For Aaron, however slim, this represented an opportunity to escape, to Chapultepec Park—a way to avoid the senseless deaths that all would befall who stayed.

The prisoners huddled around the doorway, ready to spring on the first Soviet or Japanese soldier who trespassed. They were hoping to acquire a weapon before they tried to escape. The Big Swede was closest to the door, his enormous hands shaped like battle axes ready to wreak havoc on his prey. In his hands was a black-smeared fire stoker large enough to roast a man on a spit. As a former Navy corpsman he was trained in hand to hand combat and was a match for anyone. The Russian or Japanese soldier who had to deal with him was going to be in for a rude awakening.

"They're coming," someone in the back whispered. Aaron tried to peek out and saw a Russian soldier rummaging through some barrels, looking for something to eat. Aaron next saw him shove some scraps of food into his mouth. Once inside the camp many of the soldiers were searching for food being so starved that they were half enlisted in the battle—many ran towards the commissary instead of following the attack plan.

Unfortunately for him, one of the soldiers tried to get into the men's dorm. He rifle-butted the door until he shattered the locks. Aaron never forgot the image of the man's face when the Big Swede drove the long spike into his mouth and impaled him on the wall of the hut. Horror shifted to a quick death.

While this was occurring, the rest of the men were shocked with what they saw on the grounds. The entire compound was in shambles, many of the walls looking like Swiss cheese instead of the solid fortress that they had been before. The Japanese were in some cases locked in hand-to-hand combat and looked like Hobbits compared to the taller Russian force. The compound was starting to flood as the intense heat from the battle was starting to melt all of the ice. Fires raged everywhere, thick smoke clouding every person's view. Puddles turned into streams which turned into rivulets---soon there were running rivers throughout the entire camp. Torn timbers lay askance and were being pushed by water in all directions—creating an obstacle course for those engaged in the fighting, the risk of being clobbered by large chunks of debris was as great as being hit by a bullet. While they were foraging for food, the Soviets rounded up the Japanese forcing them to stand in the bitter cold with their hands above their heads. From a distance a large plume of smoke was emanating from the camp turning the early morning sky into a mottled cloud of black smoke fragmented with debris.

Aaron and his men realized that this smoke could provide excellent cover as they tried to flee the camp. Overjoyed by a sense of freedom, Jingles made a run for it leaping towards the new opening in the wall. Had he looked back, he would have seen a Japanese guard taking aim with an AK-47 fat on his back. He was at the wall, trying to slide through the hole in the ice, when the bullet throttled his skull. A sense of loss swept through the men as they realized Jingles was not going to be jingling anymore.

Seeing this, Aaron thought better of just moving forward on an impulse. He would lay low a little longer as others tried to make their escape. Some would make it through, but others would be picked off like Jingles. He was hoping to see a pattern that he could take advantage of. Each man would be on his own as trying to escape as a group would draw too much attention and be foolhardy.

So he remained calm as each man in turn tried to depart. The Big Swede could not fit through the opening Jingles planned to escape through, he was too big. Instead he went to the far side of the camp, having the advantage of being armed, he managed to slip through before he drew notice.

Patches, like Aaron, waited things out. He went under his bed to remove a knife he had made from scrap metal—it looked like a Bowie knife and he had a scabbard for it he had clumsily constructed. Despite it not being a gun, the knife gave him more confidence as he made his way towards the area where the Big Swede exited. Aaron would find out later that Patches' escape, like the Big Swede's, was successful. But what lay ahead was totally unknown.

These success stories, however, were more the exception than the rule. Many prisoners were either lost or recaptured as the Russian took further control of the camp. Those that did not die were held as prisoners, by the new regime.

Lifetime-enforced captivity weighed on Aaron's mind as he plotted his next move. If he faltered, he might never again regain his freedom. He had heard of a hidden trail composed of several connected narrow paths that winded south. Some of the camp hunters had stumbled across them on one occasion, but they were never able to find them again. Aaron did not know where the trail started but it did have a series of small cairns that marked it, if he could find it. He reasoned that he could shadow the trail, keeping off of it, using it as a guide to make his way towards the *Warm Zone*. What worried him more, aside from capture, was how he was going to find enough food along the way to feed Sam and himself. This would be a 300 mile journey before he found any sort of relief. The other option, staying, with the new Russian leadership, was not possible; this is what eventually drove him to action. The Russians were known to be more ruthless than the Japanese.

A veil of sooty darkness blotted the morning light. Smoke continued to billow out all over the grounds. The chilly moving water was mounting all over the camp and men were wandering about in total disarray. There were areas of high and low ground, where the soldiers were either trying to stay dry or splashing around in large puddles. It was at this point that Aaron decided to go. His window of opportunity was closing. Several Russians had cornered a group of Japanese and were encircling them. The camp's attention seemed to be focused on that spot—the Japanese were firing from behind a small stockade of frozen garbage---losing men with each passing minute as they were picked off by sharpshooters.

Aaron peered beyond the door. When he was satisfied the coast was clear, he tucked Sam under his trench coat—only the dog's black snout peeked out between the upper buttons of his master's outerwear. Both man and canine breathed heavily, Aaron with mortal apprehension, Sammy with a dog's fearful intuition of things about to go awry.

Stepping out into the cold, translucent air, Aaron cursed his dreadful visibility. *How in God's name did we reach a point in time like this?* All of the advances that came with progress in history and civilization seemed to be reeling backward in slow motion since the advent of the *Big Freeze*. Humanity was waning; only the polar bears and the flora and fauna that thrived in the planet's coldest reaches were gaining ground.  Aaron missed his family; he ached for his former way of life—the lecturing and close ties with his students and the soul-stirring consultation and debate with his colleagues while tackling difficult conundrums.  He grieved the stifling of his creative self's imaginings and felt disconnected from his real self.  No one knew him for who he really was. He roamed alone on the tundra, surrounded by slumbering strangers. But no man truly walks alone, he had his faithful dog Sam.

While in this reverie, a chilly breeze hit him full force, sending pangs of icy needles shooting through his entire body. New and old fears crept into his unsettled consciousness. The length of the trek, his inability to keep warm, the potential confusion from acquiring hypothermia, his lack of any sort of weapons, and the prospect of being unable to find the right way—they all gave him further cause for hesitation.

Not far away, the sound of gunshots and muffled voices rang out. Aaron shot out from the shack clambering alongside the building on all fours struggling to keep his balance while holding Sam tightly to his body. During this time he did not realize he was an easy target. He had unintentionally arched his back like a cat during his hurried exit from the shack rendering himself a good target if someone happened to gaze in his direction. Craning his neck around the corner, he saw nothing but a white expanse stained with the battle's bloody remnants. He sprinted across an icy field, endeavoring not to trip on any of the small fissures and phantom forms that marred the crystalline surface. Already soaked from all the melted ice, his boots provided flimsy protection from the penetrating dampness. Assessing the best route out, he decided his next goal would be to get past the commissary on his right.

Aaron hid behind some steel containers that had been stacked high enough to afford him some cover. When he thought no one was watching, he ran around the corner of the commissary where an opening in the stockade existed—the same one his previous cellmates had either successfully gone or unsuccessfully attempted to go through.  There lay before him a few bodies; some face down in the mud, others he could not distinguish as being bodies anymore, having been splintered by mortar fire. Without further inspection he could not tell who they were, *I hope there weren't any that I knew;* Sam twisted under his coat as he pondered this.

Not much underbrush lay beyond, but Aaron spotted some bramble that looked a little thicker than the rest. *That might offer a temporary hiding place,* he mused.

Again Aaron studied the landscape. No voices, nobody in sight. He and Sammy quickly dove through the hole in the wall of ice. They slipped more than plunged, the ice having long been transformed into "slip and slide" mush. Reaching the underbrush they rested a short while before starting out again.

A strong sense of wretchedness washed over Aaron. The combination of coldness, hunger, and sadness over the death of some of his friends overcame him, rendering him spiritually wasted. But he was still physically strong. And he had resolve. In the end, that's what would drive him further than he thought possible. He had no other choice but to attempt the impossible.

Before he and Sam could grow more chilled, he started forward again. Even relatively mild temperatures like those found in the White Mountains of New Hampshire, where Aaron used to live, could be lethal in the wrong situation, especially with that area's fickle weather systems. Men wandering on clearly defined hiking paths in relative safety could become afflicted with hypothermia from the sudden decreases in temperature brought on by freak storms. The conditions for that happening here were more acute, even though they were at a lower altitude. Their normal was already very dangerous.

He pushed Sam's face farther down inside his burly jacket. There was nothing more he could do to help his campmates, but with any luck, he'd catch up to the Big Swede or Patches on the way to Chapultepec Park. Aaron knew they would probably stand a greater chance of surviving if they could combine forces, much the way wolves and hyenas work symbiotically in packs in the wild. However, had they attempted to escape as a group, it's probable that none of them would have survived or they would have been tracked down shortly after escaping.

They would have to travel miles before they could stop safely and break a camp. Aaron knew he had to find some shelter and warmth before nightfall.

The bioengineered dog could survive longer in the cold than he could, that Aaron also knew. The sticking point was that the relatively open wound on his arm was still healing from his accident. The prolonged coldness could complicate things, inhibiting circulation in his arm. That potentially was a cause for alarm. He would have to watch for that.

From his days at MIT Aaron learned that volcanoes were once active in central Texas, some, in fact, not far from San Antonio. They looked dormant when you visited them but some were still geologically active. Because of this, there was a small chance of finding some thermal springs that had been activated by the earth's changes that were connected to the line of volcanoes Aaron also knew slight changes in its vertical axis since the freeze had made one end of the planet heavier than the other, bringing about a metamorphosis to the landscape.

In addition, the mantle had begun uplifting in spots across the globe, reactivating dormant volcanoes and creating more geysers on the scale of Old Faithful and even hot springs like the Boiling River were turning up in unexpected locations. One had already formed in the Grand Canyon and another had started to spout in what used to be downtown Las Vegas, near the Golden Nugget. These were natural hot tubs that warmed the body and were great for circulation; some aficionados claimed they were even useful in improving overall health.

The warmth that could be derived from these hot springs was a deciding factor in the location of many of the camps. The problem for Aaron and Sam would be the lack of knowing who could be lurking nearby; most of these outposts were run by international thugs or visited by criminalized elements of a new breed of roaming kidnappers. There also was no way of telling where to find them. No maps existed, and for that matter, snow and ice inundated the roads that led to them. Indeed, the grid that had once served as the nation's infrastructure had devolved into utter shambles. The only locational tool Aaron had at his disposal was a compass. He had pulled it off the soldier the Big Swede had killed, who no longer had any use for it.

Aaron's first obstacle lay ahead. A small fortress of ice was situated off the nearer side of the camp. He needed to scale it quickly to get clear of it if he was going to give himself and Sam a chance. The incoming and outgoing hail of bullets and mortar fire had fractured part of it, just enough so that he could walk through a channel that rose about thirty feet off the ground. It dawned on him that he did not think to take the dead soldier's boots when he pinched the compass out of his pocket. This was an unfortunate oversight as his boots were worn and full of holes that he had sealed with duct tape. Insulated with GORE-TEX®, they had withstood the colder climes when new but they had been worn down into disrepair. Swapping them out for a newer pair had topped his wish list. A new pair of boots would have provided traction to climb uphill and scale this impediment.

He hunched his body very low and scuttled across the field in front of him. He had to untangle himself from a pocket of thorny thickets on the way, which slowed him down a bit, but he was not seen. Looking back the thickets resembled stone stalagmites rising off a cave floor.

He started up the hill of jagged ice. Holding Sam off to one side, he balanced the dog on his hip under his coat jacket and used the stub of his arm to keep the animal upright. His right usable hand and arm he kept on the ground, clawing the snow while relying mostly on the force of his leg muscles to work his way upwards. The effort proved slow-going but manageable. Within about twenty minutes, he had climbed the thirty feet and somehow lumbered through to the other side.

An unforgettable sight now lay before him. Men of all shapes and sizes lying in heaps littered the landscape. Faces, frozen to the earth, contorted in the early morning sun, gazed at him-- their bodies fused together into shapeless piles. *So this was where they buried all the casualties of the camp*, Aaron thought. It was without ceremony or fanfare. Envisioning himself a member of this dead society gave him the courage to go on.

He walked around the killing field, mindful of staying in the shadows of the ice wall. The way looked clear ahead. He only saw a group of buttes in the distance, basking in glowing morning amber light. Could it be the *Lost World* ahead? Arthur Conan Doyle's novel immediately sprang to Aaron's mind, the only difference being that today the prehistoric beasts were human not a collection of Jurassic dinosaurs.

Now that his initial adrenaline rush had passed, Aaron cogitated more clearly on his situation. Using his compass, he plotted a way southwest from his present position. This would lead him to Interstate 35 (more likely the remnants of it), which he could follow to the vicinity of Artesia Wells. This location was in an area that he had heard might have what he was looking for: hot springs. From there, he could continue on to Laredo, also in Texas, and later on, further south to Mexico.

Artesia Wells was once a water spot called *Bart* on the International-Great Northern Railroad routes. It took its name from the numerous Artesian Wells located beneath it. Even though this area of Texas had its own water source, it had never really attracted much of a population. Before the *Big Freeze*, only about 35 people had lived there—that number had grown dramatically due to the hot springs. Aaron knew he would have to be careful. A prison settlement or two might very well have been established in the area. Most of the camps lacked hot water and took great pains in melting ice frozen wood, burning it, and heating water in large basins. He trusted Sam would alert him for scents of smoke or other signs of human habituation.

Was he 52, 53, or 54? Aaron hardly remembered. The calendar meant nothing; the sheer will to survive had displaced time. The last three years of the *Big Freeze* had made him feel both timeless and locked in time. He felt like a flickering permeable human-tissue mass floating on the whimsical gyration of an unintelligible universe. In his subconscious, he sensed life was more than that, but he reckoned that what you were shown was merely the roll of a dice; your belief system is what set you apart and made you different.

On the subscript below his name in the Hall of Records, he did not want it to state that "Aaron Griffin had died in vain, trying to save his faithful companion, Sam, on an Interstate 35–bound journey to Nowhere Ville, Mexico." If he had any say in the matter, his life would not be reduced to a pointless epitaph.

He would have much rather it read, "Aaron Griffin famed MIT scientist, miraculously found alive in Chapultepec Park, a soldier of fortune, after having saved his loyal dog, Sam, perished after a long illness at the Chapultepec Park Center for the Aged." This obituary was more to his liking.

Aaron began hearing some noises behind him. *Perhaps the camp's getting back under control and men are now fanning out looking for escapees*, he conjectured. He decided to pick up some speed to put some distance behind their location and any potential trackers.

Trudging several miles through snow, ice, and large mounds of desiccated soil and amorphous rock formed by the climate changes, it seemed to Aaron that he had found every ditch and gully in Texas. Twice he fell down, once dropping Sam out of his jacket onto the ground. He was lucky neither he nor the dog broke any bones. In Sam's current situation, that would have been lethal for the dog. Likewise, fractured bones for Aaron would have meant a slow, tortuous death in the subzero cold.

The noises behind him seemed to be diminishing. To Aaron's knowledge, the pursuing Soviets had no bloodhounds, and with all the melting around the camp, it would be hard for them to pick up anyone's trail through the water and changeable debris fields. Water would also disfigure or erase the footprints making them indecipherable.

In time, he came across a wide valley with a small clearing that seemed to have the beginning markings of a road. Two bright orange twisted cones and some yellow and black caution tape caught his eye in the distance. In the old days, these objects would have indicated a break in the road for a traffic accident or for some road construction. Now Aaron wasn't so sure what they signaled. They could represent a hole in the ice, perhaps restricted access to a fishing pond or some other anomaly a camping party had detected. In any case he needed to find out. The last thing he wanted to do was to cross the road and get taken off course and have to backtrack in this intense cold.

So he ambled on.

His legs had grown warm from all the exercise, but the tips of his feet pricked from numbness. Red pockmarks marred his face where the cold had seeped in through his mask. He did not realize that small scabs had begun to form around his eyes and that water droplets were crystallizing on the lobes of his ears. He needed to get warm soon and get some food into his belly before nightfall or it would be a very uncomfortable if not unrelenting night.

The effort of each step became a drag on his entire being. Every step forward was like walking in deep mud. Eventually closing the distance, the cones materialized into Aaron's field of vision. The lip of the valley, where it got rocky again, lay not far off. As he approached, to his great relief, he discovered a road, and by the look of its size it was a substantial one. The road seemed to cut through the valley and disappear into a notch, snaking past vertical inclines on both sides as it ascended. Aaron checked his compass again. The way ahead pointed southwest, so he followed it, as this was the direction he needed to go.

Before Aaron left, he investigated the reason for the cones and caution tape. He was saddened to learn they were a makeshift burial marker for a woman and her young child who were half-immersed in a blanket of snow and frost. The girl looked to be about six, the mother perhaps in her late forties. The daughter's long, braided ponytail eerily whipped about in the wind. He also spotted what could have caused their demise: parts of a snowmobile strewn across the road. *A tragic slip on the ice perhaps, or something more complicated?*

Aaron sifted through the rubbish and found nothing of value to help him. Other visitors had ransacked the site. As he piled a bunch of rocks on the bodies, his thoughts turned again to his family being buried alive in an avalanche. The memory brought great grief and tears rolled down his cheeks. He would have to be more careful about expressing emotions in the future; survival of the fittest required gumption and ruthless behavior. The ivory towers of MIT had shielded him from the marginalized of society and he had to remember that grief could cause more harm to his face.

During these sad moments his thoughts continued to revolve around his position in the universe. Did any religion have a monopoly on God? Or did each just own a piece of him or her? Since the *Big Freeze*, his reflections had become more radical. There were those in his department at MIT who did not accept any divine deity or its existence. They thought the high science they practiced was as an extension of man's quest for God or that science was a replacement for God, even that God put trust only in science. *In Science We Trust.*

Aaron believed a certain unbridled mathematical elegance ran through all things which required intelligent control. Whether this tendency was "God's creation" or the result of some other form of external intervention remained to be seen. His current situation had begun to shift his belief system more toward the latter. In his view, men's minds were small repositories of knowledge that needed to be cleaned out every so often and refitted. Perhaps we advanced towards God or an understanding of God's mind with each successive evolution.

Sammy started to shake again. Aaron had stopped too long, the dog could withstand the cold but perhaps he was nervous about the mental gymnastics he perceived his master was struggling with. The dog sensed his owner's internal struggles. It was time to move on as far as the dog was concerned.

But what could he contribute to the maelstrom that existed before him? A dog's mind operated on the fringes of survival, knowing only a master's love, a quest for food and warmth, and the partaking of biological necessities. One characteristic, however, stood above all the rest when it came to dogs, and that was loyalty. Loyalty—the word had petered out of existence long before the *Big Freeze*. He had seen this in the mini-Depression of the 2010s—and it had never really improved. The *"Me"* culture having reached its apex, people scrambled to save themselves in every way they could. A few good eggs guarded the gates but they were overrun by the "Me-sters."

Aaron stooped down to grab a stone. He had missed it before—a piece of flint, rare for these parts, but serviceable enough to start a fire. Perhaps the decedents were out of matches and had used it before they crashed. It looked like it had been struck a few times. He slipped it into his pocket and zippered it shut. *This could be a lifesaver.*

A large gathering of seasonal birds passed overhead. It looked like they were heading south towards the Gulf of Mexico. Small and yellow, they had the field marks of American Goldfinch, perhaps confused by the lack of seasons. This movement could also mean there were humans or wildlife in the area that were advancing in Aaron's direction.

The weather had begun to turn too. Small snowflakes drifted down and were swiftly covering the ground. The road ahead was already painted white. With new snow coating it, the footing would be difficult and the hiking time-consuming. He started to move forward again, following the contours of the road. He would have to find a walking stick soon to establish constant asphalt underneath him. Otherwise, he might get drawn off course.

He passed through the valley and into the notches. Steep cliffs flanked him on both sides; giant crags of limestone lined the path. Some boulders looked loose, as though they might fall. He avoided these and moved to the far side of the road. *This might be a good place to set a trap for a passing convoy,* he thought. *Or in my case a passing escapee.*

Aaron traversed through the rough and uneven landscape without incident. By using the heel of his worn boots every so often to create a wedge in the frost and snow and validate macadam, he was able to follow the changing path of the road. He knew he couldn't keep this up for long, so he ventured off the main road when he was about a mile away from the notches in search of a stick he could use as a poker.

About forty feet from where he was, he sighted a Western Mesquite that was partially abraded and flash frozen. With some precarious maneuvers, he was able to grab one of the overhanging boughs and snap it. He fashioned a cane from a long lash that could be used to check the status of the road. It was more like a long icicle than a walking stick, but it would serve its purpose.

Aaron estimated he was still a good forty miles or so from Artesia Wells. At his current snail's pace, that would mean he would have to stop for the night at least two or three more times on the road before arriving at his destination. It was much too far for a forced march before nightfall, so he reasoned that they would have to find cover. The snow continued to fall and it began to mount up. He knew from geology books that many caves were present in the Texas badlands. The trick lay in how and where to find one. And if he did find one, he needed it to be one that was not occupied. The migration and explosion of wild animals from the north had made certain that most potential dwellings already served as homes for creatures large and small. Aaron couldn't help thinking about the larger such critters, polar bears in particular.

Aaron's other overriding need was to replace his waterlogged boots. He could get *trench foot* in a day or so if he did not find a way to keep his lower extremities better protected and dry. He did not have a change of socks with him so he would have to watch his feet closely. Discoloration of the toes, instep, sole, or heel could indicate trouble. He remembered reading about the condition in World War I manuals, where entrenched men fighting in close quarters during prolonged periods of wet and snowy weather had spawned the nickname for this condition. The pictures of discolored, sometimes blistered, bloated feet had remained seared in his mind. For some, it meant losing all or part of their appendages. For others who were more fortunate, it meant a way to leave the battlefield with at least their lives intact, even if it left them handicapped.

The late morning sun hung in full view overhead, emanating a powerful golden radiance over the fields. The snow had almost subsided with the remaining flurries being whipped errantly about by an inconstant breeze. Aaron continued down the path of Interstate 35 searching for a way to survive first the afternoon and then, more pressingly, the evening hours.

Conventional shelters, like homes and buildings, were a thing of the past. If Aaron could find one, he would gladly take advantage of them. With the advent of the *Big Freeze*, massive, fast-running glaciers, on a scale never recorded before, moved north to south. As they passed, they basically decimated everything in their path, including a huge chunk of the population. Land mass that was once flat formed hills and mountains. The rising glaciers and the constant snow had created a North American snow base of several hundred feet.

A few outlying cabins had been restored outside the confines of the prison camp system by survivors, but by and large, places like Texas had been reduced to vast snowfields with not much in the way of sustenance or accommodations. Even tall buildings like the Empire State Building had been either badly damaged or engulfed by snow and ice. There were occasional outliers where parts of a town or a nest of buildings were spared, but that was not usually the case.

In some areas, where dams had been broken, the water had frozen and created gigantic palaces of ice. The gulag-style prison networks now mined these areas for freshwater. They carted large chunks of this permafrost back to camps then heated it for drinking and cooking water.

The water had to be boiled to an extreme temperature after the ice melted. The animal feces that had been frozen within it needed to be distilled before it could be considered safe to drink. Still, even after treatment, some people came down with E. Coli or some other unmanageable bacterial or parasitic infection, like Giardiasis that often proved fatal thanks to both the short supply of medicine and medical knowledge. Antibiotics could be transported from the *Warm Zone* to the U.S., but only at great risk and expense, usually via black market enterprises. The prisoners in the camps were expected to die within an allotted period of time, there was no one looking out for them.

Once the U.S. lost its leading commerce position, its resources became that of a third world country. On the other hand, the African continent because of the cold snap had actually emerged into a thriving group of colonies. Many of its impoverished countries had been repatriated with immigrants from the North. The Africans were now known far and wide for their ability to reconstitute land into arable properties. Studies from UNEP (United Nations Environment Programme) in the early 21$^{st}$ century had advised that the African nations were only using a portion of their arable lands--the *Big Freeze* had changed all that. With their full potential now realized, they had a sevenfold increase in production over their former baseline. International food conglomerates all over the African continent buzzed in ardent pursuit of business deals as a new age of agriculture took off in the region. Poverty and starvation were all but eradicated. *The world really had turned upside down.*

Aaron stayed on the lookout for mesas. Small habitable caves where people could stay were often nestled at their base. Stony overhangs that provided protection from the cold and wind also frequently accompanied them. So far he and Sam had had no luck. They kept trudging on, immune to hardship, focused on the task at hand. Aaron found Sam to be the perfect companion; if he were under stress it escaped his master's notice.

The dog shivered ever so slightly, probably more from nerves than from the cold temperature itself. His body was inured to freezing temperatures, but his respiratory tract totally was not. Sam's tolerance to cold was quite remarkable. *Moreover his sense of smell was off the charts.* His olfactory nerves having been bio-engineered to the extreme, his sense of smell was about twenty-five times better than that of a bear. And bears could smell 2,100 times better than humans.

The only drawback to his uncanny sensory ability was that Sam could not communicate his findings to his master. His creators had worked on "paw sign language" with him, but it had not gone too far, the apocalyptic events that shook the planet put his education to an end almost as soon as it had begun. Despite a shortened stint in the classroom, Sam had been a good student, better than most of the chimpanzees that had learned sign language in research labs. Under different circumstances, he probably would have gone to school and been enrolled in a Maltese astronaut training program. The animal rights activists had tried to ward off this tinkering of animals' genetic codes, but the greedy interests of corporations and political wrangling had obstructed them.

This lonely pilgrimage that was Aaron's was bearable because of Sam. His will to live was not just founded on self-preservation but had a twin meaning; he wanted to save Sam from the rotisserie spit, a likely end if the dog became captive. He had great passion for Sam; he was the family he no longer had. Much of his emotional resilience sprang from this love between dog and man. Sam grounded him.

The afternoon went fleeting by and the boys (dog and man) had not found their overnight stop yet. But they were starting to make better time now that the snow had stopped. They were both very hungry and had not eaten since the night before. Aaron had a few crumpled cookies left in one of his coat pockets that they shared. He had kept them hidden from the guards on his last outing at the camp. These calories would not sustain them for very long and more concerning was that they were in danger of dehydration if they did not find some water soon. As a last resort they could eat snow and allow it to melt in their mouths but that would decrease their core body temperatures. It was a risk Aaron wanted to avoid.

Ahead and to the left of them, Aaron saw movement across the road. He noticed there was a frozen stream of water atop a large bank of ice and near it were some small crevices, the size of junior footballs, dug into a wall--*not large enough to contain a human, but large enough to house some small critters*. Aaron was a bit confused. How could anything survive in this frost when they were that small? He looked around and saw some hollows beneath some transplanted arctic willow shrubs. He also observed pockets of mountain avens and even some wild crocus. Perhaps this creature was surviving by feeding off of bulbs and shoots where the ice was thinner? *That must be it* Aaron thought. Sam had other ideas. He was ready for the chase having smelled a rat a while back.

Aaron approached the opening cautiously. He did not want to disturb the inhabitant of the hole quite yet nor did he want to precipitate an unwanted skirmish. He saw what looked like whiskers jutting out of the hole. At least then it was not a fisher, a vile beast he knew from New England that could successfully hunt porcupines. But what was unsettling was that the creature might be bigger than what he presumed.

With one swift motion he brought his walking stick's mast down on top of the beast, holding it firmly while pushing it forward with his boot to take a look. In point of fact it was no beast, only a brown lemming--a garden variety of fat-looking rodents that can masquerade as large hamsters. Aaron assumed it was edible as he knew other predator species engorged themselves on lemmings. It did not offer a super-sized meal, but anything that he could put into his and Sam's stomachs would be beneficial.

He held the rod tight around the rim of the lemming's neck and after a few little whimpers it suffocated. It was the best he could do to simulate a mercy killing. Great African tigers used similar methods to asphyxiate their prey. At MIT he would feel squeamish about performing this action; in a survival situation he allowed the laws of nature to take hold.

The next step would be the hardest. How was he going to prepare the lemming for a meal? Eat it raw? Sam would prefer it that way, but for Aaron that thought was revolting.

He still had the flint. But could he start a fire? Nearby there was loose detritus that could be used to start a fire, but could he round up enough from where the lemming had been digging? He was a bit skeptical but he would try.

He started to scour the ground taking what he could of the dry stuff and crammed it into his right pocket. He needed to find more cover where he could get a break from the wind before he tried to light a fire. The road ahead looked clearer although he saw more hilly terrain about five miles away. He continued in that direction. With any luck he would find a shelter and a chance to cook the lemming. He had no way to carry the lemming so he tied its tail on the top end of his walking pole so that the body of the animal swayed continuously back and forth as he walked. This was unnerving to Sam but Aaron was not going to put the still warm creature in his pocket.

One of the fears about being on the open road was the risk that over-flights would pick them out and report their presence to a local hostile force. Because of the total breakdown in the electrical grid and lack of landing fields airplanes that passed over the continental U.S. generally were not landing, but they could pass along damaging information. Single engine Piper aircraft were common sights flying in the sky on targeted missions. They dropped nefarious supplies to contracted camps, especially arms and ammunition. This was a large-scale operation that supported a military black market in arms trafficking that was surreptitiously sponsored by *Warm Zone* countries. There wasn't a camp that was not armed to the hilt; the country had been transformed into an Afghanistan-like feudal system with warring tribes.

Back on the trail, Aaron and Sam moved over to the west side of the road since it provided better cover. Petrified, oversized Prickly pear cactus afforded some protection from above. They continued along this natural barrier by following a rough trail that ran alongside the road. Although the clearing was patchy in spots it was manageable. Aaron avoided anything that looked sharp on the ground as his boots had reached their breaking point.

Besides fire and food, he desperately needed a pair of boots. He had eyed the dead woman's boots but they were way too small for him to make use of. He should have taken her coat, though, and then he could have torn it up into small pieces and plugged the holes forming in his boots. He could have also used it too for fire-starting material or for extra bandages. He needed to think more clearly; he hoped his judgment was not getting impaired by the cold and exhaustion. He would have to exploit every opportunity, however small, in order to survive.

The way ahead remained clear. He constantly looked for a sign of a cave or natural cove that would provide a place of protection for them to stay the night. Looking back from where they had come, he saw black billowing clouds smudging the horizon; they looked like dark phantoms dancing at a masquerade ball.

The entropy of the universe had changed for Aaron. He felt closer to the stark facts of existence. Time was at a premium; collective past and present moments a stream of indelible photographs etched into his mind and floating through the collective unconscious. The book of his life was burning like a flickering candle, close to being snuffed out. All he could do was go forward and have the will to live. He had no control over his circumstances; he could only double-down by making *intelligent choices* in the face of adversity.

Since the advent of climate change the Middle East had overtaken vast parts of Europe. The French who had been in decline for a long time eventually succumbed to Muslim rule of law. They had become a vassal of Iran. Italy was involved in a civil war as the last loyalists of Christianity in that country were now fighting at the Vatican to save it from destruction at the hands of an invasion from Syria. Spain was relatively secure, but with Italy and France losing or on the verge of losing independence, Spain was the next domino to potentially follow. Most of France, Spain and Italy miraculously had avoided the Big Freeze. The cold did not stretch its arms that far South into Europe as much as it did in North America. France was partitioned into two different climate states, one hot and one cold. The Muslims controlled the warmer region and were spreading their influence wherever patriotism and love of country were weak. In this strife, extremism had taken roots in many quarters. The general populace had taken refuge in strong-armed dictatorships that promised to provide security and sustenance in a less sustaining environment. The global and poorly sponsored climate manipulation had produced a bounty of dividends, long lines of hopeless people who were starving or who had lost life or the will to live.

There were also numerous Middle Eastern camps sponsored in the U.S. The less patriotic Muslims in Europe had been banished by extremist sects and shipped over to the U.S. for life. They had formed their own camps. Unlike the vast majority of the other camps, they did not house prisoners. They worked together to support themselves and were community-minded. They were not anti-American or really against any other group. But when it came to survival they were very ruthless and were not bashful about what they dined on. They were accustomed to beheadings and the killing of women and children from radical sects in their former countries so they had hardy and strong constitutions already acclimated to survive in the new normal.

Thus, encountering a Muslim camp, for Aaron, who was in any case a devout Pantheist, would be a bonus. However, trying to find a "friendly" camp in such wilderness would be like finding a way out of a labyrinth. He felt like he was fleeing a bull in a maze with no apparent exit.

If they did run into trouble, he could always release Sam so the dog could hide; his camouflaging white fur and lack of a bark would protect him. However having only one useful hand really handicapped Aaron; if he needed to fight anyone he would be at a distinct disadvantage. Foraging with one hand was extremely difficult and time consuming too. As it was right now, the dog was still under his coat, an added weight and encumbrance above his waistline. The lemming on the stick was also a burden; he frequently had to reposition it and tighten the tail into a knot. Having the use of one hand also made this a tedious process.

Aaron's face had become increasingly red and it was streaked with ash from the fires in the camp; his clothes were torn and shabby and he had unsightly puckers all over his exposed skin. Rubbing the sores made everything feel worse. The incessant cold wind was also taking its toll. Save the raw beauty of the wintry countryside, there was not much to get excited about.

He was in a state of constant mental turmoil, dipping between highs of hope and the nadir of despair.

Something was amiss; he saw movement out of the corner of his eye. He couldn't be sure if it was something smaller scrambling along the adjacent rocks or something larger not wanting to make its presence known. It was yet too far in the distance for him to discern. He had bad eyesight to begin with and had been wearing the same pair of eyeglasses the last three years. They were scratched and much of the anti-glare on the lenses had peeled off and created "dead spots."

Sam seemed disturbed. Not a good sign. Aaron picked up the pace nudging closer to the road each time he took a step forward. He decided to squat down behind a wide-bough bush to take a look.

Sure enough, it was an errant Polar Bear scavenging the land looking for food—it had a plump appearance and seemed occupied in one particular spot, using its massive thirteen inch paws to dig out an area near a clump of vines. He knew about the strength of Polar Bears; one had escaped its paddock at the New England Aquarium while he was visiting. The bear had jumped into a Beluga pool and ripped a young female calf to shreds before the keepers could tranquilize him.

Aaron noticed that the bear had dried bloodstains on its white coat especially in and around some of the large teeth in its gaping mouth. One or two teeth were black and broken off and resembled fish hooks. The stench of the bear is what occupied Sam; it had the unpleasant smell of raw fish and death. Aaron guessed its last meal was not that long ago.

While the bear was busy, Aaron silently crossed the road about 50 yards north of the bear. The wind was blowing northerly, so Sam could smell the bear, but the bear would have trouble detecting them. That probably saved them from a very dangerous encounter. Aaron had no firearms and a charging bear would be impossible to stop. Pepper spray could halt its charge but he had none in his possession. He also had to drop the lemming off the line, as the bear would now be able to smell it with their change in direction, with the wind blowing past them into the bear's direction. He hoped this would detain the bear as they put more distance between the bear and themselves.

Their situation was becoming grimmer and more critical. Leaving the lemming was necessary but it was their only source of calories. They were still freezing, in need of shelter and rest, and fast reaching a state of exhaustion.

His mind raced back to his carefree days at MIT, Aaron was regarded as one of the most gifted academicians. His students loved him. His lectures were interactive, engrossing, and "out of the box" in the way they attempted to go beyond the bounds of standard topics and interpretation. He had developed a reputation for being bold and thoughtful. Almost every year he was the leading candidate for the *MIT Excellence Award for Teaching*. The Nobel Foundation recognized the work he did on climate change and he was nominated for the Nobel Prize. To his dismay, he did not win. A priggish Malaysian academic, Alfred Menses, won it for explaining the wave dynamics of Tsunamis, this during the most terrible hurricane season in recorded history. Aaron did win the second place prize, but this was below the cash award he was expecting to assist him in expanding his research lab.

Adrift in a maelstrom of emotions, Aaron continued to review the high and low points of his life. In Hebrew, his name meant "Mountain" and he had climbed mountains, literally and figuratively, during his time on the planet. He had also moved them. He had met his lovely wife during a national conference exploring climate change. She had been trying to pitch her publisher's academic magazine to his colleagues, "The Journal of Geologic Markers", when he had first cast his eyes on her. She had sparkling green eyes and an effervescent personality that was crowd pleasing. Her freckles were subtle and attractive and imbued her with beauty. She had long legs and an athletic build. He found out later she ran the NYC and Boston marathons every year, training at a local New Balance Armory. She worked at Elsevier, an elite scientific journal publishing company that specialized in scientific journals and science books.

They had a wild romance during that conference and were married a few months later. Lola bore him two children. They had a happy life in New

Hampshire for the brief time they were together. That was all in the past now. A series of memories cast ashore, driftwood in the cosmic sea of life. He wished she was still here.

*Anxiety*, a now familiar friend to Aaron, was starting to creep in. Sam sensed it. The dog looked longingly at him, eyes of sorrow and pain mixed with high intelligence. Both of their stomachs were rumbling. Once they were a safe distance away from the Polar Bear, Aaron looked back to discover that the bear had found the lemming and was gnawing at it while glancing in their general direction, several hundred yards away from them. Aaron picked up the pace again.

"This is not a time to be scared," he kept repeating to himself. "It will turn out all right in the end. I always rise to the occasion. I am confident we will survive." The frazzled inner workings of his mind continued to blur his consciousness and his judgment. He just needed to stay calm. Solutions were nearby, he would find them.

He reached around Sam and hugged him tightly, more for his own reassurance than for the dog. They would continue the fight. They would not be defeated by the elements or by themselves. He pointed his stick to the heavens and shouted in protest to the circling birds overhead, "I will conquer!" They peered at him closely, looking for more signs of weakness.

Aaron stayed on the road, every so often using his poking stick to make sure there was pavement underneath. They were lucky that this part of Texas was not as ice covered as other parts or there would be no way they could follow the road. After a time, they passed a frozen stream that wound its way under the road. There appeared to be an ice hole that was dug out for either fishing purposes or to get at the fresh moving water. The dog and Aaron were dying of thirst and he had a suspicion some of his spooky feelings were the result of the beginning stages of dehydration or hypothermia.

They scampered down the side of the hill where the culvert opened and advanced slowly onto the ice. The hole was about six inches by six inches in diameter and was directly under the road so it was not exposed to snowfall and was easy to access.

To Aaron's delight, it was a working water well they could use. Someone had recently been here the last few days and used an auger or a similar tool to dig out the well. He reached down and was able to work through the newly formed surface ice with his hardwood pole. He needed to find a way to draw the icy water up. Nearby he found an old aluminum can, the surface markings were worn clean, so he could not see the original label on the can, but it could serve as a draw bucket. He untied one of his boots and tied the lace around the top of the can so he could remove water from the hole. Before using the can he used fresh snow to clean and rinse it out. In this way, for the first time in a long while, Sam and Aaron were able to drink until they were full.

To carry a can full of water while they were moving would be cumbersome but also impractical, as it would freeze on the way and add further weight to his load. Aaron guessed if they found hot springs they could mix the warm water with ice to make it drinkable. He could also boil some game in the pools of thermal water if he could find some along the way.

The water rejuvenated them and provided a revived sense of vigor. Aaron was still afraid that the bear would follow them so they did not tarry. He threw the can under the bridge and tried to conceal their presence. He put Sam back under his coat and climbed the side of the culvert carefully. He nearly slipped and landed on the ice but he used his poking stick to grab into the ice and he was able to hoist himself up.

He could smell the cleaner air now through his mask and the sun was shining, its silhouette producing dark shadows along the edges of the frozen stream. The circling birds had moved on, looking for other foundering prey. Perhaps they would feed off the scraps of the lemming, if there were any.

The landscape was starting to change its shape again. It was becoming hillier and there were now more ravines and valleys with scrub brush and hanging trees—all weighed down by the snow and ice. They were making good time now. It was starting to get late in the afternoon, they would have to search for a place soon to pass the night.

Yellow line road lane markers were becoming more visible. A steady breeze kept the snow from piling up on the road. Aaron observed that it preferred to accumulate in snowdrifts near the side of the mesas that enclosed the valley. There was a wide plain in front of them. Visibility was quite good. Chances were that prairie dogs once roamed here. Also several different species of venomous snakes probably inhabited the area. Mountain lions and even cougars traveling from Mexico were once commonplace in Texas. It was hard to imagine with the valley as depopulated as it was. In ice ages wooly mammoths, saber-toothed tigers, and other beasts of prey were dominant. But in those cases animals and man had more time to adapt to gradual changes in temperature. Many died. Sudden climate change like this was more akin to extermination.

Even so, they had caught a lemming. If small creatures could somehow survive, there was hope for other types of smaller and larger creatures, really a whole range of possibilities. Polar Bears, penguins, and walruses had cold weather adaptations that evolved over thousands of years. They would be expected to survive. Most of the Texas wildlife evolved to withstand heat not bitter cold. It would only be the more intelligent or serendipitous inhabitants that were able to modify their genetic code to the climate that would live on. Most would have migrated by now, but others, who knows. The fate of many species was in the balance. Aaron did not know enough about the biological life in Texas to hypothesize too much.

On the right side of the road, the wind had sculpted a long ridge of snow that looked like a shark's fin. Sand that had been whipped up by a windstorm was sprinkled on top of the snow.

There was also a line of rocks, forming jetties that lead to a large mesa that was about two thousand feet high. In between, a natural waterway formed a sluice that seemed to extend in all directions from a large opening in the rocks. Farther on ahead, he eyed a large crack in the side of the mesa, tall enough to get through standing up, but only wide enough to accommodate a person with his body turned sideways. It looked to be an archaeological site. There could be small paintings on the wall perhaps made by Coahuiltecan Indians that once inhabited the area. He needed to get closer. The Coahuiltecans were known around the area of San Antonio as agile survivors who thrived in the 1700's and whose varied diet included deer dung, worms, spiders, rotten wood, and snakes. They held ceremonies called mi-totes that celebrated many rites of passage including puberty. During the mitotes they smoked peyote and played drums and danced. They inexpli-cably disappeared once the Spaniards conquered South Texas. Perhaps the Spaniards brought disease or cross-bred with them, it was hard to tell. A genetic study would need to be commissioned.

As Aaron approached the wall, he saw that these were in fact pictorials of Indian life. The Coahuiltecans did not usually use caves, but preferred the outdoors where they built-semicircular tents out of reeds and straw. Perhaps this was a sacred site. He knew just a little bit about Indian history from a summer program he took at UCLA, entitled *Anthropological Origins of Native Americans*, when he was thinking about changing his major to cultural anthro-pology. This was a short-lived notion, a flight of fancy that never material-ized. He would instead become the consummate climate expert that he was.

He peered into the crack in the wall. Sure enough it was a cave. About six feet into the opening it turned into a sizeable cavern. It smelled a bit peculiar. He wondered if wafting through the cave was the remains of age old burnt peyote that had become a permanent feature of the cave. He really did not concern himself with that at this point. He was just glad to find some solace and refuge from the cold. There was enough light coming through the open-ing to alight the front end of the cave. Beyond the front, it was total dark-ness. As nothing was visible he could only conjecture how far the opening stretched back into the side of the mesa. Aaron suspected the cave formed through long-term erosion spurred by an underground river. The famous site at Mesa Verde had cliff-dwelling houses, caves, and priceless paintings and artifacts. The residents of Mesa Verde also carved petroglyphs in stone that marked seasonal positions of plants and other social activities. They were a people linked closely to nature, as most native peoples were. They marked time by the changing seasons and the location of the sun in the sky, and by birth and death. Man-made conventions like time of day were foreign to them.

It occurred to Aaron that if he was a cultural anthropologist or an ar-chaeologist he could find real treasure here. Given his current state and more poignantly, the state of the U.S., this was an unrealistic dream. What the cave did provide, though, was a means of survival. He could make use of that. It showed no signs of animal bedding. The smell of smoke most likely had a human origin. On the way into the cave, he discerned no footprints or animal tracks, which was also a good sign. They were in a fairly remote pocket of land southwest of San Antonio that was once arid and was known geographically to be inhospitable to humans. Of course now, it was inundated with snow and ice and the topography suggested more the Alaskan tundra. Guests should be far and few in between. His only worry was that a camp patrol would haphazardly stumble on the opening of the cave and try to explore it—a risk he would have to take. The entrance was small enough and cloaked in enough snow to make that unlikely. The only melting was around the rock paintings as if they were meant to be discovered.

Sam made himself at home near the front of the cave. He had found some old shredded straw probably part of a discarded native tapestry and had snuggled on top of it. It was still brutally cold and they needed to address that first if they were going to last the night. Aaron remembered the flint he had picked up at the crash site and was thinking about how he could use it. He recalled from survival training when he was in the ninth grade that they had practiced striking flint with steel to produce a spark for tinder. He took out some tinder he had piled in his pocket. But he had no steel knife to use. He was wearing a heavy belt buckle. He wondered if that could produce enough friction to create a spark. The only way to find out was to try it. He removed his belt and rubbed the buckle against the stone that lined the front edges of the cave to wear down its shiny edges, to make it coarse for striking. He reasoned that if the belt buckle offered more resistance it would be better at starting a fire.

He moved the tinder and placed it in a small pile near Sam. He also took bits of straw that were matted to the stone floor and prepared a secondary pile of tinder to use once the main pile got started. As luck would have it, stored near one of the walls were clumps of old branches and dried wood. *So, somebody had used this place before.* Still it looked like it had been a while ago; the place was in disuse except to a lost, intrepid traveler like he who stumbled upon it, either by luck or necessity.

He started a fire, striking his flint against the belt. It was primitive but it worked, although it took several tries. He disrobed and put his clothes in a pile by the hot fire including his soaking boots. He was glad that he couldn't look and see himself in a mirror; he was sure that it would not be a sight to behold. Someone happening upon him at this moment would probably regard him as alien to the human race.

*The warmth from the fire did wonders for reviving his spirits.* He nestled himself near it and the heat engulfed him while he napped for a while, not before putting some additional wood on the glowing embers. He had enough wood for several hours. He would have to ration what he had and then try to find more wood he could de-ice and use. That could wait for later. Right now he earned some rest. Sam snored alongside him.

In his dream he recalled a tale a friend told him about an underground base hidden in Dulce, New Mexico. The base he was told had several levels and had been holding alien life forms in its tunnels for thousands of years. The Apaches had discovered the cave before the English came to America, and had fought with these small creatures; they were called "Greys" who functioned like worker bees defending a colony. The fighting was intense and lasted several days, the superior alien technology had scared and frightened the Apaches and they never returned to the site. In fact they avoided all mesas for centuries as this was where they thought additional bases were hidden underground.

His dreaming went on for quite a while and then it abruptly ended. He had no sense of time. His only real timepiece was the rising and falling of the sun. They were close enough to the earth now to know that time was an illusion; days and calendars were manmade measurements that provided security in a universe that respected order but whose natural pull was always towards disorder. The chaos created by the climate change was to the earth a natural transformation, part of a greater metamorphosis that was inherent in the universe. For man, these changes were a harbinger of unwanted change and further insecurity about his existential state.

Sam woke up. His master was muttering in his sleep, having a bad dream. He smelled something rotten. There were shadows where there shouldn't be shadows and they were moving right towards them. Sam started to paw Aaron's unshaven face to try and stir him. Something was amiss as far as the dog was concerned. The shadows circled around them and then moved back into the recesses of the part of the cave that they could not view. Aaron did not wake up. The danger had passed for the time being. Sam was still uneasy but would have to wait until his master awakened. The dog shrieked inside unable to voice his fear.

The light from the outside was starting to dim. Late day was bringing in nightfall when Aaron finally awoke from his slumber. He felt achy and stiff, from all the walking. He needed to stretch a bit and get his bearings again. He peered outside and realized daylight was in short supply. His clothes were dry and he got dressed. The fire was simmering. He put a good portion of the rest of the wood he had on the remaining flames. He made a note that he would have to look for more wood and find some food soon.

In the back nook of his mind he remembered something unsettling but could not put his finger on it. He noticed Sam appeared shaken and nervous. He did not know why. But for now he had more pressing demands. They had shaken off hypothermia for the time being but her ugly sister, starvation, was an imminent threat. He put on his warmed coat, gloves, and winter mask and stepped outside. He walked back through the paved way of stones and surveyed the horizon. The air seemed crisp as much as he was wanting and hungry.

He saw a small stand of tall trees that provided some cover on the ground where there was an area of less snow. It was perhaps a hundred yards away down into the valley across the other side of the road. He reconnoitered the distance and figured it was a ten-minute walk through the windswept snow and ice. As he was beginning to feel weak, he was starting to analyze every one of his actions and calibrating them. This change of behavior was not a good one; it was the sign of the slow downward spiral from physical and intellectual alertness to a demented state brought on by either dehydration or hypothermia or both.

He walked quickly; it was invigorating and got his blood moving again. It felt good. He was on the lookout for interlopers, both man and animals.

This valley, before the *Big Freeze*, had the imprint of a vast prairie park that he imagined was teeming with thousands of lizards, snakes, and scorpions slithering in and out of amorphous rocks and into narrow crannies and passageways. Today it was a vast frozen wasteland, devoid of life, silent, rife with discord. He and Sam were strangers on this landscape, lonely, forlorn, witnesses to its intrinsic beauty and cold grace.

The stand of trees was as he thought. There were some branches and small twigs he was able to collect from the dry area of ground beneath the ring of trees. The stand had formed a kind of umbrella on top that shielded the area because it was weighted down with snow. It was an oasis in an otherwise wintry forest. He carried back a chunk of frozen snow he intended to put near the fire; Sam could lap some up and get a drink. Besides starvation, hydration was always an ongoing concern.

His stubbed wrist was still tender and was beginning to sting. It was bandaged and the spilled blood hardened by clotting was also beginning to throb. In addition to his other losses, he had lost significant blood during his accident—this had started to take its toll. The camp surgeon did not have an IV to give to him and his intake of liquids since had been low; his escape had put greater strain on his lymphatic and circulatory system. He would need to make water from ice tonight and drink a great deal of fluids to infuse his system.

*He would also have to inspect the wound. That process worried him.*

Aaron returned to the den without incident. He dropped the wood and then went out again. Sam seemed fine and appeared to have settled down. He had thrown some more branches on the fire as a precaution before he left. He was concerned about the thin line of smoke drifting out of the front of the cave but the life-supporting heat was paramount. The increasing darkness would also conceal it.

He was intent *this time to find something to eat*. Earlier he had noted some small tracks in the snow, not too far from where they were encamped. The lemming was a prize they had lost. His hope was to find something else he could cook before they retired for the night. The tracks had more of the look of a bird than a small mammal. He would have to follow the trail and stake it out to see. He had his long staff and had sharpened its end between two rocks in the cave. It was now pointy and spear-like, and could be used as a harpoon or lance.

He stayed close to the ascending walls of the mesa, away from the road, right of where the cave entrance was. He walked slowly and deliberately, avoiding making any unnecessary noise, back to the area where he had seen the tracks. Any bird would vanish at the first hint of unfamiliar sounds and even the slightest noises would make them flee.

There was not one but a gaggle of Canadian geese sunning themselves on the snow, on a precipice about ten feet off the ground. They were probably migrating to the border of Mexico where they habitually went for the winter months, down past Laredo, Texas. The geese were resting comfortably and honking and were totally unaware of any threat.

Aaron knew he would have one shot at this; they would be gone in a flash if he missed. He aimed and calibrated his throw several times; there was a particularly fat goose that seemed very distracted preening its broad feathers and looking absentmindedly at the ground. He jerked his one good arm back and fired the spear. It was a bull's-eye; the goose ran around a few times in a circle then fell sideward, mortally wounded. The rest of the geese formed a wedge in the air and quickly left leaving their friend to his fate. Aaron who did not have any affinity for killing caught the goose by his spear and impaled it further until the bird was still.

He felt bad for the goose. In his own way he hated the whole process. He was an intellectual not a butcher. He avoided going to the meat market leaving that to Lola.

Back at the cave, he added more wood to the fire. He estimated his supply of wood would last through the night. They would have to move again tomorrow. The smoke would be unseen during the night, but by day they would be vulnerable. He set the goose more firmly on his rod and used it as a rotisserie to cook the entire goose. He de-feathered it before cooking and peeled off what he could from the carcass after they ate—he rolled away the scraps and put them away for safekeeping. It had been a long time since they both had a full belly and they soon fell fast asleep.

Before he slept, however, he remembered he had to inspect his wound. The throbbing had persisted during the day. He removed the bandages carefully, taking care not to pull the gauze off too quickly so that he would not aggravate the wound. He unwrapped each of the three layers until his flesh was exposed. What he found startled him. Areas along the ridge of the stub were becoming blue-black, a sign of gangrenous tissue. Yellow pus was suppurating along the edges. An acrid smell was also palpable. It was not a good sign.

He would have to cauterize the wound, a necessary and painful process. It was not going to be pleasant. He just hoped he did not lose consciousness before the task was completed.

Aaron placed the butt end of his rod into the fire turning it around for several minutes heating the end until it had a ring of glowing embers. He then pressed it on the wound—cauterizing it to stanch the bleeding and sterilizing the field of infection. He did not leave any area untouched that looked suspicious. His muffled screams could be heard throughout the cave. Aaron had placed his belt in his mouth to prevent him from biting his tongue. He carefully rewrapped the wound and soon passed out from his effort. Sam's unease grew with each passing minute. He felt his master's pain and witnessed his anguish. And Sam was smart enough to remember they had not yet investigated the rest of the cave.

The night passed slowly. It was pitch black outside. The only light emanated from the small fire on the floor of the cave. Sam and master were both asleep. The day had been a nightmare, a grueling episode that had finally drawn to a close. They were in an awkward spot but conditions were far worse back at the camp. The Russians had taken over and summarily executed the Japanese. The remaining surviving men had been corralled and were under heavy guard. Most of the camp had been destroyed and the Russian commanders were discussing whether it would be worthwhile to rebuild it. The Russians had killed the only medic, who was Japanese; so many of the wounded were suffering and lay untreated, moaning in the increasing cold. Many men were dying from exposure and still wearing wet clothes. Their food supplies had been pillaged and what remained was soaked and spoiling fast. Shelter was at a premium. If they went on a forced march, many more would succumb on the way. Finally the decision was made to stay the night, build a big bonfire, and those that survived until morning, would be relocated to the Russian installation. This, unknown to Aaron, was a move beneficial to him, as the Russian camp was in the opposite direction to where he was going. So the risk of being followed was greatly diminished.

The risk, however, of being picked up by another camp, was still a present danger. There were many camps in and around Texas and an ever-present Mexican border patrol keeping undocumented U.S. refugees out. Generally from what he had heard, you needed a sponsor to get into Chapultepec Park, you weren't automatically admitted. Though there were cases of exception for those who needed asylum for specific circumstances, Aaron had no idea what they were.

So the risks would be magnified as he traveled closer to the border. He would have to build up his strength and stamina if he was going to have any hope of succeeding.

If he made it through to Chapultepec Park, the Mexican border patrol would be his biggest obstacle as well as bandits like *Whitewater* who were involved in continuous human trafficking. The border was sealed with barbed wire and they used attack dogs to keep intruders at bay. Some areas could be passable, generally those that were in more barren or frozen areas. The newly revived Mexican army provided large numbers of jobs to their populace and they took their roles very seriously. There would be no mercy if they came in without proper documentation. It was ironic, as America had given clemency under a democratic regime to many of the illegal Mexicans residing in the United States before the Big Freeze. This was a peculiar twist of fate.

Something was stirring in the back of the cave again. Sam awoke. Aaron was in a deep slumber, his damaged left arm charred in spots, resting on top of his torso. He was using his right arm as a pillow. The fire was barely burning and was giving off a pale luminescence. There was movement near the far wall. Sam was frightened and started frantically digging into his master's right side. Aaron woke up just in time to see an object flash across the fire and scamper outside the cave. He followed the form outside, using a lighted branch that he quickly pulled from the fire to illuminate the ground. The tracks looked like an overlarge rodent, perhaps a large kangaroo rat, which was known to frequent parts of Texas. If the rat reappeared before sunrise, Aaron thought he would make a nice breakfast of geese and rat omelets.

They had about an hour before dawn. Aaron threw the last of the wood onto the fire. He was much warmer and felt better after a night's rest. They would have to move soon. He shared the rest of the cooked geese with Sam.

His main concern was detection. The morning light was not their friend as it illuminated the sky and showed the smoke filtering out of the cave. He wanted to avoid trouble. So they gathered up their things and started on their way. The brisk air felt like whiplash on their bodies. After the fire's warmth, it hit them like a block of ice. They searched for a few minutes to find the road. There had been a light snowfall during the night. It was nothing he was concerned about; it consisted of a soft blanket of fleece that caressed the ground. Aaron put Sam down and let him walk a while. Now that he had become acclimated to travel, Sam would have to carry his own weight unless they found themselves in a crisis situation. The arm was healing but it was still very uncomfortable throbbing periodically where his hand had been shorn off. His senses were flaring.

Aaron began wondering what happened to the Big Swede and Patches; he imagined them sturdy fellows that would manage in the wild. Too bad about Jingles, he had fond memories of the merry-maker. Aaron was thinking that the others in his bunkhouse would be surprised at his sagacity so far in lasting as long as he had against the elements. They viewed him as a "soft person" with a large intellect who was designed more for peregrinations of the mind not of the body. They liked Sam but considered him to be an experiment gone wrong; after all a dog's signature was its bark, which Sam could not perform. They were not aware of Sam's other supernormal properties.

The mesas cast a soft metallic glow over the horizon. The view ahead was very Alaskan, snow pouring over the cliffs, deep snowdrifts and icy domains dotted by tangled brier. The road had relatively shallow snow. Aaron assumed that the hard base prevented snow from accumulating as much as the surrounding areas. Although refreshed, Aaron knew they would have to keep on a strict timeline to stay alive. He hoped they would reach the hot springs by the day's end so they could be assured of another restful interlude. They would have to keep up the pace and avoid any lengthy interruptions. "Next stop on Interstate 35 is Artesia Wells!!!" He was feeling better and offered Sam this bravado shout. Unfortunately this was not the railroad where most trains get to their appointed stops. And come to think of it, he really didn't know how far the Artesia Wells really were. He had no map. And travel was going to be utterly slow.

The day wore on quickly enough. Overhead were bright blue skies and puffy white clouds that had a fine sheen to them. No sign of anyone save a lone man walking alongside his tiny dog. Sam had his nostrils flared but if he smelled something he had no way of communicating it. Aaron realized yesterday he had a lapse of judgment. He should have checked the snowmobile more thoroughly. He really needed a container to carry water and preserve fire. He also should have searched to see if there were any quantities of gasoline left in the vehicle. He was not thinking and resolved he would be more thorough in the future. Their lives depended upon him being ever vigilant.

Their march continued. They tried to stay near the boundary of the road but far enough away from it to be unseen. They wanted the option to swiftly conceal their presence should anyone or anything cross their paths. It was rough on Sam. He had soft pads on the bottom of his feet and couldn't work through the snow that well. Eventually, after a few short miles, Aaron had to carry him in his trench coat like before.

During the next few hours they passed through several valleys and were once again on what looked to be snow-drenched prairie desert. The intense cold was only bearable because they had the promise of a warm destination in mind. As far as a strategy for getting food and shelter they were depending entirely on the wings of serendipity.

The better part of Texas was not hit with as much ice and snow as the rest of the United States. This is what gave Aaron cause for hope. Areas like NYC were literally sideswiped by huge glaciers that came down from Canada. Only the tips of the very tallest buildings including the Empire State Building and the Freedom Tower in the World Trade Center site were visible. Chicago was a sheet of ice with water from the Great Lakes encasing it. Long Island, which was formed by a glacial moraine, was now just a long stretch of arctic land—its barrier islands a sea of endless icebergs.

Many people escaped on boats during the Big Freeze. Others were buried alive by the sheer volume of debris that was generated by the changes. The amount of denial and inaction on the part of many islanders was beyond comprehension. Families were just erased from the face of the earth. Even the wealthy movie actors and directors in the Hamptons moved too slowly. The rugged fishermen who harbored in Montauk were able to get out ahead of everyone else. While many of them were departing Fort Pond Bay they became witnesses to a migration of Orcas, black and white killer whales, coming into the Long Island Sound. The Montauk Lighthouse was the only structure still standing on Long Island. It was a testament to what once was.

The coming climate change had been a source of great debate among the planet's scientists. What the public knew was a small fraction of a larger story. As a climatologist Aaron had been given access to information that was considered above top secret, the highest clearance level of the U.S. Military. There was never any agreement as to the cause of all the changes. Some scientists argued, led by an Australian climatologist, that the changes were part of a larger cyclical process on earth that occurs regularly, so called "mini ice ages." He argued that this was initially offset by the industrial pollution which began in the last two centuries--producing a tempering effect on the incipient cold by raising temperatures. This was part of a natural cycle of icing that would then be replaced again by de-icing later on. Ice core analysis provided data that supported this type of thinking.

Another group, represented by the combined leadership of Greenpeace and the Sierra Club put forth a scenario similar to that depicted in "The Day after Tomorrow" where changes in temperatures in the Atlantic Conveyor Belt and Gulf Stream destabilize underwater currents that control the planet's weather via the Jet Stream. This triggered mind-numbing superstorms that ravaged and eventually chilled the planet.

A third thesis, put forth by Aaron and others at leading edge climate research institutions felt the changes were multi-factorial. Yes, the carbon concentration in the atmosphere had been increasing and causing some greenhouse effects. Yes, we were due for a "mini ice age." Yes, currents in the Atlantic conveyor belt had been weakening and causing some changes in the distribution of warm salt water and changes in wind direction and the distribution of fresh water. But the intensity of the sun was also increasing and decreasing, and photo flares and sunspots could have been playing a greater role in the evolution of climate than we were realizing. Also ozone depletion could have been a contributory factor to the creation of a hothouse then a boomerang cold climate. This was one of the areas Aaron was investigating before the Big Freeze.

He was also part of a working group testing Edward Teller's proposal to create a sun shield to block untoward effects of the sun on the surface of the planet. The fellows at MIT had vigorously studied Dr. Teller's proposition in a pentagon document entitled: "Global Warming and Ice Ages: Prospects for Physics-Based Modulation of Global Change." The U.S. government, under the auspices of the Pentagon, as early as 2010, in its Quadrennial Defense Review, had inextricably linked climate change with national security. These facts were not lost on Aaron as a young scientist considering the consequences of this unadulterated change agent. The DOD (Department of Defense) had this to say:

*"Climate change will shape the operating environment, roles, and missions that we undertake. Assessments conducted by the intelligence community indicate that climate change could have significant geopolitical impacts around the world, contributing to poverty, environmental degradation, and the further weakening of fragile governments. Climate change will contribute to food and water scarcity, will increase the spread of disease, and* **may spur or exacerbate mass migration***."*

The wind was picking up again and the clouds were thickening. He started shaking his head to Sam. Soon before them, they saw a bent sign on the side of the road. It was green on one side and badly banged up. Aaron could barely make out the white letters "Pearsall" and the number "20" faded on one of its sides. Pearsall, Aaron realized, was still some distance away from the Artesia Wells, so they were further away than he thought. Unbeknown to Aaron was that Pearsall was at the heart of "Hunter's Paradise", better known as the

Golden Triangle--when it came to hunting deer, wild hogs, turkey, and quail among other game. How many of these animals were still resident remained anybody's guess, probably a small number if any at all, but if there was somewhere that he could find something to eat, this would be the spot.

As if on cue, he detected some tracks that were leading across the road. He peered more closely, hoping that they were the tracks of another small mammal that they could hunt down and butcher for a meal.

This time, though, the tracks were a bit more unsettling. They showed the signs of a larger animal, a bear or even perhaps a larger cat like a cougar or mountain lion. It was hard to tell, the blowing snow played tricks with footprints. Aaron was not an expert on tracks. He had some outdoor amateur experience but it paled relative to that of more seasoned hunters. There had even been rumors of black leopards migrating into Texas from Mexico before the *Big Freeze*. They had started to populate the hinterlands according to some wildlife experts. The abundance of food near the border towns and corpses of the dead who did not escape the U.S. provided a continued source of sustenance.

Sammy also did not like the look of the tracks. He sniffed over them and gave Aaron a quizzical look that spoke volumes. Sam was worth his weight in gold. It was hard for Sam, though, at times. His sense of smell was so developed that it was hard to differentiate all of the sensory input he was receiving. Imagine, being in darkness leaning back in a comfortable chair in a living room, and being bombarded by a kaleidoscope of different colors, forcing their way into your field of vision. It could lead to confusion and sensory overload-- likewise sometimes Sam's power of smell was a hindrance. When he could interpret what he smelled he had trouble trying to communicate his findings.

The good news was that the tracks were leading away from where they were going. But they would have to stay on high alert. The bear encounter was still lodged in Aaron's mind. Aaron knew that hunger was a perpetual state of being on the cold prairie. He was actually forced to eat Polar Bear when he was in internment. As they were now multiplying and plentiful, hunters often shot them for food; they actually tasted like chicken, but a tad gamier. He had learned their livers contained lethal doses of Vitamin E for humans and should not be eaten under any circumstances. Usually vitamin E was a useful supplement for individuals with heart disease and diabetes, but overdosing was not recommended.

The prisoners were forced to skin the bears and degut them, which was not a pleasant task. The final product, which was protein-based, was worth it. Otherwise, they would usually eat plant-based food that was grown in their greenhouse. It was drab, mushy stuff rolled into gruel that was served on large, dirty spoons. It was like eating seaweed that was in a slow cooker for a week. Aaron wished he had some of either now.

When it was first conveyed to Aaron that he was selected out of a small group to do an Environmental Impact Study on the earth's ecosystem he was surprised. The project he was asked to review consisted of clandestinely placing small aluminum particulates airborne via commercial airliners to deflect harmful ultraviolet rays from hitting the planet's surface and to reflect the sun's rays. By reflecting the sun's ray's back into space, the hope was that this would slow down the heating of the atmosphere and the planet. It was a solar radiation management project.

When he learned more about how long the project had been in existence, he was stunned.    Apparently people never bothered to look up at the sky and notice these unusual trails.  They were virtually everywhere; their signature was a chess board configuration in the sky.  They were spread right before rainstorms for maximal effect, as they would stay suspended longer in heavier air.  Aaron had seen them all over the country, first in New England, and then in Montana, later over almost all of the metropolitan cities he visited.  Commercial airliners were retrofitted to release them in contrails; it was all done in secret, and highly classified.  The pilots were threatened to stay quiet or lose their career or their families would be smuggled away to a detention center.  No one said anything. Any brave pilots were muzzled.

He had a top-secret clearance but this was *way above top secret* according to his contact at the NSA. He was told that he and anyone else that agreed to participate in the project were expendable. If they spoke about what they had learned their families would be apprehended and they would never be seen again.

Two of the U.S. government's most urgent security concerns were climate change and the increasing scarcity of fresh water needed to support the burgeoning population. They had a program of weather modification underway since the 1960's. The quest for fresh water could be solved with mass desalination. One of the primary hurdles in transforming salt water into fresh water was the excessive cost. It was being done, with some success, in parts of Asia and the Mideast. According to government consultants the bulk of the work in improving that technology still needed to be done. In the meantime, the U.S. government funded many of their projects by selling water to China from the Great Lakes. This occurred before the *Big Freeze*.

On the climate change score, key figures in the U.S. security apparatus had determined that Edward Teller's proposal (the same man who invented the Hydrogen Bomb) was one of the least expensive options for protecting the environment. However, discovery of this, would lead to panic and possible civil chaos, including the disruption of national and international financial markets. So containment of this project was crucial for this to work to succeed. This required Aaron to take frequent trips to Caltech to get updates and to analyze data from the sprayings. No one from MIT knew where he was going; a cover story was arranged with the MIT president that Aaron was on retainer and loan to the NSA to study the ever expanding Ozone Hole above the Antarctic, which was one of his academic interests. He became a paid consultant for the government. The extra money was being channeled towards his hobbies of dirt biking and buying antique books.

The winding road was tiring them out. It passed through many types of terrain, dipping and clawing its way through the hollows of Texas. Somewhere, in the early part of their hike, they had passed near the old Lackland Air Force base outside San Antonio, Texas. This was both a strategic and tactical command and training center for the Air Force. Known for its harsh training curriculum and for launching newly minted first lieutenants for post commissions, it was a highly prized center of the military air command. Most of its graduates went on to important posts in the Air Force including working as intelligence agents dispensing disinformation about the reality of UFOs.

The base had eventually fallen out of favor and was defunded which hurt the economy of San Antonio. Area 51 in New Mexico became the preferred training site for advanced aeronautics and warfare using mind control and strategic satellite disruption.

When Lackland was in operation, weekend passes had provided airmen the opportunity to spend their saved up monies; and they spent lavishly and freely during their leaves. Rumor had it that many of the aircraft at Lackland AFB were the absconded property of a bounty hunter group called *Whitewater.*—a portion of which was a non-affiliated group of ex-pilots and ex-airline mechanics that transformed aging fleet into lower-flying surveillance aircraft that had hydroplaning devices to land in snow. Many Cubans who had worked secretly for the CIA were now in charge of the material and planes at the abandoned air force base. They were paid with commodities like gold and silver that were still being mined, and they were hired to capture runaway prisoners and to occasionally firebomb various unpopular camps by rivals. There was also an international cartel that was part of *Whitewater* specializing in human trafficking.

Aaron had nearly forgotten the Whitewater group, so-called because the men wore heavy white uniforms to camouflage themselves; they also painted their planes a glossy white to shield and hide them. Once airborne, all this stealth was a bit redundant as the roar of the planes could never be mistaken for anything else. If the Russians made contact with this group, that was another source of consternation, as their reconnaissance would include his coordinates, of that he was sure. He just hoped that the paperwork on the camp's census had been burned during the devastation.

As they approached the outskirts of Pearsall, night was unleashing her bony dark fingers. They found another road sign, as broken up as before, citing 2 miles to Pearsall, another 46 to Artesia Wells. Signage evidently was still in some working order in Texas. If he was in Chicago or Minnesota, farther North, he doubted he would have the same luck in uncovering any buried signs; the snow was deeper and piled up much higher.

The problem, tonight, again, was the quest for shelter and food. His left arm was still a medical issue. It was no longer pulsing around the stump but it had started to lose its feeling, either from the numbing cold, or perhaps because of some collateral nerve damage brought on by the initial trauma and amputation. It was beginning to unravel him and it was becoming more of a distraction. He was holding Sammy against his chest with his left arm and he couldn't gauge how much pressure he was exerting on the dog. But no matter how tight he squeezed, Sam knew his master loved him.

Rolling hills, featuring sienna and sinopia hues, were starting to dominate the landscape. Out in the fields, a feral cry from a great horned owl and a lonely falcon echoed through the prairie. He knew they dwelled in this habitat but could not distinguish one cry from the other. Birds, whatever their pedigree, were turning to scavenging to survive.

The way ahead looked blocked. A big yellow school bus was lying on its side in the road. It was badly crumpled on one side and had dirt and snow firmly matted to the other side. Aaron felt hollow. Seeing a school bus reminded him of his own children and his family's deaths at the hands of an avalanche. As they got closer, carefully trying to stay out of sight as they did so, Aaron spotted a bus driver's cap. It was frozen to the ground, blue and bloodstained. He tried to pull it free but was unable to do so. He was able to dislodge it with his walking stick. He read the emblem on the hat. It read "Laredo School District." His heart thumped. He guessed the bus had been going south when it careened out of control. Aaron hypothesized it was going back to Laredo from San Antonio on a field trip, perhaps after visiting a tourist site like the Alamo. Whatever the reason, it probably occurred during the onset of the Big Freeze, or else state or local authorities would have removed the bus and the debris. He calculated that this accident was at least 3 years old. There was slim hope that there was anything he could use but he would poke around.

He peered inside the dilapidated vehicle and saw that the seats were in total disarray with bent steel hinges and rusted door latches. The roof was caved in from the impact and the windows were cracked in assorted spots but had not broken free. The steering wheel was disconnected and tilted downwards. Some snow had worked its way into the vehicle through the retractable door but for the most part the bus was still weatherproof and its hull intact. He judged this might be a good place to hold up for the night. It provided shelter and there was the potential to find some needed supplies for his journey.

He exited the bus and looked around. What he saw next was a disturbing sight. On the perimeter close to the bus was a ragged pile of bones. They were old and cracked and barely visible because ice had baked into them. Leaning down on all fours, he examined the bones finding that many had teeth marks on them. Some of his worst fears were realized--the bones were smaller than adult's. He also noticed strands of white fleecy fur embedded in the bones and on the surface of the ice.

Aaron intentionally focused on retrofitting the bus into a more comfortable short-term abode and started his search for food. He needed to control the ebb and flow of emotions that were streaming into his consciousness. Activity would cure that.

His first priority was to look for a first aid kit. Most buses carried them, especially if their cargo was school kids. He crawled into the cab of the bus. The entrance was now on top, as the bus was on its side. He tried to avoid any sharp edge caused from all the buckling. He proceeded slowly on his hands and knees, sweeping the chassis with his eyes for useful implements. In the back of the bus, Aaron found what he was looking for latched onto the bottom of the bathroom door. It was the square white case with a red cross that caught his attention. He carefully removed it from its mountings and carried it out of the bus. Curled on a flattened tire, Sam was waiting patiently for his Aaron to return. He was exhausted and hungry wondering what his master was up to. He thought maybe this kit was full of dog food or at least some yummy dog biscuits. The dog crowded Aaron as he tried to pry open the plastic clips that held the kit closed tight. Pulling with some difficulty the jammed clips off, the mystery was soon revealed: antiseptic wraps, hydrocortisone cream, Betadine, Band-Aids, gauze, and surgical scissors comprised most of the first aid kit. It was a bounty as far as Aaron was concerned; a disappointing find for Sam.

Aaron redressed his wound with clean gauze and plenty of antiseptic. Feeling was beginning to come back into his arm and the area that was exposed was no longer pulsating and the fact that it was draining was a healthy development. He was pleased, as these were good signs that pointed to not only improvement in the arm but an eventual recovery.

He decided to go back into the bus and scrounge around some more. He noted that the area around them did not offer much in the way of sustenance nor cover. He calculated that the substantial snow piled around the bus provided enough cover with the evening coming on. So he decided to stay the night, figuring he could work out more details tomorrow.

When he retired, he coaxed Sammy inside the bus. He placed the dog near one of the seats close to the entrance. He checked the driver's area for supplies. He opened up the glove compartment box and found some maps. There was a detailed Rand McNally roadway map of Texas that he could use. He folded it up so that it fit into the first aid kit. He also found a multi-tool Swiss Army knife that would be useful; it had a can opener, little rip saw, corkscrew, two different types of screwdrivers, (flathead and Philips), and a few different retractable blades. The only thing missing was a gutting knife. He also uncovered some old batteries that were leaking and a stained Dallas Cowboys coffee mug. Also there were some pictures from a calendar shoot of the Dallas Cowboy cheerleaders; these warmed up his otherwise dampened spirit. Apparently the driver was a football fan or at least an aficionado of well put together women.

Exploring further, Aaron unearthed the mother lode. Underneath the driver seat wrapped inside an old Navajo blanket was a box of flares, a rain poncho, and some tins of Spam and Beef Jerky covered by saran wrap. Apparently the driver had a yen for salty snacks; perhaps he was a native Indian. This would sustain them a few more days if they rationed the calories wisely.

He knew the flares could be used in a myriad of ways for defense or in emergency situations. The knife could serve to start a fire used with his flint. The blanket would provide additional warmth and could be converted into a makeshift knapsack. It was a good haul.

Before it was dark, Aaron reminded himself that he should rip apart some of the seats and use the padding as tinder for the fire. But for right now he opened the Spam with his Swiss knife and scooped out a small feast of salted beef he shared with Sam. This *mystery meat* never tasted so good—even the fact that is was over-saturated with sodium nitrite did not bother Aaron, who definitely preferred organic products before the Big Freeze. He recalled a little known fact that sodium nitrite at certain concentrations can be used as an antidote for cyanide poisoning—a fact that was not lost on Aaron but one that had no relevance to his present situation. What did have relevance is that the strong scent of Spam could attract unwelcome visitors that he needed to be wary of.

Teller's proposal for the sun shield was mythologized and popularized by U.S. conspiracy theorists as *chemtrails*. This was a very different entity from contrails, which are vaporized trails emitted by high-flying aircraft. Chemtrails, according to the conspiracy crowd, was a global program administered by the U.S. government using high-flying commercial and military aircraft to disperse sun reflecting compounds in the upper atmosphere. One of the more troubling ingredients was the use of barium as it was known to have nasty effects on human beings. There was a gap between what the public knew and what was actually true. Being that all the work around this Top Secret enterprise was compartmentalized Aaron did not have full disclosure himself. He did know that the "shield" seemed to be working; global temperatures were decreasing, but weather patterns became increasingly erratic. Drenching storms and hurricanes were fiercer, wildfires were more common, especially in the Pacific Northwest and Canada, and flooding became a global problem. There was a nonhomogeneous impact on weather systems. It was attributed to natural earth cycles.

Weather modification was in its infancy and much was yet to be learned and determined. His job was to monitor not so much the health consequences to people by these government actions, but to investigate the interaction between the fallout from the atmospheric Chemtrails and the effect on the ecology of the landmasses. Citizens on various web sites in the public domain were reporting strange anomalies on the ground. Unknown to the public, these were being monitored by clandestine agencies, like Aaron's, around the globe.

They huddled in closer, man and dog, intently watching the men in the helicopter using binoculars to survey the area. Thankfully, it was getting dark, and their footprints would be hard to see, unless the helicopter came in for a closer view or decided to land. After a few minutes, however, they disappeared as suddenly as they came. They did throw down a red marker not too far from them, but other than that left no hint of their arrival or departure.

The red marker, Aaron conjectured, was either to mark the spot as being worthy of further investigation, or just the opposite, that the site had been checked and was secure. In either case, he planned to leave by early morning's light.

Aaron shredded some of the seats into fire tinder and fashioned others to make a comfortable bed for the night. They slept near the front of the bus and kept the door slightly ajar so smoke could escape easily into the night air. He also burned the wood trim that was around the seats to sustain the fire longer until morning. It gave off a slightly noxious smell, but the warmth that the fire provided was worth the risk.

Nighttime was quiet with the exception of the rustling wind and the occasional spooky sounds that one either really hears or imagines when sleeping out. They awoke without fanfare and Aaron refreshed the fire. He stepped outside and started towards the rear of the bus when he saw something. There was a ring of large, fresh footprints--that had circled the bus. They were unmistakably polar bear tracks due to their size. A new conundrum emerged-- was this the same polar bear that they had left with the lemming? Or was it another bear stalking them? Aaron was unsure. His decision to leave was heightened. They had some Beef Jerky and leftover soup then gathered their belongings and headed out. He would have liked to stay another night but the twin risks of discovery by *Whitewater* or being stalked by a bear was too great a gamble.

In case of an encounter, he would keep a road flare handy. Hopefully the bear would disengage, razed by 1400 degrees of burning fury. *Whitewater was another issue.* He did not have a plan to contend with the *Whitewater* thugs. Hide and Seek was his best ploy.

Up ahead, he could see that the sky was dominated by an azure glow. Solferino etched hills cast crazy lazy shadows on the snow. Images of beasts and mythical creatures like Charybdis edged into Aaron's mind.

It was a short walk to Pearsall. He wrapped up his supplies in the blanket that he found in the bus and constructed a sling to carry it over his back. This way he could still hold Sammy if needed, when the dog could not walk. Even though he was a bit harried, he made a point of bringing along what he could retrieve from the bus. He brought the empty can of Spam to act as a water ferrying and cooking container; he also checked the bus's gas tank but found it punctured and emptied of fuel. He did take some of the wiring out of the engine to act as rope or as hanging lines should he need it.

They left the safety and comfort of the bus and returned to the trail. Before starting out, he studied his new toy, the Texas roadmap, which also contained a significant chunk of the Mexican border. He noticed that Interstate 35 bypassed what was left of the main part of the town. That was a good thing, he did not want to be ambushed or surprised by any interlopers. With the extra weight he was now carrying, his ability to run and flee was diminished. He was also starting to feel chronically exhausted. The rest he had the night before had helped him recover to a degree but he found he lost energy much quicker than he had in the past. The constant exposure and ceaseless walking had taken its toll. He struggled to keep hold of himself. The cache of food and supplies he had taken from the bus was a bright spot in an otherwise uncertain future. He knew any choices he made would be critical in determining their destiny.

In the early days of the weather modification experiments, Aaron had traveled strictly in the U.S. He went to locations in Wisconsin, the Dakotas, Washington State, West Virginia, and Long Island, NY to assess both inland and coastal impacts of the spraying. He was part of a team that included a botanist, marine biologist, microbiologist, etymologist, industrial toxicologist and forensic biologist. After a year or so, they were also asked to go to foreign nations to do environmental impact studies. There was another team that studied the human effects. Aaron's team focused on animal and plant studies and its interaction with the aerial spraying, although occasionally their work overlapped.

The spraying was done usually before a forecasted rainstorm. It was believed that the particles would remain airborne longer and then be neutralized and filtered by nature's most abundant substance, water.

All was quiet, in the beginning. Then there came a spate of reports about honeybees not being able to reproduce, the so-called colony collapse disorder (CCD), frogs being genetically altered born with more than one head or more than four legs; strange deformed dogs roaming the desert (nicknamed chupacabras by the locals); and a whole list of other oddities that went unexplained.

Something was not right with the planet. Aaron, as a principal investigator, was designated as part of the early warning system to pave the way towards greater understanding of the climate and environmental problems. Their goal was to assess whether geo-engineering interventions were working, including positive effects and unintended negative consequences.

The scientists hailed from all the great research centers in the U.S.: Caltech, MIT, Princeton, Harvard, and Johns Hopkins University. This brain trust had the best possibility of finding the answers to the problems afoot. *The alternative of not knowing was not an option…it was felt by powers high in a clandestine part of the government that the planet was in serious trouble. These power brokers were taking care of themselves, building vast underground structures to survive the oncoming hardships, but the list of people to be saved was a closely guarded secret.* As far as Aaron was concerned, the thought of living underground in bunkers held no pleasure; it would have been another sort of imprisonment.

They arrived at Pearsall without incident. In the distance, they could see what was left of Main Street. A cell tower poked its head out from among the snow and rubble and a few stray telephone poles, wires and all, were leaning, ready to fall down. This would be a find for someone, as most of the telephone poles had been removed for firewood. They burned for a long time and the decoupling process of removing ice from wood went very smoothly compared to the frozen timber that was hauled from the open fields. The only problem with the poles was that many had been chemically treated and contained wood preservatives that had dioxins which were harmful to humans. Before the freeze, there were still 135 million poles that had these compounds on them. About 3% of them were replaced yearly in an effort to meet newer, stricter EPA guidelines.

Unfortunately when the first storms arrived on the plains, towns like Pearsall had become kind of a backstop and collection point for the glacial flows that followed. The inhabitants as well as the towns themselves were thoroughly buried by an onrush of wind borne sediment, dust, and snowy effluent. Many of the residents were buried alive while sleeping in their beds much in the same way many New Orleans residents drowned in homes during the floods from Katrina. Other folks perished in transit. Over time a few that survived were able to form small communal camps. These camps, sparsely dotted over the land, were a potential haven for Aaron. Unfortunately their locations were secret and not coded on maps. There were also a small number of people who escaped the cold by taking boats off the U.S. mainland to South America and to other warm countries beyond. Their safe departure only further hastened Aaron's desire to succeed in his mission. Only the words "Chapultepec Park" ringing occasionally in Aaron's ears, sustained his sanity, promising an alternate version of Shangri-La, *a new horizon if you will*, that promised sanctuary from the apocalyptic U.S. mainland and the start of a new life.

He mulled over going further into town to climb among the rubble and search for useful implements and supplies. But in his view, the risks clearly outweighed the benefits. The slopes that had formed around the buildings were treacherous and he would expend large amounts of energy trying to dig through this frozen encasement to find anything of value. He didn't know if the polar bear was tracking them; and he anticipated Whitewater patrols could be nearby. The dog was also uneasy again, trembling with trepidation; Aaron looked for telltale signs of trouble as he cautiously moved on.

The town was not very wide or very long and they passed around it easily, keeping a wide distance between themselves and the outskirts of Pearsall. All seemed well until Aaron spied a small figure mounted above the ground several hundred feet away. From his vantage point Aaron could not calculate the distance between his position and this lonely outcrop. He elected to go further "off-road" and climb a large boulder that provided a better view.

Aghast, he was now able to see a man with both his arms and legs dangling off a crooked telephone pole. The posture of the body looked eerily familiar. He was large and appeared well-built with small streams of blood curdling out of one corner of his mouth. Aaron climbed down the boulder and grasped Sam tightly under his coat as he walked forward towards the man. He tried to keep out of sight as he went along, scuttling among the many mangled scrubby bushes that were scattered along the road. His fear was starting to grow, welling out from the innermost parts of his body. His heart was racing like a thousand racehorse fish fleeing a trawler's deep-water nets. Seeing the cold, pallid man had sent goose bumps up and down his spine. He started to shiver and his vision started to waver.

It was the *Big Swede*, impaled in part by his own poking stick that he had used a few days ago to batter a Russian. His hands and legs were fastened to the poles by nailed clasps. He looked like a gladiator on the Appian Way, eyes oozing a purulent discharge, completely in shock.

Amazingly, he was alive and trying to gesture. He weakly pointed towards the middle of town trying to articulate a word. Aaron, attempting to hear him, leaned in closer. *"Whitewater,"* he gurgled one last time before caving in to his injuries. To Aaron's horror, *"Whitewater" had been tattooed in bloody letters across his chest,* a final act of barbarity, *or was this a warning?*

Aaron did not know what to do. Greatly saddened, he realized he could not tarry; he needed time to think but it was more important at this juncture to act fast. He could not cut the Swede down, as that would raise suspicion and could lead the Whitewater bounty hunters to him. He didn't understand why they didn't keep the Big Swede alive and sell him back to another camp—after all; bounty hunting was their business. He speculated that the Big Swede had been entangled in a mishap or was ambushed by one of the Whitewater guards and this was payback. Whatever the case, Aaron was not going to ignore the warning, he carefully stole away, heading further south down Interstate 35, and did not look back until he was many miles away.

The day proceeded peacefully enough, although a dark feeling of dread constantly drove its ugly spikes into Aaron's mind. The earth, ultimately, was a friendless, savage place. Mankind and womankind had elevated the planet into a swirling, commercial enterprise that masked its inherent brutality. Now, *on the road,* Aaron realized the taming of the planet was a cruel joke played on everyone. We were never in charge, our status as the dominant force on the planet was always suspect and under siege; we were slowly slipping off the highest steps of evolution into the darkest holes that historians could possibly imagine. The *Big Freeze* event was so different from what people previously experienced in the last two thousand years that the minds of most people were in a state of perpetual torpor. But Aaron and Sam were highly evolved, light beings in a field of slumbering souls.

They were still a considerable distance from Artesia Wells. They stopped in a sheltered area to light a fire. Aaron rubbed the flint against his knife to create some sparks that after several tries resulted in a small fire. They chewed on some Beef Jerky and melted some ice for water. The sky was a crystalline blue, extending outwards like a swan swimming in a never-ending river of life. The cold was constant, but the fire made it more bearable. Aaron thought once or twice that he heard the drone of airships or some other flying vehicle in the distance. He was a little spooked, he admitted, from the encounter with the Big Swede. *The Swede's lifeless eyes stamped were into his consciousness.*

He was wondered if cargo jetliners were still dropping their fusillade of chemicals into the stratosphere south of the Cold Zone where it was warmer, but much hotter than the previous normal for those latitudes.

The original intent of the team Aaron was part of was to study habitats including the ocean ecology, as well as assessing livestock and crop effects to safeguard the food chain for living things. It was a tall order and it all had to be done surreptitiously. Land rovers and ocean-going vessels were leased in secrecy. Aaron was given leadership of his group, responsible for collating data from the others, and delivering summary reports to the Pentagon and the NSA.

The anomalies that were being reported seemed to have a common thread. At first, it was not readily apparent what that thread was. Phytoplankton that was the foundation for the ocean food chain was steadily decreasing. On the land, the collapse of honeybee colonies was having a similar pronounced negative effect on the food chain and the production of crops. The crash of one or both of these vital creatures would have insurmountable global repercussions on the food supply. This was a very serious conundrum that needed solving. Unknown to the public, huge amounts of resources went into trying to solve the problem. Many folks thought that the near financial collapse of the U.S. economy was due to a housing crisis in 2008. It was due to the CIA and NSA pouring huge amounts of money into black hole operations like Aaron's, in an attempt to stall the near collapse of the ecology of the earth. The government deficit was being buttressed by U.S. financial institutions that were borrowing large sums of money from the World Bank. The ripple effect was toppling markets internationally.

The data that was collected from fifty states eventually seemed to shed some light on the matter. The weather modification aerial spraying and the food supply problem were inextricably linked. Unintended substances that formed in the highest layers of the atmosphere were infiltrating critical life support systems of earth. We were poisoning ourselves and nobody seemed to notice except in the highest levels of government and for a few activists. This was going on for years before anyone really made the connections.

Night was approaching and Aaron started feeling anxious again. Every day on the road had its ups and downs, the grueling and tiresome walking, the constant need for evasive maneuvers from *Whitewater and animal predators*; the iridescent brilliance of the winter wonderland, all having profound effects on his psyche. There was an inescapable albeit ironic harmony to this land where life was played out in all its intricate details. Birth and death were converging life forces that steadied the chaotic junctures. The passage of time was like the stillness on the water's edge, rippling into infinity and nothingness. He often reflected back on his stable past and how now he had slowly lost his grip on the series of future events that seemed ready to engulf him and Sam. Would they survive? What horrible fate would befall them? Could they make the long haul down to Chapultepec Park? Like barrages out of a Gatling gun, questions like these forced their way into Aaron's consciousness. In the new apocalyptic U.S., freedom was an exquisite luxury, a solitary reminder that without it everything else becomes unbearable.

He looked at his map. He estimated they were about 20 miles away from Artesia Wells. They would need to find another stopover. For this to happen, they would have to either get lucky, like when they found the bus and cave, or they would have to brave the cold in an open less sheltered environment where they would be pounded by cold winds. The second scenario scared him. The wind, when blowing strong, produced wind chills that could quickly lead to hypothermia.

Overall Aaron felt his constitution was stronger than before but self-analysis in these conditions could be deceiving. He was in more of an anabolic state than he was when he first escaped, but the amputation was working incessantly stealing precious reserves. Most people with his level of exposure would have already succumbed to the elements. Only his tremendous drive and high emotional intelligence were keeping him and his dog alive.

The wind, originating from the Northern zones, was starting to swirl in concentric patterns. It was becoming colder. In the new ice age that had emerged, it was possible to get a new brand of tornado that packed ice and hail that was more punishing than the warmer weather driven variety of tornado. Virtually any object in its path, whether animate or inanimate, was disintegrated by the icy foment. It left huge telltale cicatrices on the land, a series of undulating impact craters.

Aaron was afraid that this was the beginning of one of those storms. He sought shelter immediately. They were still a distance away from Pearsall at this point. He saw through the snow several varieties of cacti. Atop one of them he saw a torn sheet and some confetti, which looked odd considering the snowy landscape. Ahead of them lay several hundred acres of open wasteland marked by drifting snow and windswept terrain. He felt a powerful wind pushing him forward causing him nearly to slip. A slow surging wind had now turned into a crying squall. About a mile away, he spied another culvert, between intersecting roads. They hurried towards it, hoping to outrun the escalating wind. Tornadoes in Texas were commonplace and an overpass provided some protection against its fury. With the wind pounding their backs and the cold sending chills down their spines, Aaron and Sam navigated down the culvert into the comfort of the overpass.

Someone had been here recently. A pile of ashes revealed bones that could have been the remains of any small creature. Smaller fragments of bones were also scattered outside the fire. Relief soon turned into fear as Aaron considered the possibilities. Was this another runaway? Was *Whitewater* on this person's trail? Although an unlikely scenario, this could put them into further jeopardy.

Peering further into the snow, he saw the profile of something bright and shiny. He took out his knife to dig it out and uncovered an object, both blunt and bloodied. Twirling it a few times in his hand, he was able to remove the snow from its surface. It looked chillingly familiar. Then like the torrent of water released from a dam, Aaron recognized it as Patches coarse knife. "Sam, we are not alone," he stated. Without knowing the circumstances, Aaron hoped that Patches was still alive, wherever he was. Any tracks that were visible would be long erased by the pitching winds. The discovery of blood on the knife, however, was vexing to Aaron.

They still had a little bit of dried beef left and some canned stew devoured. Out over the horizon, Aaron could see that harrowing winds were zigzagging across the land. It started snowing again, but thankfully the overpass blocked out most of the precipitation. Aaron found some small twigs and a few slender branches that Patches evidently left behind. In a short time, he started a small fire along the sheltered edge of the concrete walls of the overpass. Aaron and the dog circled the fire to shield it from errant drafts. Aaron knew it was going to be a *long night* if the bad weather continued. Fortunately, after an hour or two, the storm subsided and calm was restored to the darkening land. Aaron excitedly remarked to Sam: "See, there is still hope, if we look hard enough for it."

His run of luck continued when he found some old, crumpled rags which he tossed into the fire. There were enough dried-out branches stockpiled to pass most of the night in relative heat and comfort. They sat close to the wall where the fire burned and were able to rest for quite some time, their only bed being the hard earth underneath them. It was a moonless night, utterly quiet. Still in the morning, they awoke cold and shivering. Aaron rekindled the fire. Although refreshed they remained miserable, tired, and were not looking forward to another long day in the wilderness.

The heat shield did its job for a while. Median temperatures across the globe had steadied. Some areas even saw a small downward slide in temperatures. The geo-engineering of the weather became a practical possibility for the first time in the history of mankind. The inner circle of scientists slapped each other on the back, praised their ingenuity, and started to consider military applications for this technology. Not much time passed, though, before the strange reports started to circulate catching the scientists' attention.

Citizens were reporting a skin lesion that was later called Morgellons Disease. It included intense itchiness and formation of lesions on the skin at various points on the body. Physicians who treated it categorized it as "delusional parasitosis", a complex form of mental illness that manifested itself physically on the body. Over time, as more cases were discovered, first identified by concerned laymen then by government scientists, another culprit emerged. During the time of the aerial spraying strange white fibers were being discharged over the land. These fibers were being breathed in by the unsuspecting populace and were severely compromising the health of their human hosts. One of the industrial toxicologists who worked later on Aaron's team made the connection. These fibers were also being linked to the destruction of the oceanic and terrestrial food chains.

The government soon went into a panic mode and that was when Aaron was first contacted. He had heard some disturbing information from one of his MIT associates that the aerial spray contained living microorganisms that were spliced to nanorobots. This provided a platform for the chemicals to stay afloat longer in the upper atmosphere. The longer the particles remained airborne the longer the shield worked in reflecting light off of the earth's surface. These were bio-engineered by Caltech and some private corporations like DUPONEX to withstand the colder temperatures of the stratosphere where the aerosols were released. Some of the early testing was done on Long Island, over Montauk Point, where there were less people and where a military base that specialized in covert operations was located that could provide cover.

Unfortunately, many of these nanoparticles were reassembling themselves on the ground and foraging on people and animals, where they bore into tissue. After several weeks, they would re-emerge on the skin as unusual moles or pustules or as infected fever blisters, not before causing much internal damage to their hosts. People had either very severe autoimmune responses to these invaders that sometimes ended in coma and death, or they suffered from septic shock that was equally as debilitating, some people even developed leukemia and rare lymphomas. These effects were tied to the overall syndrome of Morgellons disease, but were not limited to this new ailment; they sometimes operated independently without causing skin eruptions.

If this wasn't bad enough, Aaron's team discovered that bees were picking up the nanoparticles during the pollination process and they were brought back to the beehives where they systematically destroyed the queen bee and her colony. Also, the nanoparticles were dropping into the ocean and attaching themselves to phytoplankton, the basic nutrient in the marine food chain for many types of animals, including whales and other fish, putting extreme pressure on the marine ecosystem, causing slow but systematic phytoplankton extinction.

Many foreign countries were finding the same phenomenon across the globe. A tremendous cover-up was put in place to silence any whistleblowers. The rash of mysterious scientist deaths around the year 2001 was a point of mystery in the academic community that had its roots in this cover-up.

It was very difficult for Aaron to separate what was fact and what was fiction as every department within the government was compartmentalized. No one had access to other teams' data files unless there was "a need to know." Much of the information Aaron amassed was in the variety of "filling in the blanks" by looking for connections between what he heard from the proverbial scientist rumor mill around the water cooler and what he observed in the field.

All he really knew for sure was that there was urgency to the work he was doing and that the fates of many peoples' lives were at stake.

By the time they got up and were ready to move on, the sun's bright rays were in full view over the horizon. The past evening's cold had winnowed itself into a bearable day. Sam seemed heavier under his coat and for Aaron each step forward was a painful reminder of their predicament. The light at the end of the tunnel would be crossing the border into Mexico and reaching the *Warm Zone* that could be found after Monterrey. Their final victory would be their march into Chapultepec Park. For now, they had to content themselves that Patches was still alive, possibly nearby, and a potential ally in the case of danger. Aaron presumed that *Whitewater* could also be stalking them while looking for Patches. The good news was that the Big Swede did not know about their escape, so any interrogation of him would have yielded no clues to their whereabouts.

Their latest goal was to make Artesia Wells by nightfall so they could spend additional time recuperating. They still had a few cans of food left, but they were meager provisions compared to what they needed in caloric intake to withstand the cold and to escape starvation. The intensity of the cold and the impediments while walking they encountered made their caloric needs soar.

Aaron knew Artesia Wells could be a double-edged sword—a place to revive oneself and gain strength but also a destination for other travelers, who might have more malicious intentions than he and Sam. They would have to be wary of wayward strangers and keep a watch out for fortified, unfriendly-looking camps.

More snow-covered fields lay ahead of Aaron as they followed the interstate to the left around several small, sloping hills. His feet were very sore but he had new boots. The Big Swede would be happy to know that his shoe size was close to Aaron's. He had buried the old shoes under some shrubs well off the road. If his wife could see him now she would hardly recognize him. He had one stubby arm, a shaggy beard pleated with frozen snow, and an unkempt, anorexic appearance; he was a shadow of himself. His visage would undoubtedly send shock waves down The Ray and Maria Stata Center at MIT where he once roamed. In its present state it could be found in the Charles River, driven deep into the mud by an advancing glacier. The once proud white palatial marble stone that formed its base was frozen solid and cracked in several places by the force of outside elements.

MIT and many other great learning institutions in the U.S. had been destroyed by the onset of climate change. Most of the information from these centers was lost, only that which was stored in electronic databases in South America was retained. The first storms had mauled buildings and people, catching both unawares and unprepared for the onslaught that followed. Institutions were swallowed up; their libraries were entombed by a frozen mix of snow and sleet. There was not enough time for data back-ups or any opportunity to transmit information elsewhere. The advancing snows were a nightmare eventually making formidable ice cauldrons of all the major cities.

The turn before them banked and then climbed a steep hill, at an unusual ascent for Texas. The air was crisp and purified by the constant driving snow. The lack of industrial pollution had eliminated the smog; only the smoke from fires and incendiary battles continued to foul the atmosphere.

As bad as he felt, Aaron would give anything for a strong cup of aromatic coffee. The coffee at the camp was like drinking blackened campfire soot. One of his daily habits before the freeze was having a morning cup of coffee with his wife Lola. She was an early riser and he remembered how the White Mountain Coffee she served would waft into their bedroom while he was still dozing. It provided comfort and a jolt to jumpstart his day. One of his upcoming desires was to find a way to make a good cup of coffee in the wild. The food and beverages at the camps were notoriously bad; perhaps they would stumble upon a settlement that could supply this wish.

They marched up the hill to get a panoramic view of a vast winter-scape. For miles as far as the eye could see, the countryside was marked by vanilla-coned hilltops and flat congruous land. Initially, Aaron's eyes were fixated on the breathtaking scenery. Then appearing at first dimly then sharply into his field of vision, Aaron saw some smoke rising in the distance. He reasoned this could either be an indication of a lone survivor or the demarcation of a camp or some other settlement in the area. Aaron made the decision to slowly move ahead and investigate. Just in case of a close encounter, he pulled the flares from his haversack. They could be used in a pinch as defense in close combat but were principally designed to function as signal flares. Aaron had learned some self-defense from one of his comrades at the camp, but he was a long way from being classified a Navy Seal. His internment in the camp had been a learning laboratory for many things: how to ward off starvation, how to compete for bunk space, how to avoid scuffles at the latrine and the development of physical survival in subzero temperatures. It was the physical rigor that tested his mettle now.

"Sammy, we can't survive by ourselves, I just hope we are making the right decision," Aaron remarked as they strolled towards the black wisps of smoke. He held a canister of one of the flares in his good hand. He was prepared to pull the starter plug if necessary, and scald an attacker. He would have to grab the starter coil with his teeth to do so. They haltingly made their way down the road, turning off to perch on some large rocks where they could see more clearly the terrain ahead. He felt his breathing, realizing the veil between consciousness and unconsciousness, was merely his ability to take in oxygen. Life and death were on either sides of this curtain.

Five men sat in a circle below them, dressed in bright, lively colors. It reminded Aaron of the Nigerian native clothing he had seen once at an African religious festival at MIT. That was a merry occasion; these men looked mean and miserable. Each one of them looked battle-hardened and was carrying a machete and had ammunition bandoliers crisscrossing their shoulders. The rifles looked fairly modern and powerful. They all had long, tangled dread-locks. He noticed some type of insignia embroidered into the back of their jackets, but at his current distance, Aaron was unable to identify it. He had heard of a few African camps composed solely of gunrunners who competed with the Cubans for business. These men were vicious and had experience in the Civil Wars in Nigeria and Mozambique which were some of the most politically unstable hot spots on the planet. Without hesitation they had massacred women and children and had a long history of extreme violence. In short, they were tough customers, not the type of people you would want to share a friendly campfire with and have a sing-along.

And in the midst of them, to Aaron's dismay, sat Patches. He looked far removed from the Southern gentleman he once was. He was disheveled, disoriented, and not bemused. His silver white hair was bloodied, like someone had slammed him on the side of the head with a baton. He had his hands tied behind his back and a tether attached to his waist. One of the men was jerking it occasionally trying to discourage him from falling asleep. *Was this a torturing action or were they trying to keep him awake for a pick-up?* Aaron could not be sure. He speculated that the smoke trail was designed to alert another party to their presence.

While watching the man pull on the tether again, Aaron noticed something else. The tether was attached to the ring of a hand grenade. He was terrorizing Patches, there was no doubt about it, but for what reason remained unclear to Aaron.

It was about midday and getting colder not warmer. Shapeless and ugly clouds inebriated the sky. Hidden behind a wall of boulders, Aaron and Sam were situated about thirty feet above the group of men. It would be suicide to make an approach during broad daylight. They would have to just wait it out. It would be easy to track the men if they moved off. Aaron hoped it would be in a southerly direction, because if the marauders went north, they would surely see his tracks. Then he would be in more serious trouble.

He calculated from his map that they were about 3 to 5 miles from Artesia Wells. There was relief in that direction, but if the men headed there, that would also pose a problem. He imagined the hot springs cleansing his body and spirit, suspending him above the cold land with heat spiraling off his body in every direction; the thought of it sent him into a reverie. Close to passing out, he awoke suddenly and realized that these dreams would have to wait until he found a way to rescue Patches. Sam was looking at him quizzically, seeing in his mind's eye a different vision, a flickering image of Aaron burning at the stake.

Eventually the men packed up their belongings and headed out in the direction of Artesia Wells. They tied Patches' hands behind his back with the tether and removed the grenade. Aaron kept a safe distance behind as the men methodically followed the contours of the road ahead of them. They had large cleated boots that left indelible marks in the snow. As they were top-heavy with arms, they travelled at a plodding pace. Aaron had no trouble keeping up with them. They looked constantly at the sky, either anticipating an ambush or waiting for a friendly aircraft to guide them to an as yet undisclosed location. One of the men was limping noticeably and constantly falling behind the others. Perhaps he had slipped on the ice and had an injury or had a congenital deformity it was hard to tell. The others frequently turned around and exhorted him to move faster. With each passing minute, he seemed to be slowing his pace, falling farther behind. He was older than the others and sported a grey shaggy beard that was also twisted into a tangled mess of dreadlocks.

They went on for another 2 miles or so, in a long, ragged single file: the elder statesman ever drifting further away from his comrades. He was getting weaker and seemed to be pointing towards his mouth; Aaron thought perhaps he was thirsty. He proceeded to shout something loud in an unknown language towards the other group and started to gesticulate wildly with his hands when out of the corner of his eyes Aaron saw a large, lumbering form moving towards the man. It came out of the brush, at breakneck speed, and grabbed hold of the man with a gigantic claw. The animal flipped the man, slashed his sides, and put its enormous weight on the man's chest caving in his ribs and puncturing his lungs in the process. The man started bleeding profusely and had only seconds to live when his companions rearing back reacted to his terrified screams.

Aaron realized immediately this bear was the one that had been stalking them since their overnight stay at the abandoned school bus. They had precious moments to act and take advantage of the situation.

While the African men went to assist their friend, Aaron ran across the road and carefully advanced along the opposite side towards Patches, who was now sitting alone on the ground. He avoided coming into the open until he reached Patches. The Africans were busy warding off the bear. He cut

Patches' bonds with his knife and gestured for him to be quiet as they stole away along the brush line.

They looked back to see the Polar Bear facing off against the men. They had started shooting the bear but the bear had managed to take hold of another one of them, and they had to be careful for fear of shooting each other instead of the bear. It was starting to take the look of a blood bath. The last thing Aaron and Patches heard was a mixture of snarls and high-pitched screams that echoed over the valley. They hurried on.

Despite the joy of reuniting with Patches, Aaron was upset as new calculations proved Artesia Wells was still a distance away. He had wrongly estimated the town's location. The topography of the land had changed so much it was next to impossible to judge distances. His map needed updating for all of the earth changes.

Road signs had been moved or abandoned, large chunks of soil and concrete had been broken apart and entire highways were shifted due to erosion and moving glaciers. The ceaseless snow had covered many familiar landmarks. It was like navigating in the dark. It had also created hills and mountainous terrain where before there was flat land.

Patches looked haggard. His shirt was ripped in several places and his pants torn asunder. His hair was in a tussle and his fingernails were ravaged and blackened by the cold. He was also still in a state of shock having spent several days with the renegades. At this point he was not ready to disclose his experiences. His Southern veneer had been besmirched. His eyes had that glazed look a fish gets after being tossed out of the water for a few minutes. Sam peered with recognition and understanding and nuzzled against Patches leg. Forcing a smile, Patches mindlessly scratched him around his neck. The clan of three quickly moved forward afraid of the renegades but more concerned about the Polar Bear that they could hear whimpering along with several men's muffled screams reverberating through the valley.

They walked several miles along "the trail" as Aaron had started to call it, following what was left of a road sauntering through a few more valleys with menacing hills that looked like small citadels accompanied by an ever-expanding skyline that extended south of the border. Far ahead of them loomed a huge flock of birds that seemed to be feasting on something. Feasting might not be the right term; Aaron's mind was dominated by graphic images of violence and carnage, as his new normal was reset by the events of the past few days. Also, in the distance stood some buildings, a derelict gas station, and a large central plaza, curtained by large mounds of snow. He noticed the stumps of some telephone poles and the glimmer of what looked like steam coming from an area not too far from the center of town. Aaron was hoping that this would be Artesia Wells, an oasis in the wintry freeze zone; he needed to check it out just to make sure.

Since they rejoined forces, Patches had been carrying Sam. He realized Aaron was partially handicapped having only the use of his right hand and Patches had always liked the dog. The warmth and vitality of the dog provided Patches with a sense of comfort that had been missing from the past few days.

He told Aaron of his escape and subsequent unfortunate capture. He had run from the compound to escape the Russian invasion only to be surrounded by the African gunrunners a few miles outside the camp. Apparently the Africans had been trailing the Russians hoping to collect some of the spoils of their battle with the Japanese. They waited around for a day or so, out of sight, until they determined that all the Russians had departed. They then entered the camp and looked for guns and ammunition. To their dismay, the Russians had taken everything, including sweeping the greenhouse of all remaining edible food. The bunker houses had been razed and the commissary picked clean. All they could find was a few unexploded grenades that were still attached to some of the dead soldiers.

They then marched south where they camped on their second night at the culvert where Aaron found Patches knife. Patches had intentionally planted this in case Aaron, the Big Swede, or someone else from their group came across his trail. Lucky for Patches, Aaron was able to make the connection.

Artesia Wells, for all the hope it provided, was a nondescript place. The buildings consisted of a general store, a small post office, a tiny tin-foiled gas station with barely enough room to pull alongside the pumps, and a central square. Piles of rubble lay everywhere, including a high one-story dumpster filled with tires. The general store was ransacked and had little to offer. There was evidence of a big bonfire near the central square; perhaps gas was siphoned from the gas tanks below the ground as the pumps were clearly damaged. The post office was in ruins with myriad papers and packages strewn about the ice-logged carpets. This was small town Americana reduced to shambles. There might have been a vibrant, thriving community here before the freeze but now the town was a mere shell of itself. It was best suited as its present purpose, a stopover for survivors and vagrants heading to other destinations.

"It would be best if we move on," Aaron said. "I saw some steam come across the snow about a mile from here, it could be what we are looking for, a place to warm up."

"Agreed. I overheard some stories about there being some hot springs on the way out of Texas," remarked Patches. "I could really use some warming; I hurt like hell all over." Sam was between them, rubbing against both their legs, trying to garner some attention. Aside from the cold having a negative impact on his health, Patches was inflicted with rheumatoid arthritis, which currently was not being treated. Walking was a chore for him. The pain was unceasing and he had developed knobby nodules on all his fingers. Back at the prison camp he could occasionally get some generic anti-inflammatory medications or low dose medications like Aleve that would provide some temporary relief. He had to steal them when the guards were not looking. Pre-the-great-freezing he had access to potent infusions like Humira that kept his disease in check. Now he was at the mercy of chance and the elements.

"I don't think we can stay very long. This road is very traveled and near too many crossroads and I am afraid of interlopers like the ones we just left." Aaron could not allay his fears.

"Let's keep off the road then and try to stay near cover," Patches interjected. They both thought that if they kept a low profile they could find the springs, get refreshed, and then move on. Patches was starting to get back some of his fire even though his health status was marginal. His pedigree came from a long line of soldiers who sucked up the pain and went on with their business.

"My greatest hope is that we find a way to cross the border before we are apprehended. I will do what it takes till then for us to survive," he finished.

They pushed forward having discovered hope in the nick of time. Would this be another vanishing oasis in the storm? Or were their imaginations starting to run wild, full of the vagaries of a declining life force? Aaron did not have much to live for anymore; the collapsing mountain had squashed his family and the Big Freeze had jettisoned his profession into extinction, his will to live went through wild swings of disillusionment and despair. Sam was the positive life force and a steady companion who kept him on track towards safety and sanity. Now that he had Patches, Aaron found another reason to stay alive to face the onrush of difficulties that still remained in their path; he would be a steady rudder as they made progress towards their goal.

That day of reckoning would come soon enough. If captured a sure death sentence awaited them. If unable to gain admittance to Chapultepec Park and they were deported, they could expect a life sentence of hard labor. Both options were untenable to Aaron and would have to be avoided at all costs.

The first place to purportedly show the effects of the nanoparticles was in the area around Lake George, nestled in the Adirondack mountain range. Summertime visitors were reporting unusual baitfish, having two and three tails with a mossy white protuberance on their backs. It was more complex than ICH. He also read stories in the local gazettes of enormous Lake Trout, five to seven feet long that were terrorizing kayakers. The NSA sent his team to investigate and to document any irregularities that were occurring in the area.

His team was booked at the best resort on the lake, the stately *Sagamore* that gave them a breathtaking view of the pristine scenic mountain lake. To everyone's surprise, no deformed or overgrown fish were discovered. The scientists concluded that the articles that were written were meant to attract curious tourists, as the Lake George region was in a depressed economic state and way past its heyday of the early fifties and sixties when it was frequented by the rich and famous.

The next alert was not so benign. This was occurring in his backyard. Black bears were no longer reproducing. Many of their young were found in their dens unattended and adults were wandering around the White Mountains in New Hampshire as if they had forgotten that they were bears, eating poisonous berries and mushrooms that by nature they typically avoided. They had, in a word, "Food Alzheimer's", unable to distinguish the edible from the bad. A kind of stupor had set in and the population of black bears was in serious decline. Aaron's group started to investigate; they used MIT and Harvard laboratories to analyze their data. They collected numerous specimens and autopsied them sending a variety of skin, organ, and bone samples to both academic institutions.

The findings were nothing short of alarming. Nanoparticles, of the weather modification origin, had invaded their reproductive organs and had taken residence there. They were genetically altering sperm and eggs of both sexes in such a way to nullify their fertilization potential, damning evidence of an experiment going awry. Apparently the nanoparticles could inflict damage at the chromosomal level of their hosts. They were making species infertile by reorganizing X and Y-chromosomes at the cellular level! This begged the question whether these super-intelligent particles were systematically attacking the plant and animal life to insure their own particular type of survival on the planet. This could also account for the honeybee collapse disorder as well as the reduction of phytoplankton in the oceans—an organized attack on the flora and fauna of the planet! The nanoparticles were also attacking the central nervous system and altering brain patterns of these creatures.

The impact on humans was more blunted and seemed to be much slower in progression. It had found its main expression in lower sperm counts for human males and a sudden onset of autism in children.

The immediate impact of this research resulted in the temporary stoppage of the aerial overflights around the globe until they could formulate a new technology and methodology, eliminating all use of nanoparticles and finding a more suitable substrate to keep the shield airborne.

The ironic part of all of this was that in an attempt to save the planet from global warming, another, uglier problem emerged--*intelligent nanopar*ticles had found their way into our lexicon and were trying to find a way to *hijack the planet.* Not all of this information was known to Aaron because most of the data was compartmentalized. But in science as in life there are sometimes unintended consequences of any selected course of action.

Nearing the area where they thought they saw the steam, *their dreams were realized.* Directly ahead of them were several fissures in the ground where hot, bubbly water was undulating in magnanimous sunshine. Small geysers gushed upwards towards the sky releasing a translucent mist that loped over the llano. Except for some small rodents and an old bear's paw print, there were no signs of recent life visiting the site. Sooty indentures in the ground indicated some recent fire activity but Patches estimated that to be several weeks old—no cause for concern.

They basked in the sun after diverting hot water into a circle of rocks that formed a small pool. When the water cooled, they dipped their aching feet into the water. It was very soothing and revived their spirits. The water was fresh and clean and having been boiling and filtered below the ground, it was suitable for cooking. Aaron had kept aside one can of minestrone soup he had taken from the bus for this occasion. He placed it on a large rock in the middle of one of the smaller whirlpools. After several minutes he removed the can from the scorching water and placed it on the ground to cool off. He shared the soup with Patches and Sam; it was the first hot meal either of them had in a while.

They draped their socks over the tall grass near the hot pools. A warm mist emanating from the water blanketed the entire area. It was delightful to indulge in after their long journey. Seconds turned into minutes, minutes turned into hours, time was standing still and they were in her divine embrace.

"If I knew we weren't going to be followed," Aaron remarked, "I would make a camp here after what we have been through."

"Me too. I haven't been in a hot steam bath since I was a little boy. I used to go with my father and his friends to the sauna after we worked out. I remember their old, droopy bodies, filled with sweat, faces flushed, with a look of exhausted contentment that still strikes a fond image in my mind today," Patches added.

"Where I lived in New Hampshire, the water was always cold, even in the summer. It was the refreshing shock of the cold I remember, growing up, when we waded into frothy rivers and fought the icy currents. Also, I recall Arethusa Falls, a hidden cascade of water you needed to hike into that was a state treasure."

"To be free again, in mind and spirit, seems like a pipe dream compared to where we are today."

"Well, we do have one small hope we can live for, Chapultepec Park, who would have thought the U.S. citizen would be reduced to begging for lodging in another land?"

"Sad but true," Patches finished, sniffling slightly through his leporine nose.

They both agreed they needed to be moving on. It was not wise to tarry especially since they were at a crossroads, known to frequent travelers. This bleak and desolate road seemed to swallow them up whole. They encouraged each other and the newfound companionship was having a very positive effect on Aaron's state of mind. He also no longer had to carry Sam; Patches had taken over that responsibility.

As they departed, Aaron pulled out the map from his pants pocket and studied it closely. This time, he estimated accurately the distance between Laredo and Artesia Wells. They were a little over 50 miles from Laredo, which was on the edge of the Mexican border. He imagined the traverse to Laredo would be harsh, but the opportunity to cross the border heartened him. They would have to re-supply themselves along the way and also get exceedingly lucky to avoid contact with patrols or settlements. Aaron felt Patches' quiet confidence and knew he would not panic and would be an asset in time of trouble.

He was more nervous about Sam. The dog seemed out of sorts the last day or so. His tear ducts were constantly draining and he had developed a small ulceration on one of his paws. The dog was impregnable to the cold but something had worked itself into his left paw. It might have been one of the sharp branches from the cave that scratched him. Every time they stopped the dog began licking his paw. Aaron would have to watch him more closely.

Aaron's own medical condition was still shaky and vacillating. His left arm throbbed unceasingly. The wound had scabbed over and formed an overlay of new skin. It was dark pink and tender to the touch, the tissue had granulated in many spots, a sign that it was mending. He kept it wrapped up and exposed it periodically to air to help speed the healing when he was around a fire. He dared not immerse it in the hot springs for fear of the sensitive skin rupturing. His wife, who liked to gamble, would have called him a "one-armed bandit' if she was alive to see him. She had a macabre sense of humor. Aaron wept as these and other memories of her flooded his mind. As a tribute to his family, he resolved that he would overcome all odds in his quest for survival.

The way became more difficult, deeper encrusted snow impeded their progress as they trudged alongside the road. Their supplies had dwindled to a few morsels of food and they would really have to think about trapping some small game to supplement their diets. They were starting to survive just on heart and guts alone. Patches determination was contagious and his calm demeanor reassuring. They took turns watching the skies as they walked; the white snow sharpened their visibility from the sky and made them easy targets for pursuers. But choices were few; if they traveled further inland they could lose their way and the going would be even rougher. They had to balance the likelihood of *being seen* against the speed of making good progress by shadowing the reliable path of Interstate 35.

They passed a large roadside lake that was completely frozen. It was to the left of the road and smaller tributaries seemed to feed it from the West. The whole surface seemed frozen except for a tiny area near the road where there were a series of small holes punched in the ice. As they moved closer they noticed the openings were frosted over with a thin veneer of ice, apparently someone had accessed them not too long before. A feeling of danger crept over them. *They looked for more signs of visitors.* Close by Patches noticed some shoe string that somebody had rigged as a fishing line with a pierced earring. The earring, snarled in the shoe string, was very shiny and had small brittle scales intertwined with it. Aaron wondered why they left the fishing line if they were successful catching fish--unless they left in a hurry. *That must be it.*

"I think we should test our luck," Aaron said. "But I don't like the fact that they left this line behind, it makes me nervous." The feeling of dread continued to build.

Patches replied, "I know what you mean. Our food supply is running low. Let's give it a quick go and leave as quickly as possible." They both agreed to work together in untangling the line and Patches weighted it by tying a piece of his shattered Bowie knife to the line. Any larger fish would be towards the bottom of the sink hole. Patches had experience with ice fishing in the Canadian Rockies where he often went with his younger brothers on vacations--so he assumed the role of the lead fisherman. Aaron and Sam kept close watch. Aaron was wary of fishing lines after his incident with the unruly fish.

Patches tried several times dropping the line into the ice hole. He drew the line taut then let out some slack, trying to mimic the movement of a baitfish. In the chilly water, it was hard to think anything could be alive, but creatures in the sea could survive at cold bone crushing water depths and there was life in thermal pools even at abnormally high temperatures. *Life finds a niche in the most hostile of environments.* Aaron thought their survival was a testament to this postcard from the edge.

A slight pull of Patches line gave him cause for hope. He thought he was imagining it but when it occurred again his hope transformed itself into an emerging sense of glee. After a few more minutes he really had something tugging hard on his line. Far underneath the surface of the water, a longnose gar had attached itself to the shimmering lure and it was not letting go. It was about two feet long and slim enough to pass through the opening in the ice. One last long tug and Patches was able to bring the fish to the surface; Aaron grabbed its side, being careful not to get cut by the armored scales that coated the fish's body. He already had one fishing accident and did not need another. Not too far away from the hole, they placed the fish on its side in the open air and let death run its natural course. Using their knives, they first scaled then gutted the fish. They had no time to start a fire, so they cut it up into small chunks and devoured it sushi-style. They fed some of the choicer innards to Sam who did not seem to mind. Any edible leftovers were wrapped in scraps of cloth and burlap. They put the guts that were not eaten back into the ice hole, in an attempt to conceal their presence from predators that could be in the area.

They marched into what was left of the day. Shadows were forming around the horizon as the earth was rotating slowly in the full force of the sun. All three comrades, two men and a beast, were comfortable with their bellies' full, which triggered a renewed sense of optimism. The road became very circuitous at this point and they found themselves divagating across a bleak landscape in front of them. They walked into shallow valleys and passed by ornate hills of snow sunlit by the fading day. Incandescent beams of light scurried along the rippling waves of snow that scored the foothills. Ghostlike shadows weaved themselves seamlessly into the tapestry of light. It was the land acting like a screen for their innermost fears, scattering their projections that were seeking refuge in the boundary of twilight. They slithered along trying to avoid the pale void that was always inches away from engulfing them. Their fellowship was tenuous, based upon mutual fear and a quest for absolution. Mayhem could race in at any moment and turn its cold shoulder upon their pilgrimage, ripping off the temporary mask of confidence that they now wore. Under the snow, all that remained was the final resting place of fallen soldiers and prisoners who had lived in the light, for a short period of time. They treaded lightly to avoid waking them up and prayed for their resurrection. They also prayed for the miracle of a spiritual redemption to shield them for what lay ahead. The air had become thick and heavy imposing another barrier for them on their way to the *Promised Land*. Impregnated by months of frost, the ossified ground had slowed their passage to a crawl. Sam, who was being held by Patches under his overcoat, was the first to sense strange clouds ahead. His olfactory system was ringing on *high alert*.

In their exuberance about being able to suspend a sun reflecting shield around the planet, global leadership had fallen asleep at the wheel. By the time Aaron and his group recognized the *nanoparticle problem*, the damage had started and it was too late to turn off the switch. Carbon dioxide levels had swelled across the planet. The smaller numbers of Phytoplankton could no longer produce enough oxygen to sustain marine life support systems. Phytoplankton served as the base of the food chain of the ocean so huge populations of fish and other sea creatures were decimated by starvation. Countries like Japan and China, who depended on harvesting the sea were having a terrible time feeding their populations. Terrestrial animal life was also affected. Vast herds of cows and other live game were having trouble reproducing. More humans than ever before had asthmatic and respiratory conditions; these were often lethal for vulnerable populations like the very young and elderly, and those with compromised immune systems. The nanoparticles' ability for bioaccumulation in organisms remained an unsolved puzzle. It concentrated in mosquitoes and caused Zika virus.

The inability of bees to survive was also leading to worldwide food shortages, as fruits and other food-bearing flora could not propagate.

Vast killing fields had emerged across the continents--this occurred while before the severe climate changes that took place.

Beset by so many different problems, world government was in chaos. Countries retreated back into nation states and went into further isolation. Many countries had civil wars and became ripe for religious fanaticism.

Because of all of this, Aaron's findings continued to be held in the *highest secrecy*. The sad part was that the nanoparticles were not the root cause of the changes; they were an attempted solution to catastrophic change caused by mankind. The primary cause started with the onset of the industrial revolution and man's ever expanding desire to consume all the limited resources of the earth. *Unbridled greed had caused the crash of many civilizations in the past.* The difference this time was that mankind had unprecedented power to change his environment and he did now with impunity-- without worrying about the residual consequences.

The attack came suddenly, out of the blue, without provocation. A massive paw grabbed Aaron's left boot off of the ground, driving him backwards off his feet while knocking the breath out of him. He crashed sideways, sliding for a few feet, tumbling till a crusty snowdrift stopped him. His boot was shredded and a long gash from the tongue of his boot up the side of his leg appeared. He was lucky it was not that deep, a graze wound; it was long and jagged but not oozing too much blood.

Patches backed away slowly, with Sam dangling in his arms, in time to see an old, maimed polar bear start working his way up from a gully alongside the road. He was of immense size, perhaps fifteen feet long; his coat sullied by blackened blood and dark earth; his eyes as choleric as a chimera.

Favoring his left back leg, the giant polar bear limped slightly. The leg looked like it had been broken in the past and then re-healed out of alignment. It featured an ugly bony spur that reminded Aaron of one of the Gargoyles he had seen in his excavations in Greece. The bear had been following them for days; staying in the shadows, silently stalking them and feasting on any scraps they left behind. He was an advance guard for a pack of bears that had attacked various Texas camps during the past few months. After killing the men who had held Patches in captivity, he had stayed on their tail. Only Sam had sensed the bear following them but he was unable to communicate his premonition. He was an old, wise bear—and he knew how to use surprise to his advantage. His old age brought on a physical handicap; he was slow on his feet which was his only Achilles heel.

Speed is what ultimately saved them.

Aaron recovered to his feet quickly and noted a large dendroid cactus field in the distance. He calculated that if he zigzagged through them he could potentially get the bear snared between two of the large cacti. Even though the bases of the cacti were frozen solid, the spines were still attached and they protruded eight to twelve inches out, forming lethal icicle spears. He also banked on the fact that the bear was earnest in catching some dinner, and would be careless.

He waved his arms in the air and shouted at the bear, trying to gain its attention. The bear looked once at Patches and Sam then decided to lunge towards

Aaron. Aaron was fast on his feet and traveled quickly through the cacti, changing directions often and with great agility, the one quality the great bear lacked.
He was lumbering and slow, no longer a youthful bounding bear cub.

Even so, the bear started to gain on Aaron. Bears in their prime could
easily outrun a man, sometimes reaching speeds of 40 mph. They also were
great climbers, except for the Grizzly who preferred to stay near the ground.
What it lacked in agility, it made up for with determination and quadruped
speed, leading its big body across the cacti patches and carefully avoiding
their prickly spinal appendages.

Aaron, seeing the bear gaining, tried to outmaneuver him. He danced
and dodged more than he was capable of and finally twisted his ankle and
fell to the ground. He noticed large streaks of blood in the snow acting as
trail markers for the bear. He realized then that his arm had been pierced by
a cactus spine which when he had wrenched it out caused more bleeding. He
was also still bleeding from the shallow wound on his foot and leg.

Aaron was lodged between two large barrel-shaped cacti, about six or
seven feet high; he could hardly stand on his feet. The bear saw it had an
advantage and came stampeding towards him. Aaron, in pain, backed away
just far enough to see the bear try to squirm through the opening and have
its flanks impaled by the icy daggers protruding from the cacti. As the bear
reached him it became more and more enmeshed in this spiny net. Each time
it twisted or turned shrieks of pain and rage emanated from the bear's mouth.
This was the perfect bear trap—the animal was sandwiched in and fettered
by the cacti, in a death trap.

Aaron and Patches were more unhinged by the ferocious noise emanating from the bear than from the bear charge itself. Patches helped Aaron
back out slowly and they made all haste in getting back on the road. So that
Aaron could walk better, Patches cut some patches of cloth which he wrapped
around some small sticks that acted as a supportive splint for Aaron's ankle.
He also dressed the wounds, which were relatively shallow on his leg; deeper
on his arm, but they closed quickly and needed no further attention for now.

Still, weariness was starting to settle on Aaron. He was walking wounded. He was starting to feel the weight of his circumstances. His leg hurt, his

arm hurt, now in two spots, he felt dehydrated, and newfound anxiety was starting to cast pallor on all his thoughts and actions. He felt like he was naked while tugging a heavy chain across the desert and wearing only a straw hat as protection against a fiery sun.

"It's getting harder for me to stay the course, Patches, I almost think that at this point it is better for you and Sam to go on alone," Aaron said as Patches finished working on his arm.

"We can't do that. You are the keeper of the map. I could never find my way to Mexico without you. We both need to see this thing through to the end. Besides that, Sammy would be lost without you." With sad, coaxing eyes, Sam stared at Aaron. Aaron was struck by their clarity and uncompromising kindness.

"I guess I can go on a little further. I can reassess my health as we go on." Patches and Sam appeared brighter in Aaron's eyes the longer he cast his gaze upon them. It was as if their fellowship was a ring of light that needed all three to complete the circuit.

Echoing across the flats, they could still hear the fading screams of the bear, undergoing the last agonizing throes of death. This gave them impetus to move on and not to debate the issue.

The internal nanoparticle debate raged within the halls of global government. It had been an international group of hand-picked scientists that had made the decision to use nanoparticles in the heat shield formula, so no one government was being blamed. However the U.S. as the principal architect of the project was now taking most of the heat from the other powerful leaders from around the World.

The pressing, thorny problem was how to stop the nanoparticle chain reaction. This hybrid life form, part biological, part artificially engineered, was out of control, and *intelligent*, able to outsmart the scientists that had created it. No simple fix was available. The best thinkers from a variety of different fields could not find a solution to the problem. A vote to bring this to the public domain to try to enlist private sector assistance did not have enough support; this was deemed too desperate a measure and one that

---

could exponentially create panic. Instead, clandestinely, government agencies searched databases and perused journals like the *Journal of Nanoparticle Research* for scientists that were intimately involved in nanoparticle research to get input and counsel regarding this matter.

The sad facts were that even though they wanted to stop the nanoparticle chain reaction, the climate, unbeknownst except to a few, was already speeding on a highway way out of control. High carbon levels had hurled the climate into a freefall that could not be stopped. The Meridional Overturning Circulation system had virtually shut down, decreasing the amount of heat that went into the North Atlantic, fostering much colder temperatures in Europe and North America. Both mainstream climatologists as well as marginalized thinkers like author Whitley Strieber, in his book *The Coming Global Superstorm* had discussed this as a real possibility. Now that it was occurring; they were getting their due recognition.

A proposed solution was to restore this important configuration of ocean currents that controlled temperatures over the planet. But this was never implemented nor fully addressed as it was beyond the scope of capabilities. The new earth climate was here to stay. And the nanoparticle problem further worsened the situation.

Not too far away from where the polar bear had been hopelessly snared, Oviak stirred in his sleep. He had a very peaceful night of dreaming, except for the last part of his dream, where he saw a large polar bear impaled between two rocky shelves trying, in vain, to remove his leg from a narrow crevice. Shrieking in blood-curdling pain, the bear was pulling his leg apart as he was trying to escape. As he awoke, the bear image was imprinted indelibly on Oviak's brain.

Oviak was a native Alaskan who had moved into Texas after the Big Freeze. He had founded a "friendly" camp of like-minded Alaskans who lived in close proximity to the border of Mexico, and who remained undetected by the other work camps in the vicinity. They knew how to live off of the land and could survive cold temperatures better than any other human beings. They ate raw fish and hunted bears and other carnivores to sustain their group. They were well armed, having negotiated some deals with gun-runners who occasionally came into the area to offer them services, which included revolvers, shotguns, and rocket-propelled grenades for their protection. The gunrunners were never taken to their camp; they met well outside the perimeter to keep the exact location a secret.

Oviak was the clan leader and was much respected among the Inuit tribe. He bore the markings of high rank: craggy, high cheekbones, twisted nose, and a disarming incongruous smile.

He craned his head outside his igloo to listen to the soft mutterings of the wind. He reckoned the bear was about three miles from his camp. He draped himself with his bear fur-lined anorak and crept silently into the night air. Before leaving, he pulled his well-traveled spear off of the blocks of wood that held it tight against the side of the snow house's entrance. The spear's shaft was composed of hard ivory and strong baleen. He also slipped a revolver into the side pocket of his parka, just in case he met up with unfriendly strangers who were overly aggressive. He looked at his beloved wife, Iluak, and kissed Adlartok, his daughter, whose name meant "clear sky." She was unusually tall for his people; she measured five feet eight inches in height, and was lighter in skin tone than any other Inuit.

Standing five feet tall Oviak was known for his ferocity as a hunter. He was also heralded for his ability to lead and provide for the clan. To Oviak, hunting had a spiritual quality to it, one that transformed him where he could experience the sublime undercurrents of nature underfoot. He could feel what he could not see. He preferred to hunt by himself, he could travel much faster and problem-solved better when alone, he would not have to worry about another person's fumbling.

He could also call for help. The 21st century had brought a new tool into the Inuit's culture, the cell phone. Satellite communications were still possible in the frigid climate—phones were manufactured to withstand lower temperatures and improved voltaic cells kept the inner workings of the device charged and heated.

He un-tethered his lead husky, Willie, to accompany him—the dog was pearly white with patches of creamy gray, he loped after Oviak like a wolf cub following its mother. Bringing Willie clearly had advantages and disadvantages; he was a great trail dog and could follow a scent. Unfortunately, Willie was a "wheezer", some of his breed having a congenital deformation of the larynx that caused a wheezing sound during the dog's normal breathing. This alerted prey to their presence and made him a liability during the hunt. On the other hand, the wheezing kept predators away due to its shrill intonation. The blood bond between the two was also an asset.

They followed a well-traveled trail out of the camp that lead away from the center of the encampment. When they were a few hundred yards away from their living quarters, Oviak could no longer see his igloo—in fact the whole village was so well camouflaged that a passerby would need to be almost right on top of it to make out its contours and notice a settlement was there. This natural camouflage served the village well in perilous times. The Inuit were excellent at situating their villages in obscure areas and blending in with their surroundings.

The area they crossed was pimpled with small-truncated cacti and covered with thick, stubborn sage brush. Markers made of carefully erected piles of windswept stones pointed the way out of the Inuit territory. Oviak walked carefully trying to avoid any awkward obstacles in his path. A month ago one of the villagers had lost his balance and twisted his ankle a few miles outside of camp. While limping back, a pack of wolves ambushed him. Only the gnawed bones of his body, picked clean, were found a few weeks later.

Oviak's nephew's funeral had caused great sadness in his family and in the settlement. They dropped his remains into a popular sink hole, hoping that his spirit would attract fish to this site at a later date. They could not afford to provide any telltale signs of their existence. They knew that the underground current ran south, away from them, into the far reaches of a wilderness, which was considered a virtual "no-man's" land of bramble and uninhabitable terrain.

Oviak had eulogized his nephew and had warned his Inuit brothers about the dangers of going it alone; ironic as that was what he was now doing himself. Potentially his actions could lead to a foolhardy death—not a respectable ending for such an esteemed leader-- "an eater of raw flesh."

The polar bear to Oviak, was a magnificent creature, a work of art, to be admired, but most of all *to be hunted.* It was a test of manhood, the soul's quest to pit death against the glorious gestalt of living. The Inuit did not find sport in deer hunting where meek beasts are ambushed without the ability to fight back—that type of hunting would be repugnant to them and below them unless it was a question of survival. They believed in fair play with a balance of power in worthy battles that challenge and uplift the soul. A wounded bear was by far one of the most dangerous animals, a force to be reckoned with. This kind of encounter was what made life worth living, a chance like what the ancient Spartans longed for by a glorious death.

Aaron was feeling better. They were making progress on the road and his wounded body seemed to be miraculously mending itself again. Interstate 35 was still very windy but relatively flat on this part of the route, which enabled them to keep up a good pace. Aaron still wore the look of a wounded soldier returning from war, but Patches' incredibly upbeat disposition kept depression at bay. The farther they got away from the trapped bear, the more relaxed Sam seemed to be. His fluffy white hair was matted into a dirty disheveled pelt that covered his body. His pugnacious black nose seemed offset from the rest of his countenance—*seemingly having a life of its own.*

A few hours later, they decided to take a rest near a frozen pond that had a stone cordon around it. The reason for the stone enclosure was not apparent. Aaron could not determine if it was designed to keep people out or whether it was constructed to keep something in—in any event it made a nice place for them to stop and contemplate their next moves. The wall provided a place for them to sit, if only for a while. The snow was actually starting to thin in spots, reminding them that they were making some progress towards their destination. Aaron couldn't determine if the snow was less accumulated due to the winds or because there was less snowfall, it was still very cold.

Once again they felt famished and were in serious need of food. Aaron had suffered some blood loss and needed to replace the lost nutrients. His usually stable demeanor had been replaced by a scowl. He felt permanently encased in one of Jack London's stories, such as *To Build A Fire,* or *Call of the Wild,* tales he certainly never considered would be moving parts of his living history. He also thought about Jon Krakauer's *Into Thin Air*, an adventurous tome about uphill climbing in the Himalayas, home of K2 and Mt. Everest, where experienced guides and hikers succumbed to the elements and unpredictable avalanches. At least he and Patches were on level land, which made for easier hiking, and had less of a chance of being exposed to howling mountaintop blizzards.

The brutal cold continued to take its toll on all three of them; a screeching and riveting wind accompanied the sub-thermal temperatures. As much as they kept moving to stay warm, this was offset by the daily bombardment of cold and constant exposure they experienced. Only Sam, who was bioengineered for this climate, suffered little, but he was totally dependent upon the men for his survival. Without their protection, he would quickly become tasty prey for many of the scavengers that roamed these desolate plains.

Trying their best to keep shadowy thoughts from entering their minds, Patches and Aaron discussed their situation. *They did not want to but had to face the cold, brutal facts that without help their survival limits had almost been reached.*

"I'm getting weaker rather than stronger," Aaron said. "My arms are hurting as well as my leg, I feel like I am slowing you down. Why don't you take Sam and go on. You will make much better time without me."

"I can't do that," replied Patches. "You saved my life." Sam looked wearily at the two men seeming to realize that this was an important crossroad.

"I can show you on the map where you need to go, it is pretty much a straight run from here. Keep to the brush, probably near Laredo you can find food and shelter." He pointed south with what was left of his stubbed arm. "I can give you my haversack and all its contents, with any luck you will find help along the way."

"I can't do that," repeated Patches. "With all that we have been through, you want me to leave you like an old, farm animal to die on the trail? Absolutely not. We go on together, or die together; I won't have it any other way." Patches' tone was adamant and he was not going to take no for an answer.

"I can't be responsible, then, for any more slippage. I will try my best to go on. If you change your mind I will understand."

"Consider it final."

Sam eyed them both again, sensing their torment and pain, acutely aware of their strong bond, one borne of hardship and familiarity.

The lion inside Aaron was very strong, a tall mast that was lashed by a taut rope. He submitted unwillingly, not caring for himself, but more concerned for the welfare of his comrades. He did not want to impede them in their quest for freedom. It was the second time in a few days that he decided not to talk about his misgivings.

They turned their attention to the pond. It looked promising—a tidal pool of food. They cleared some of the snow off its surface and looked down into the ice. It seemed like there was movement underneath.

They followed the edge of the pond around to the southeast where there was a pronounced bulge on the ground. They chipped away at it with the blunt sides of their knives, using their hands to whisk away the snow and ice. Under the snow, a steel marker revealed itself "U.S. Fish and Wildlife Services, Fish Hatchery." They were hoping to land on a gold mine. Perhaps there were some remnants of a colony of fish still alive, enough anyway to support a few small meals. At this point, they would be glad for anything that was nourishing.

They hacked away at an area of ice that was close to a mixed stand of brush and cactus that had some good tinder partially exposed through the snow. The ice was hard at first but then gave way under increased pressure from above. They formed a crack in the ice several inches in diameter and broke the ice to form a ring that was large enough to see their faces reflected in the dull sun. Aaron was barely able to recognize himself. His face looked gaunt and his head matted with unkempt hair. His countenance was a mask of dark, deep furrowed wrinkles. He looked away not wanting to see more.

They passed the line they acquired before into the water, attaching first a small piece of beef they had left from their stash onto a makeshift hook. Minutes passed. Nothing was biting.

They tried again. And again. Each time throwing out the line until their arms hurt. Time started to stand still. All their focus and energy was directed at the task at hand. Soon it would be dark. And they would have to consider shelter and passing another vulnerable night on the trail. Losing hope they continued to ply the line and jiggle the bait where it was dangling underwater. When it seemed they were at the height of despair, something chomped on the bait. It gave a long pull and almost snapped the line. Patches drew the hook up into its mouth and dragged onshore a large, pouting Black Bass that weighed about 4 pounds. On any other day, the men would have been proud of their accomplishment and taken pictures. Today, on the brink of starvation, they were just intent on cooking the fish and erasing the hunger from their bellies and their souls. They used the tinder they had discovered to start a fresh fire and cooked the fish hastily.

The deepening cold enveloped them like a tumescent shroud discharging the warmth from their bodies. As the fire waned, their cold reality returned. The food had filled their bellies and for a spell of time sated the nagging hunger that plagued their every footstep. Darkness was coming and they needed to formulate a plan for the evening.

The dog sensed something. Patches and Aaron, both of their eyes bloodshot from the cold, could barely discern the silhouette of a form emerging from the cover of some heavy brush. The figure seemed to be dragging something behind him, something large and inert. It became clear that the person was straining as he was arching his back while moving the object with a sleigh made of hastily constructed wood saplings, an unusual find considering the resources of this area. A large dog was leading the figure cautiously patrolling the ground ahead of him avoiding uneven patches and peering side to side for objects lurking in the dark shadows. A gurgling sound emanated from the dog, a noise that seemed to broadcast a warning that was both menacing and ambiguous.

The stranger's dog was now staring at them and starting to move aggressively in their direction, when his master commanded him to stay.

Oviak looked at the men and pitied what he saw. He could see that these were not people who were accustomed to the travails and perils of the wild. One of the men was especially painful to look at, with a bloodied-stumped arm, bedraggled hair, slumping spine and a noticeable limp. He also noticed a small, frail, white dog that had little fight in him; he was amazed that such a dog could exist in these extreme climate conditions.

Although Oviak's English was shaky he shouted: "Hey there!" to the men, followed by "Kutaa" (hello) in his native tongue.

The old leader moved forward with his Dog. Patches came over and offered to help him drag his cargo sled which was ingeniously designed to offer little resistance to the ice and snow. Further communication was done with rudimentary sign language – the old man offered them some bear meat as he saw the fire was still ignited and hot enough for cooking. The smell of the bear meat filled the air, titillating their nostrils and sending messages far and wide that meat was being prepared for consumption. Aaron was worried about pack bears but the sumptuous food was irresistible. They ate voraciously. It made their bellies warm and they became momentarily content forgetting the unforgiving rigors of their ordeal. The earth certainly had become a harsh mistress; light years apart from the pleasantries of the luxurious college campuses Aaron formerly inhabited. The cold zone was not for the squeamish. The men were far afield of their comfort zones. They had grown rugged, yes, but were still were learning the native wariness needed to survive in the wild. They could tell that this old man had an understanding of the environment far deeper than them.

Willie and Sam seemed to hit it off. The small Maltese was no threat to the larger husky and they seemed to form an immediate bond. They chased each other around in circles while the men ate. This served as entertainment for the men as they became better acquainted. The dogs' game of tag went on for quite a while before they started panting from expending so much energy. Their tails wagged wildly, especially when they were given scraps of bear fat and meat scraps by the men. All seemed well as they slowly ceased playing and started to nap.

The sky was turning a deep, ragged purple and a light snow was beginning to fall on the ground and on the men. Overhead, steep ridges of cumulus clouds looked like ski banks unblemished by human touch. Unbeknown to them, they were being watched. Raiders from the south, travelling from the rough border towns along Mexico, had a fix on their position. They had been systematically tracking Patches and Aaron for the last ten hours and were waiting for an opportune time to bushwhack them and make them captives. The older man who was with them now did not look that formidable and did not concern them. With time, they would be able to carry out their plot. Some of them were pirates, others were bounty hunters who kidnapped travelers and sold them into the naval slave trade...here the prisoners would work until they died on ragged ships owned by pirates that ran guns and other sundries to the work camps. This was a thriving business and a throw-back to the dark ages when people were treated as commodities. Being on one of these slave ships was worse than being imprisoned in the U.S. Cold Zone.

America had indeed become a collection of prison sites losing its identity in the process. The Northern Hemisphere had lost much of its mercantile and political clout; the Southern Hemisphere was where the real seat of power was located and a central staging point for most of the planet's commerce. Former third world countries were growing exponentially, flooded by refugees and also new money. Any land around the equator was considered prime real estate.

The bandits eyed the men with watchful eyes, carefully weighing each man for the best time to strike. They were patient men and were willing to wait a long period of time if they had to-- having stalked quarry many times before. They were known for their calm in the face of danger and were regarded as silent barracudas stalking colorful reefs. Their leader, Gigulta, dispersed the men in three groups of three completely surrounding Aaron's position and cutting off all routes of escape. Even though they were hungry, they did not feel hunger; even though they were cold; they showed no signs of being cold. These men were gladiatorial; fearless and immune to pain. The odds were heavily stacked in their favor. They were perfectly adapted to their new Frozen World. They were conditioned to the wild and unpredictable patterns of Nature and were able to withstand pain that normal individuals could only think about. They were heavily armed and were not afraid to use their weapons; they even looked forward to it, like a pack of hyenas stalking and then taking apart their prey. They were the new warrior Neanderthals of the tundra.

The men sat slumped next to the fire. It was getting dark and the thought of traveling into the cold reaches of the night was becoming more of an after-thought. Food brought comfort and complacency and soon brought shallow sleep. Around the fire, the only vigilant member was Willie; he had sensed something amiss in the environment, even though he could not name it, he still felt it. Pricking his ears to hear deeper into the silence, his eyes though half-closed, were scanning the topography looking for changes in the land-scape that only a highly-skilled hunter would notice.

Gigulta raised up his hand to alert his men to action. He motioned for them to creep slowly along the ground in the direction of the fire. His gnarly hand was covered by an oversized black glove that gave it the appearance of a block of obsidian stone that was melted by a fireball. His face was riddled with ugly cicatrices and one of his eyes was deformed, with the iris perma-nently pointed upward, seemingly navigating the heavens. He was a grue-some sight and often sparked fear in the marketplaces in Mexico. He was "ugly man with scarred face" *o hombre feo con cara asustadora* to the people who recognized him in the city.

The journey to Chapultepec Park was at a crossroads. Patches and Aaron knew it. They still had weeks, if not months ahead of them of trudging through fields of snow and ice. The monotonous terrain ahead of them con-tinued for countless miles. Overall, the dogs were best equipped to do this, being able to survive in the worst of circumstances by foraging and trapping small creatures. Sam, of course, would have to rely on the husky's tenacity to survive, but as companions they could leverage Sam's superior intelligence for the greater good.

Aaron was a physical mess; his pulpy arm, damaged leg, and his deplet-ed energy were slowing the group down. His feeling of dependence left him feeling naked and afraid. His hold on sanity had been waning and had only been kept in check by Patches' relentless optimism to win against insur-mountable odds. That was on the verge of being challenged.

A massive arm tightened a death hold on Gigulta's neck; he was totally unprepared for the attack. Blue veins were bulging in his neck, slowly losing access to life-giving oxygen. "Call your men off," Oviak whispered. "Now!"

The wizened tribal leader meant business, that much Gigulta knew, but he could hardly breathe and he was certainly in no shape to make conversation.

If the gigantic hand squeezing his neck was the only obstacle, Gigulta might have retaliated. But he looked downward and saw a massive husky gripping his ankle as if snared in a bear trap. "I will tell the dog to chew your foot off."

Gigulta waved his arms at his men giving them the sign to retreat. They started stepping back slowly eyes focused on their leader, when something much unexpected happened. They heard a roar from behind and saw huge white shadows coming at them. It seemed as if the snow underfoot became a desert storm. Polar bears were charging them from every direction. To his horror, Gigulta's men were being torn apart.

Willie was emboldened by the activity around him and started tugging on Gigulta's leg, making him scream too.

The polar bear pack had been following the dead bear's scent to where they were located. Oviak saw this as an opportunity to escape; he let Willie engorge on some of Gigulta's pulpy leg and then called him off. He went to the others, who were terrified, and gestured for them to follow him. They worked their way into the woods leaving as quickly as possible; Aaron was helped by Patches while Oviak took command of the dogs. They followed a narrow winding path into the woods, crossing some frozen streams, and scrambled across some rocky precipices that looked like they might have been stone towers at some point in time, but were now a crumbling scattered debris field.

It was a little known fact that there were still historically significant ruins that lay undiscovered in the backwoods of Texas. There is a mysterious rock wall in Texas that is 3.5 miles wide and 5.6 miles long. The rocks are made of feldspar granite, not an indigenous rock found in the state. No one knows who built this wall; it was discovered in the 1850's.

It was a several mile hike back to Oviak's camp, but that is where he took his new friends. It was the only safe place to go.

Adlartok was the first to greet them. She was taking her turn guarding the camp. She had a quiver of arrows hanging loosely off her shoulders, this adorned a full figure that Aaron could not help noticing—it had been a long time since he had seen such a woman. Adlartok was alternately concerned and bemused by what she saw – her father dragging two wayward men beside him—both men looking haggard as men often do look after spending time in the wilderness. The object of her amusement was on the little dog that appeared to be the least affected by the elements. She immediately grabbed Sam from Aaron's arms and there was an unspoken attachment formed. Patches, as was his custom, bowed to the Inuit princess.

Oviak gestured for the men to follow him towards the main tent. People wandered by wondering who these strangers were. They touched Sam as if he was a good luck charm that had fallen from the sky into their winter paradise. Aaron had to work hard to get him back. It was finally Adlartok who intervened and demanded that they give Sam back to Aaron. She held Sam tightly as she carried him back to Aaron.

The village looked like a badly made quilt that was patched together with colorful odd pieces – simple huts with bright blue ice roofs speckled the camp. Doors made of wood without latches comprised the entranceways. There weren't any windows as that would cause drafts inside and the only venting was towards the top of the structure where small chimneys were built out of scavenged stone. To avoid any smoke being seen from passersby, Aaron was told that they only lit their fires after dusk. At this moment, the village people were streaming towards Oviak's hut trying to seek out their leader, as this was the first time an outsider had been brought back into their camp.

As Aaron and Patches entered the hut they were nearly overcome by a noxious smell. Due to the lack of fuel, human and animal waste was the fuel of choice. Mercifully the smells of pungent beef cooking tempered the smell and after a while they adjusted to the stifling air of the hut. They could barely contain their emotions when they were offered food. They ate ravenously and as there was abundant food Oviak and his men let them eat until they were full. The bear meat had been satisfying but bison beef was less gamey. Adlartok fed the dogs long strings of beef jerky that were hanging from a food dispensary in the corner of the structure. They wagged their tails and seemed at ease. That was until Sam started choking but Adlartok went to his aid quickly to clear out a piece of meat that was lodged in the back of his tongue. *It had been a long time since Aaron had felt a part of a larger group and his comfort level was high and he was starting to feel restored.* Patches too made himself at home and was also eyeing Adlartok a fact that was not lost on Aaron.

"You can stay here for the night," Oviak said, "but tomorrow we need to bring you safely out to a trail so you can continue your journey. I cannot put my people's lives in jeopardy. The raiding parties are starting to range more south and I fear we might be discovered."

Aaron replied: "It is not our wish to put you in harm's way. We will take some rest tonight and leave tomorrow. We are grateful for what you have done for us. We owe you our lives." Patches nodded his head in concurrence. "We are honored to be here."

Oviak was a simple man and accepted them for what he saw them to be. But he was not a fool. He commanded that the villagers place guards around the camp every ten paces, tightening the security for the night. He also used watch dogs at each of the security points to raise an alarm if raiders approached the camp. Their keen sense of smell and acute hearing were invaluable in sensing abnormal disruptions in the environment.

The men rolled up into animal skins that were laid across the floor. They were musty but very warm. Sam slept between the two men while Oviak and his family slept on wooden benches that used a thick fleece for bedding that was very comfortable. It must have been close to midnight when they retired for the night.

About two in the morning, Aaron heard some rustling nearby. He saw a soft dark shadow move slowly along the wall. He instantly had nightmares about the unexplainable presence they had experienced in the cave. But as the shadow came closer, Aaron realized he was mistaken.

It was Adlartok wrapped in a shallow shawl. She quietly slipped under the covers with Aaron and he felt her warm throbbing body through the thin veneer. She lifted his head and started to caress him, softly at first, then vigorously. She slowly worked her hand to his groin area and deftly massaged his testicles in her hand pinching his shaft. Aaron, caught off guard at first, moved his own hand to her genitalia. Before long, she mounted Aaron and they consummated several times throughout the night. No one noticed them as Patches was in a deep slumber and Sam awoke only once then quickly fell back to sleep. Before the sun rose, Adlartok made her way back to the other side of the hut and fell asleep. Aaron wondered if this was Oviak's idea, an ancient aboriginal custom or the result of real mutual attraction. It was hard to tell. He woke up less restless and more wide awake than he had been in a long time; he felt as if he had a new lease on life. Even his arm felt markedly better.

Aaron thought about the nanoparticle conundrum again. The earth had existed for billions of years and from what he knew about its history she had suffered terribly at times. It was a changing molten planet that evolved internally and was impacted from outside forces. There were numerous times that comets and asteroids came shooting down from other galaxies and fire-bombed the surface of the planet. Land masses frequently moved over long periods of time changing the topography and character of the planet. Ancient civilizations before the time of Noah were purported to have existed, some, like the society of Atlantis, with technology as advanced as ours. Then there was the famous Roswell Incident which suggested we had been visited from creatures beyond the stars. Or perhaps these beings were native to the planet, like Bigfoot, living in isolation, perhaps underground, in areas unexplored. Paleontologists were adept at finding new species in Wyoming and Montana; it seemed there were a never-ending variety of dinosaurs that roamed the earth.

It was hard to imagine worse times, but all of what they were experiencing probably occurred countless times before. The same events had a habit of repeating themselves in the course of time throughout the universe. Planets probably had been held hostage by otherworldly entities during the eons.

Aaron never doubted the planet would cleanse itself and start these cyclical processes all over again. But at what cost? How many species would go extinct? Aaron knew that nature's ending would eventually bring on a new beginning. But would he still be here to see the new start? What new problems would emerge in the offing? Could the cradle of a new civilization bring forth a superior society that was better than the one before? It all had happened before, of that he was certain. To think otherwise was viewing things with a narrow lens.

Oviak lead them to the perimeter of the camp; Aaron was elated that Adlartok volunteered to bring them back to the main road. The plan was to follow Rte. 35 again to Laredo. Laredo sat on the north bank of the Rio Grande and was where they would enter Mexico, if they found a suitable safe passageway. They were about 10 miles away by Aaron's reckoning or about a 2 day hike through a challenging terrain. They would still have to get to Monterrey before they found any substantial climate relief although the snow and ice were getting thinner, of that they were not mistaken. Oviak, as was his way, fully provisioned them. They had food for a few weeks; warm fur-lined coats made by the villagers, and oversized rucksacks that could hold a large cache of supplies. The local village shaman, Incanuye, had re-wrapped Aaron's stub and applied an herbal paste she concocted that functioned as a potent antibiotic. She communicated by gestures to Aaron that it would speed his healing and reduce the swelling. She was a young girl of about twenty with long, swirly hair who looked much too young to understand the underpinnings of medicine. Incanuye reminded him of the many young interns he used to see travelling the subways in Boston who frequently walked the Freedom Trail during lunchtime.

They were also given a hard wooden sleigh that easily glided over snow. It was here where they stored the bulk of the provisions.

It was still early morning when they departed; they each carried a large bag filled with food and assorted gear including fire starters, blankets, extra water and firearms with ammunition. Aaron noticed that Adlartok's pack was brimming to the top with supplies; he was wondering what she meant to do with all of this once she took leave.

The way looked clear ahead. They meandered along a few secret trails that brought them back to the main road. The sky was an azure blue and the clouds were playing peek- a-boo with the sun. Rays of sunlight spun votive candles over the horizon. The snow was soft and easy to trudge through, and the cold air seemed to radiate kindness with the absence of the unceasing wind.

A favorite James Taylor's song began softly at first then rang out in Aaron's mind:

*Way down here, you need a reason to move. Feel a fool running your stateside games.*
*Lose your load, leave your mind behind, Baby James.*
*Woh, Mexico, it sounds so simple, I just got to go.*
*The sun's so hot I forgot to go home, guess I'll have to go now.*

He hadn't felt this light since the last time he was home. He was humming along with the lyrics when Sam started shaking. He thought it was from the cold, but Sam smelled something peculiar. They were about 3 miles from the camp, close to the road, when in the distance they saw a pitiful figure hunched over near the stump of an old Mexican oak tree.

Patches took the lead while the others waited in the shadows. He dodged some small mounds of ice and then walked slowly to the cover of a large pile of crushed stones that looked like they might have come from a local quarry. In the snow he saw what was left of Gigulta, a pulpy mass of torn flesh and crushed bone. His mangled legs had huge gashes on them and one of his arms was hanging by a thin piece of sinewy muscle. His breathing was slow and labored. He was near the end. Apparently he had escaped the bears and wandered through the back country to his present location.

Patches gestured for Aaron and Adlartok to join him. In the end, rather than provide a mercy killing, they decided to leave him be and let nature run its projected course.

As they ambled up to the road, to Aaron's surprise, Adlartok did not leave. She just shook her head several times when they offered to remove the load from her pack. It dawned on Patches and Aaron that maybe she was staying with them for the full journey. At this point *it wasn't clear to them why* but Aaron began wondering about their night together. Could that have been deliberate sparking a relationship he might not find out about until later?

They found they could follow the contours of Rte. 35 without fully revealing their position. They were entering an area where Mexican border controls made forays into the United States to prevent mass migration. They did this with stern rebukes, but if they felt that you were not sincere about your intentions, they did not hesitate to incarcerate or murder obstinate interlopers. It was a cold world in so many ways. Aaron really did not know all of the conditions of sanctuary – were there green cards needed like in the old U.S.? Or did it require sponsorship? With the lack of information available, all they could do was hope for the best. They really had no other choices anyway.

Mexico had one of the strongest economies on the planet and wanted to keep their domination. This was quite the role reversal compared to what was the case in the late 20$^{th}$ century when the U.S. was a magnet for foreigners, and had control with China over most of the world's economy.

The air was becoming heavy and a thin veil of snow was making its way across the tundra. Aaron began thinking about his life again, before the *Big Freeze*. His career had been very promising; he was loved by his family and spent his days relatively carefree. His time was mostly consumed by intellectual curiosity and his research studies.

One of the features of his malaise was that there wasn't any upward mobility in his new World, just a downward spiral degrading all of mankind's achievements. History had been carved up- all that was left were hundreds of miles of white wasteland borne out of a crying earth. The civilizations that had existed before were barely a footnote in the language of time. He felt he should have done more in his previous life by thinking less and enjoying himself more. A range of emotions engulfed him. In the end consciousness was the art of making choices in a vacuum. Actions were eternal and held karmic sway; thoughts were like fleeting rainbows canvassing the night skies. His vision failing him he concentrated on the back of Patches' feet in front of him. He realized then that what he held most important was the love he felt for his comrades. This was what would last through the flotilla of time.

Beyond the outcroppings there arose a hazy sun in a wide blue sky. They trudged along Rte. 35 slowly making progress towards their goal. Adlartok looked beautiful to Aaron, and his admiration was deepening as the day wore on. Every one of her body movements was grace in motion and she reminded him of his wife in some ways except that Adlartok was built for the wild.

Patches was taking the lead and as before he relieved Aaron of carrying Sam when the dog got tired of tromping through the snow. They stayed the night at a ford and slept under a slab of rock whose ledge offered some protection from the wind. They ate well from the stores Oviak provided them, and kept a small fire going through the late hours of the night, to keep wild things at bay.

Adlartok snuggled with Aaron and Patches sensed for the first time that they were becoming a couple. Somehow in the tight confines of their down sleeper they were able to contort into various positions and make love. Their heavy love-making was like a bright votive candle in the dark sky. Sam peered on not fully understanding what was happening but seeing joy in his master's eyes.

The next day began with a heavy snow and swirling winds. They were getting close to Laredo. Patches scouted ahead while the others rested near a large tree stump that had icicles draping off of it like a large blooming flower.

Aaron was relieved when Patches came back: "We will need to be more vigilant now; I fear that Laredo is probably well-watched and there is only one bridge to cross unless we can find another passage."

Patches said: "We could attempt an ice crossing; I would suspect much of the river is frozen and then we can avoid being seen." They really had no way of knowing if there were any border guards or other outfits there. They were simply guessing. But chances were, at this crossroads, there would be people camped out or situated in an installation somewhere.

The wind continued to curl around them and was now starting to shriek. They walked carefully trying to keep their footing in the piles of accumulating wet snow. Adlartok had rewrapped Aaron's stub using more of the medicine woman's poultice which had aided his healing. Soon they crossed a treacherous pass and climbed to the top of a ridge where they were able to peer down upon the town of Laredo. It appeared quiet enough—no immediate sign of any menacing activity. It was Patches who discerned a slight disturbance in the land. It looked like tall ten foot poles were surrounding the city—this was not a usual feature of the city.

They decided to move closer to take a look. They climbed down a narrow gully in the ridge and walked back to the road. The wind was furious now, blowing their packs almost off their backs and making the sleigh bounce up and down. Sam was under Adlartok's furry coat---just the tip of his nose visible. The snowstorm was becoming unbearable.

When they arrived on the outskirts of the city they saw bollards, long slim steel poles ringed with razor barb-wire blocking their entrance to Laredo. There were thousands of sections installed across the perimeter stretching into the horizon. The clearance between rows was such that there was no opportunity to slip through and from their vantage point, no gate was apparent. The whole area was cordoned off. This was a considerable setback.

Both Patches and Aaron were exasperated. Sam didn't know any better. Adlartok actually tried to grip the wires in her hand to see if they were pliable and cut her fingers. She had to wrap them up with bands of cloth she found in the First Aid kit.

"I guess we will have to go to Plan B---try to pass around the city and make a frozen river crossing," Patches said. "My concern here besides being discovered is that we will have to traverse back trails away from the road. We don't know what we could potentially encounter there."

"I agree, "said Aaron. "But what other choices do we have? We will just have to try to keep ourselves hidden and out of harm's way."

Adlartok did not like the concern she saw on the two men's faces. But she was going wherever Aaron was going.

They plotted a route using the map that would guide them around the outer fringes of the City. It would take them longer because they would have to circumvent the bollards, but safety was paramount. Aaron calculated it would take them an extra day to cross over to Mexico. Everyone seemed up to the task, including Sam, who wagged his tail in glee.

The weather continued to worsen. It was almost a white out which worked to their advantage. However, this made for slow going. Aaron's boots were filling up with snow and his feet were getting very damp; he suspected Patches was experiencing the same thing. Adlartok had high leather boots cinched together with corded tassels that protected her from the snow. Aaron likened her to a mysterious snow princess returning to her lost kingdom. Her prominent forehead and high cheek bones added to that illusion. She glided through the tough terrain as if she was cruising on casters.

While the others were struggling, Sam sensed something. His nose twitched as his olfactory tool was put on alert. He smelled other dogs. These were not good dogs though. They were wild and hungry. They were mean and ill-tempered. There was a pack of say five to seven of them that were hunting. They were around the pass preparing an ambush. This ambush was directed at his master and his friends.

Sam jumped out of Adlartok's arms and began doing "crazy Sam"—he ran around in circles and tried to convey that they should retreat. This was where not being able to bark was a real disadvantage.

Before the *Big Freeze*, there were rumored to be hairless, bluish-skinned dogs, called *Chupacabras* that drained the blood of goats, cows, and other livestock. They roamed the Texas and Mexico prairies like vampires seeking victims. These were not them though. Aaron's party was just confronting wild dogs of mixed breeds that hunted together--brought together by starvation and teetering on the brink of survival. Dogs like Labradors, German Shepherds, Pit Pulls, Presa Canarios' and Great Danes that once had owners, but were orphaned by the cataclysmic change. They were originally bred for companionship but had now evolved into ruthless killers. All of the smaller dogs had perished---unless they were bioengineered like Sam to survive extreme conditions.

The penumbra of a large creature emerged from the blowing filaments of snow. It had a ferocious growl and its hind legs were flailing looking for flesh of any kind, dog or human. To the surprise of the Presa Canario, it became impaled by the tip of Adlartok's spear pushed into its swarthy throat. Another white shadow rushed them from the side—Aaron knocked the animal down and with surprising speed clubbed it to death with the back of his hatchet. It was a younger dog, clearly emaciated, that had lived on the margins with this pack. A rabid Great Dane leaped on Patches and started chomping at his leg.

Adlartok used the butt of her spear hitting it several times on the head until it was knocked unconscious. By this time, Aaron had retrieved the gun from his belt that Oviak gave him and started firing shots wildly around. After a minute or so, there was only silence. The snow had cleared enough to see that they were in a clearing surrounded by cairns of ice boulders. It looked calm. The snow was streaked with blood and dead animals.

Patches was clutching his leg and pleading for help. Aaron applied a tourniquet with a leather strap he located in his pouch. Patches was still grimacing when Adlartok came over and applied a gluey paste that closed the wound and made the pain bearable. It was another one of those tribal medicines that she brought with her. It also had medicinal qualities to thwart any infection that the dog could be carrying.

Patches said: "I think we were able to fend them off long enough before they were able to do any serious damage." Aaron inspected the wound and although it was a nasty gash he felt it was manageable. What they didn't need at this time were two walking wounded. Patches thanked Adlartok for her help.

Aaron asked: "Can you walk? We need to regroup and put some distance between them. With all the ice pileups here to provide cover we are easy targets." Adlartok was standing guard as they were talking.

"Yea, I think so. Will need some help though to get up." Aaron and Adlartok both helped him to his feet. He was wobbly at first, but gained his balance after a few strides. He walked around and once he felt confident that he could keep upright they moved on. Sammy's eyes were glazed from peering around the edge of every cairn and he was very nervous about what had happened, but that was customary for him.

In the distance, to the southwest of them, they saw a huge ice monolith that was askew, like it should not have been a part of the landscape. Aaron looked on his map and realized that this was the main bridge that connected Laredo to Nuevo Laredo, Mexico. They planned to swing wide of the bridge as this would be where any people would be, if they were in the vicinity. Aaron remembered reading how the rivers were drying up in Texas before the *Freeze* so he anticipated that there would be shallow water that was frozen.

This would enable them to cross at various points—the challenge would be to find the right spot that was accessible and where they could conceal themselves while doing so. They still had a long journey ahead of them.

Patches bleeding had stopped and there was a splotchy dry patch of blood on his pants. There wouldn't be a blood trail to follow but blood had fallen on the ground where the attack took place and there would surely be predators that would pick up the scent. Hopefully the carcasses they left behind would satisfy any pursuers. They had to keep moving to stay ahead of them.

Adlartok helped Patches walk by supporting him with her arm and Aaron pulled the sled. He put Sam on top of the bundles of supplies where he could stay perched and spy the horizon. They walked between the snowy outcrops keeping an eye out for more wild dogs. They reasoned once the dogs regrouped they would also be back on their trail.

The way ahead was fairly clear except for the low frozen sage brush in their path. After a few miles they noted that carrion birds were circling where they had fought the dogs. The sky was filled with wisps of straw-like clouds, the air pure, as they approached a clearing near the river.

They stopped under a huge rock protruding out over the water. It was a steep descent down to the river but the crossing looked promising. The bank on the other side did not rise precipitously and an ascent would be possible without much effort. They paused to catch their breath and to have a small meal. They could use some calories in their system as they prepared for this next task.

They heard a drone overhead. It was still a distance away but becoming louder by the second. Aaron wondered if this was *Whitewater* again, or another band of pirates pillaging from Mexico or another location. They hid under the protruding rock to conceal their presence.

Aaron was rubbing his left leg; it had started to cramp, when the helicopter dove overhead. It was not *Whitewater* this time but another outfit, with an insignia he was not familiar with—a pair of crossed hands with a dinosaur skull bone, similar to a velociraptor. He surmised it was another group looking to pick-up wanderers for a price. Human captives were currency.

When they saw the way was clear, they started down the hill. It was tenuous footing at first but they managed fairly easily to navigate to the beginning of the Rio Grande. They looked upstream and downstream, which was difficult to do, they were not able to tell which way the river used to flow. It looked like an immense ice floe that travelled on into infinity. As far as they could tell there was no one else crossing the river--the helicopter that had passed was on the other side travelling back to an unknown origin in the interior of Mexico.

Sam started to cross on his own but then started backing up and sliding on his hind feet. The ice looked thick enough to support a large animal but Adlartok slammed a few large rocks against the ice just to make sure. Once that was done, they followed Sam across the ice. It was slow going with many near slips but they threaded their way across the snow to the other side of the river. Once there, they found a clump of high brush to stand behind as they looked at the map. They estimated it would be about 150 miles more to Monterrey where there was weather relief--still a great distance, but greater still considering the current state of their physical condition. The only one aside from Adlartok who had any stamina left was Sam—and he wasn't carrying any loads.

The road they would be following, Federal Highway 85 was essentially a continuation of U.S. Interstate 35. Not that they would be following it—to do so would put them at much risk. They would use it as a guidepost as they travelled a safe distance away along the road. As they were getting ready to leave, they heard dogs barking. Sure enough the pack of wild dogs could be seen across the river. However they made no attempt to try and cross. Aaron felt like there was an invisible wall covering their retreat. Why the dogs did not want to cross was a mystery, one that gave Aaron discomfort when he thought about it again in the coming days.

There had been mutterings that when the climate experiments failed a large swathe of government employees were ferried into underground tunnels and housed in survival bunkers under airport terminals all over the U.S. It had been rumored long before the climate change that the government had been preparing to survive as an entity, regardless of what happened to the general public. Aaron had not been approached even though he was a significant player in the quest to find a solution to the nation's troubles. His generally outspoken ways and his independent decision-making sometimes made him a security risk to the government. Or so he thought.

The truth was that he didn't know if this was the case or not, in times of stress and trouble the rumor mill was just that, a rumor mill. But he wasn't totally convinced that some people had not been protected. In time, perhaps the government would emerge from hiding, but right now, as he and his comrades left the continental U.S. no one knew for sure. It had been possible to cache supplies underground without anyone noticing. And there had been reported booms and quakes throughout the U.S. before the *Big Freeze*; these were not of the magnitude of earthquakes or indications of mantle shifting but more on the scale of underground explosions. Conspiracy theorists had reported the use of nuclear-powered military tunnel boring machines, *NTBMs that were capable of melting rock forming glass-like subterranean walls.* Aaron flinched at the thought of so much money being used behind taxpayers' backs. Others postulated that many of the secret operations were financed by the drug money seized at the Mexican border.

Aaron amused himself by visualizing fattened politicians getting skinny on a staple of ready-made meals. No more steak dinners at Morton's and Ruth Chris—no extravagant parties—and they would be wilting with the lack of media airtime they were accustomed to.

As far as the Mexican government was concerned, they were making out like bandits. Their warmer climate enabled them to become more of an industrial state than they were before as there was less competition and fewer manufacturers and producers of goods. They were exporting vast amounts of crops to other countries that were in need. They also were the source of many marauding groups that were not under any government control. Drug cartels were constantly thorns in the sides of Mexican politicians looking to overthrow the Mexico ruling parties. They would kidnap and sell you if not much worse. They abducted small children, especially girls and sold them as sexual slaves. Aaron could only imagine what they would do to poor Sam—put him on a rotisserie or feed him to a Polar bear; it was too horrid to think of.

He wished he was back in New Hampshire swinging on his hammock and viewing the peaceable hills around him. He enjoyed the cool nights of the forests and the deep, rich air which he could breathe in, his lungs able to expand to full capacity. He spent many nights in front of a campfire contemplating the roots of his existence, as if the embers and the fiery glow of the wood were seers who could transport him to his comfortable past and unfurling future. There was an ache of emptiness in him now, one that would be hard to shake, but his slowly developing love for Adlartok was a reason for hope and a possible path out of despair.

Oviak had insisted they wear white coats made out of furs with fleece caps— he knew the value of camouflage and how it would be a key ingredient to their survival. In retrospect, Aaron believed this helped them cross the river without observation. Except for the small stains of dried blood on Patches leg, they were invisible to roving eyes. Every time they stopped, they spent time taking moistened snow and rubbing his pants leg to remove any remaining red residue—they then buried the colored snow in the ground before they started again. They knew it was paramount not to leave a marker of their presence.

From what they could discern, Federal Highway 85 was heavily patrolled. Tire and skid marks were very apparent along the highway. They crisscrossed it a few times and found an established side path that ran along the contours of the road. It was probably a service road that was used for maintenance or by farmers moving livestock or even an old drug runner's secret trail. There was a considerable amount of snow piled up between them and the main road which provided good cover. Patches was getting tired and they would need to find an off-road spot to spend the night. They now had better bedding and a sizeable tent packed on their sleigh that could withstand the elements quite well. So the process of choosing a site would be easier.

Before long, to the side of a rough patch of icy terrain they sighted a mangled ambulance. It was a good 300 yards away from them. The vehicle was turned over on its side and scattered around it was a field of debris. From a distance the windows appeared cracked but the main body of the chassis seemed intact. They decided to take a look. Aaron already had one good experience with a bus; he was hoping this would be another. What they viewed was distressing…there was a pile of bones of various shapes and sizes, many of them looking like they were bitten and slashed with evidence of deeper teeth marks. Nurse' uniforms lay tattered on the ground, perhaps they were moving patients from a nearby hospital when they crashed. The bite marks were too small for polar bears, but had the bearings of dog bites. They speculated that wild dogs were to blame. A stray pack probably had come upon the injured people from the ambulance wreck and made short work of them. They carefully covered the bones with bed sheets they found in the ambulance and moved on. This was not a site they wished to remain near. "Let's get out of here," Aaron motioned with his one good arm.

In Mexico, the snow they were seeing seemed softer and lighter, it was not as immersed in ice. This made for relatively easier passage as they ranged over the terrain. Adlartok was a trooper not only carrying Sam at times but becoming the principal person who towed the sleigh. She was truly a warrior princess. Aaron had taken to teaching her more English by pointing to objects with his stubby arm and asking her to recite the words to him: "Sky, snow, ice, clouds, food" and so on. Her vocabulary was expanding. "Bad and good" were also being taught as they came across situations like the ambulance or when they were pursued by wild dogs or when they made love.

About a mile away, they found some level land to lay out their tents and build a fire. They had a larger tent and a smaller tent that they also erected. Sam immediately snuggled in the larger tent where Aaron and Adlartok would stay. Oviak had also outfitted them with some kindling and small branches which they used to make their fire. Going forward they would have to scavenge wood. It would be a race against the clock to get to Monterrey where they could expect warmer temperatures. Already there was some easing of the cold which they expected to continue as they made their way further south.

They planned to take turns on watch during the night. Patches volunteered to take first watch. He could hear the wind blowing and some coyotes howling in the plains but not much else.

He was nearly asleep when he saw some lanterns in the distance, scouring the landscape, around 2 miles away. He roused the others; Aaron and Adlartok were in a deep sleep with Sam dangling at their feet. They put out their fire and sat shivering on some blankets outside the tents. The band of intruders appeared to be coming towards them when about a half mile away they veered off towards the direction of the Rio Grande River. It was hard to tell what they were doing but it seemed they were surveying the ground. *Was it a night patrol? Kidnappers? Drug lords? Who could tell?* The rest of the night passed uneasily where they shared some small naps between very watchful eyes.

Waking up, all of Aaron's party was tired. They dared not make a fire for fear of smoke detection, so they ate what dried food they had but that was unpleasant and hard to digest. They would have preferred hot food.

Another recurring problem was how to hide their waste and dog droppings. They had to bury everything. It was hard to chip through the snow and ice to make the necessary holes. They were worried that this could be another way for trackers to find them. They rolled up the tents, packed up, and started off.

After spending another night with Adlartok, Aaron was thinking back to his high school prom. It was the first time he kissed a girl. He had spent a wonderful evening at a Bostonian club and was driving Marjorie home when she started rubbing the top of his hand. It sent a chill of delight through his being, a sense of feeling wanted and a sensation of wonder. Before she departed, she smacked a kiss on his cheek which he returned with a full parting kiss on her lips. It seemed like an innocent mystery then, but now he was tumbling into love again, a freefall of firsts on a totally different planet, in a time unlike any in his life, one who's ending was unclear. Even in the darkest of times, there appeared to be light. One need only look for it.

It was late in the morning and they were traversing a gorge, when they started to hear noises ahead. It sounded like a fight of some kind…there were gunshots, shouts, and screaming coming from the valley. Adlartok gestured to the others and they lowered themselves to the ground so that they faced a ridge. Adlartok crawled on her stomach to the edge and looked down. In a vast expanse before her, she saw a high-rise prison...it was teeming with people. There was virtual chaos on the ground. This did not appear to be like the camps in the U.S.—as it was full of Mexicans. Adlartok had no way of knowing that when Aaron came up behind her to take in the view. From what Aaron could tell there had been a prison break and several guards had fired at a few men before subduing them. This looked more like a state penitentiary. He knew that in years past Mexico had many conflicts with drug kingpins, especially in areas close to the border. Perhaps this was one of their holdover prison installations that the U.S. in partnership with Mexico built.

It looked like things were getting under control so they stepped back and made a wide detour around the camp.

They were two days out from Laredo and making nice progress. They expected to make Monterrey in a bit over a week. The terrain here was hillier than Texas but the increasing temperatures were a relief. Wildlife consisted mainly of aerial creatures and the small furry ground creatures they feasted upon. Patches' leg was healing and he was walking better. It was a good sign that he no longer had to be supported when standing up. Patches' health was important especially if they had further encounters.

A few days later, near the region of Sabinas Hidalgo, Sam was out of sorts again and getting very nervous. They had made good time and were advancing without as much effort. However, on the east side of the road near some craggy hills, nestled between some cacti, they noticed a campfire. Aaron moved closer to take a look. He saw what looked like border patrol guards, but they were not in uniform, even though one of the snowmobiles had a border patrol insignia stamped on it. It did seem peculiar if these were border patrol agents as they were a distance away from the border, unless they were on route to the border on a mission.

The clue that gave it away, that these were not any ordinary men, was the young girl that they had tied up and chained to one of the snowmobile steering wheels. She looked bruised and in distress, the ropes binding her hands had caused nasty red welts on her wrists. Her clothes were partially torn and her feet were lacerated and bleeding.

There were four of them, *rapists*.....each taking turns in a quickly erected tent with another girl who could be heard periodically screaming.

*These men are animals, resorting to barbaric tactics to terrorize and take advantage of these young girls,* were the thoughts racing into Aaron's head. He wanted to shout out and storm the camp, but that would be foolhardy. They would need a plan. He went back and consulted with Patches.

One of the men, after apparently having sex in the tent, was urinating on the young girl who was clamped to the snowmobile. Making this scenario even more surreal and upsetting was hearing one of the men listening to Claude DeBussy's *Clair De Lune* in the background on a new shiny looking portable CD player. The other two men were napping against a Mexican nut pine apparently sated after extended time in the tent.

Aaron went back to take a second look with Patches. Peering through the binoculars that had been a gift from Oviak, they noticed that the men's faces were frightfully deformed. It looked like they had acquired a skin disease. Aaron remembered reading briefings about such strange phenomenon when he was doing his research work on the Chemtrails for the U.S. government. It had been reported that there was an outbreak of leprosy in some regions of Mexico. It was a little known fact that armadillos were carriers of Hansen's disease, Leprosy, and they were contagious to humans. Aaron had glossed over this not fully realizing its implication. Perhaps the autoimmune depressing characteristics of the Chemtrails aerial dispersals had spurred a larger scale eruption of this disease. Areas around Texas and Northern Mexico were serially bombarded by the aerial tankers when the program was in full operation. This could be a residual effect.

*The next question was what to do? Should they move on, undetected, and continue on their trip to Chapultepec Park?* Patches had made his mind up: "We can't just leave them here, if it was one of my daughters I would want someone to help. I hate taking additional risks, but what is right is right."

Aaron was more hesitant; he had the dog to consider as well as his new-found love interest. It was Adlartok who sprung them into action. She started circling the camp, spear ready, poised to make a solo effort to save the girls.

The man who had been urinating was especially terrifying—one side of his face had numerous pulpy folds in it pocked with ugly discolored tumors. He was now trying to rouse one of his sleepy friends so they could start the round-robin rape again. Aaron interpreted the Spanish: "Get up, it's your turn, this lamb chop is nearly dead, I will stand watch."

As he said this, a spear thrown out of the brush, pierced his torso. He went down immediately, holding the spear that penetrated him with both his hands. Adlartok worked quickly, she pounced on the two sleeping men, slitting their throats with a long curved knife she was carrying. The other man, coming out of the tent, was also surprised—Aaron and Patches grabbed him and wrestled him to the ground. Patches hit the top of his head several times with the butt of his gun and he lay unconscious. His skull had been cracked and part of his brain was expanding out of a crevice on the side of his head. The man gurgled fluids out of his mouth, barely breathing, his chest heaving up and down.

All of this occurred in less than sixty seconds. The next order of business was to release the girls, who after they calmed down, thanked them repeatedly in broken English.

Now, the group was at an impasse, *what could they do with the girls?* Their conditions varied. The girl, Lauren, who they freed from the snowmobile, though badly bruised, was relatively unscathed. She could walk and once released talked gingerly. She was the older of the two girls. The younger girl, who was 16 years old, was battered, and in very grave shape. They pulled her from the tent and rested her on some thick blankets. Her breathing was very rapid and her arms were flailing still trying to ward off the offenders. She had a long streak of blood down one side of her leg. Adlartok took a rag they had and started to clean her up. They used the fire to boil the rag first in water to make it sterile so as to limit infection.

While Adlartok attended to Sarah, they learned that the girls were sisters. They were captured while traveling from a ranch to an outpost that was deemed a safe haven near Monterrey. They had not known about the refugee camp in Chapultepec Park, but they might not have known because they had lived in a relatively isolated province of Northern Mexico.

They pooled their efforts into trying to save the younger sister. One of her arms appeared to be broken…which they set and put into a sling. One of her eyes was bloodshot and was oozing blood. Adlartok wiped that clean. Adlartok also applied her poultice to the origination wound in Sarah's left leg, but to the dismay of everyone, she stopped breathing. Aaron tried CPR several times without success. Lauren was inconsolable and had to be restrained. She wanted to mutilate the bodies of her captors. She regained more of her composure when she learned the man who raped her in the tent had died. *The rapidity of these events had deeply shaken the group and left them in total disarray.* Sam was shaking violently and had to be comforted by Adlartok—he had been watching the actions unfold from afar and was laden with grief as only a dog can be by witnessing the transgressions of humans he did not totally understand.

For Aaron, this represented a conundrum. In good conscience, they couldn't abandon Lauren and go on by themselves. But adding her to the group was going to not only put a further burden on their food supply but *create additional risks* for their party. He was starting to feel more and more responsible for the safety of the group. He had failed at protecting his family from the landslide, even though logically it wasn't his fault, but he did not want to fail again. His past losses weighed on his mind and made inaction unconscionable.

So they pillaged the camp for what was salvageable. Fire starter, extra ammunition and a shotgun, cans of dried food, water jugs, and spare gasoline they carried away and affixed it all to their sleigh. They decided not to take the snowmobile as it had a limited gas supply and they were afraid the noise would make them more of a target. They used a sharp shovel to dig through the crusty snow so that they could bury all of the bodies. They doused the fire and tried to hide traces of the coals and embers—there was no way of knowing if there was another group nearby connected to the men. Someone would find the snowmobile, but that was a risk they would have to live with.

If leprosy was more endemic in Mexico than had been reported, then this was also going to pose an additional problem for the group. But Aaron felt that it would not.

The group of 5 *(including Sam)* tramped out of the camp. They headed back to the relative safety of the side roads which were less watched. The day was wearing on and they wanted to put some distance between the camp and where they would find bedding for the night. Most likely the night would bring scavengers that would dig up the bodies and feast on the remains.

It was a cruel, cold world. People that survived did not spend time ruminating on their changing circumstances. They made swift choices that lead to decisive actions. Speed wins the day. Hesitation could lead to death.

A bald eagle could be seen in the sky above, white cropped head and pointed black talons racing in the air currents. He was far South from his normal range. For many migrating birds migration was no longer a two way annual tour; it was becoming a one-way journey to a permanent home.

Their new addition, Lauren, seemed very nimble and friendly, even though she was heartbroken by the death of her sister. She took to Sam and often carried him when the snow got challenging. Sam was fast becoming a lady's man. And he liked it.

A few days later, when the sun was shining bright and all that glistened was diamond, they arrived without fanfare in the area of Monterrey.

Doing some quick calculations in his head, Aaron estimated that he walked 600,000 steps to get here from the prison camp. *Who would have thought this was possible?* Through countless hardships, biting winds, bone-chilling weather, and insurmountable odds they had reached the beginning of the *Warm Zone!* But the trip was a little bit more than a third over; they still had close to 600 miles to trek to sanctuary in Mexico City or over another million steps. Thinking about it in those terms was daunting and made Aaron's spine stiffen. He thought it better to keep this information to himself, *why sour the others.*

Monterrey was a substantial city in Mexico and was well-populated with over 5 million people. It sat in the foothills of the Sierra Madre Oriental Mountains and was bisected by the Santa Catarina River which is a dry river on the surface, but is full of underground running streams. With the advent of the climate changes the city was depopulated to a significant degree, not so much by the cold, but because of its fringe location near several overlapping weather systems. It used to be one of the hottest spots in Mexico was and considered one of the most "Americanized" of Mexico's cities, but now it was a half-way house composed entirely of drifters, violent gangs, dealmakers, and slave traders—in short a hell hole specializing in unscrupulous commerce. Still it was warmer than other areas north, keeping a year-round temperature of between 40 and 50 degrees that Aaron and his company enjoyed. The snow melt had eventually disappeared during the last 3 day trek.

They decided that it would be too dangerous for all of them to venture into the city. They opted instead to camp a safe distance away and Patches volunteered to scout around and see what supplies and food he could procure for the rest of the trip.

The city was in shambles due to the itinerant nature of its occupants. People traveled to and fro among various assorted shops and stands dotting the streets. There was a sharp smell of partially spoiled beef being cooked and noxious odors from the numerous stray animals meandering about, some of them looking fit, others looking sadly emaciated.

Aaron stayed with Adlartok at a prominent lookout point near the foot of the mountains. They were a safe distance away from any wayward travelers. Sam stayed with them. Lauren escorted Patches while he walked towards the city; he was armed, and carried some amulets and other charms Oviak had given them. He was hoping to trade them for something useful. He was also reconnoitering the town trying to pick up any hearsay that would help them. Lauren stayed behind at the edge of the city as a secondary lookout. She, like Adlartok, had a hardy constitution.

The current population was in the area of fifty thousand people much less than the six million who lived here when the city was at its apex. One of the things Patches remembered about this city was a terror attack that occurred in 2011 that killed 150 people. Drug gangs ranged through the city using their cars as battering rams and running over innocent pedestrians for fun. He read an article about it while he was sitting on the deck of his house that summer. He shuddered to think about the type of people who would do that. He did not like the look of Monterrey; it did not look like a Promised Land. It smelled bad.

He noticed the source of the smell, rotten chicken carcasses that were dumped in piles near the corner of the roads. People were buying slabs of chicken from vendors cooking on rotisseries in the street. They were gutting the chickens in the streets and tossing their innards wherever there was open space. Chicken parts were starting to fill in all the holes and the crevices of the road, like a smelly asphalt of animal tissue.

What Aaron remembered when times were rough was that he entered the world alone and he would leave this life alone. Humans are born into space that they don't necessarily choose and inhabit the space until they die. They are taught and nurtured by institutions like schools and governments that tell them what is good and bad, what is right or wrong, and compel them to follow social contracts based upon societal and religious laws. It always struck Aaron that much of this was made up, artificial constructs, humans imposed on each other. Yes it was based partly on moral conscience and faith, but no one group had a monopoly on all the answers. We were all visitors from the dark, who lived in a space of light for a while, but then eventually receded back into darkness. Could one's life be so bright that its glow would last forever? He would love to find out.

In these many days of darkness, Aaron had yearned for light. The long trip from the prison camp had re-ignited and enlightened him. He had saved Patches and kept Sam alive. He had fought through tough terrain and discovered survival skills he was dimly aware of. He was starting to relearn what it was to love someone and to believe in its perpetuity. He no longer wanted to die; he wanted to live in the light. He never felt lonelier and he never felt stronger.

Adlartok had set up a tent and had thrown a bundle of warm blankets and furs across the opening leading into the tent. She had disrobed and was standing at the front entrance when Aaron turned around. He walked slowly towards her and wrapped his arms around her. They hurriedly went inside caressing lightly at first then more forcibly. She undid his zipper and drew down his pants. It was cold at first inside the tent, but after a while, the heat from their love-making rose like a scintillating fire imbuing the tent with warmth and a lightness of being. This went on for quite a while.

The roads were slick with mud and the sidewalks barely visible where Patches walked. He kept to the side, watching closely the pedestrians who passed by. They were mostly Mexican but occasionally he passed other foreigners he could not identify. He did notice that there were people who were talking in hushed tones, as if they didn't want to be heard. He figured they were hustlers or thugs that were looking to make a profit on human trafficking or in some other lowly occupation. He wanted to keep clear of these types of people. He also noticed some prostitutes in windows, kind of like the old Wild West saloons. They were dressed brightly, with ragged black string stockings, waving out to the male pedestrians who passed by.

"Can I help you in any way sir?" a young boy of fifteen asked Patches. "I know where you can find food, guns, and a date, whatever it is you are looking for." He seemed too young to have this much carnal knowledge. He continued: "In Monterrey we have everything; we are the gateway to the Warm Zone."

Patches eyed him suspiciously: "Thank-you very much. Right now I am fine. You could help me in one area though. Is there a pawn shop in the vicinity? Or a place of trading? I have some items I was hoping to sell."

"Yea, down on Clancy Lane, there are book shops where they also sell the articles you are speaking of. I heard people turning in items for cash too. My Mom, Gertrude, works there. Should I tell her you are coming?"

"No need. If you can direct me. I will walk there now." Cal, as the boy was called, pointed to a spot about two hundred yards away near a tall clock. He told Patches to turn right near the clock and he would find what he was looking for.

When Patches arrived at the clock he noticed it was stuck at 1:50 pm. What happened at that time to stop the clock? Before he could consider this, he saw the sign to Clancy Lane and made the right turn which brought him to the store front. He entered and waited at the counter. No one was in the store. He saw a small dog that was sleeping on a pillow and a cat that was in the window, both seemed bored. There was a variety of books in the store as well as other paraphernalia. He saw Civil War coins with Lincoln heads and small wartime sabers that came from WWI. There were a number of first editions of various titles: "Huckleberry Finn," as well as "A Connecticut Yankee in King Arthur's Court" by Mark Twain and "A Passage to India" by E.M. Forster, all favorite books of Patches. He also saw a copy of Norman MacLean's "A River Runs Through It" one of his favorite novellas. Patches loved action stories that held a message.

There, in the corner, was some of what he was looking for, food stuffs. He saw cans of soups, jars of fruits, and lumps of hard bacon and sinewy mutton on a shelf. It was hard to decipher meat-based products these days. There were also camping supplies and a large locked Sentry safe with a clear, double-plated tempered glass window that contained various firearms and ammunition. On the far wall, he noted a variety of rat poisons and insect repellents. He wondered if the city was now infested with rats and invaded by bugs as the weather had warmed. There was a large display showing Mexican war heroes, like Santa Anna, and some faded pictures of a run-down Alamo in Texas. He guessed the person who owned the shop might be a war history buff as there were other bas relief sculptures of famous commanders like George Patton, Napoleon, and General George Washington, and even Hitler's Rommel aka "Desert Fox."

On the countertop were a variety of Mayan artifacts: arrowheads, moccasins, ornate belts, and colorful head bands. The shop was braced with thick timber columns and the paneling was composed of etched woodwork. The room was lit with paraffin candles which gave off a noxious odor that was not healthy for humans. The shop had the feel of a museum, not a packaged goods store.

"Who goes there?" a squeaky raspy voice called out from an unlit corner of the room. "Didn't you read the sign?"

"No I didn't," responded Patches. "I will go back and check now." He started retreating to the front door undecided what would be the next best course of action when he noticed the sign. It read: "Out to Lunch, Be back after I have my Jiffy Pop." Patches didn't know if he should laugh or get the hell out of there…this was going to be one of those oddball encounters that would be difficult to predict an ending for. "OK, I will come back when you are ready to be seen."

"Wait, I'm coming now." That squeaky voice rang out again. Out of the corner of his eye Patches marveled at the image of the woman coming forward from the rear of the room. She looked to be about 70 years old, had a marked camel hump for a back, tangled grey hair, protruding nose, and a cane which steadied her. Her chin nearly reached the middle of her chest. "My name is Gertrude."

"Glad to meet you, my name is Patches. I know it is an unusual name but I am an unusual person. I come from America."

"That's just dandy," Gertrude rejoined. "Most Americans I know are either dead or locked up." She replied with very little warmth. "I am one of them who are neither."

"I am glad to hear Americans are still living and it looks like you are prospering in Monterrey. Any idea how many Americans are living here?"

"Who wants to know? Are you some sort of agent looking to round up Americans? If so, I want to know. I will get you in trouble in no time," Gertrude blurted out. She was used to doing the questioning and not being questioned.

"Oh, not at all. I am passing through and looking for some supplies. I am planning to leave soon. Would you be interested in some Inuit trinkets I acquired? They were given to me in trust from a friend?"

With that, Patches rolled open the small blanket he had placed all the items in and displayed them on Gertrude's counter. She started inspecting them one by one, looking carefully for any blemishes, and then announced: "I will give you 50 dollars American credit for them – to be used in the store."

Patches responded: "Deal. Can I look around?"

"Yes, but hurry, I need to close the shop again, I am on my way to a meeting."

Something was not right, so Patches was not going to wait around and find out. He grabbed the first few things he saw that rounded up to 50 dollars: 10 cans of assorted soups, some of that dried mutton and bacon, beef jerky, and some pinches of chewing tobacco for an old habit. As he was thanking Gertrude, he saw a Mexican police officer peering through the window. The kid had tipped off the cop, he was being treated as a trespasser, that was for sure, or he was being considered for something far worse. He knew Gertrude was too old to be that boy's mother.

Patches scrambled out of the store holding his pack of goodies in front of his face. His unkempt look was alarming to the policeman as well as the speed at which Patches moved. He turned the corner and started trotting between alleyways filled with discarded ash, decrepit cars and rusting dumpsters while the policeman followed him. He dodged around a few corners and felt he had successfully evaded his pursuer when the sirens started ringing. By that time he was on the edge of town following the original path he took to get into Monterrey. He met up with Lauren, who appeared frightened, and they hurried back to their camp.

For their own part, Aaron and Adlartok had packed up the tent and were ready to leave when they heard the first faint sirens. They didn't know if the alarm had anything to do with Patches or if there was another unrelated incident in town. To be safe, they packed up their belongings and put them on the sleigh which was now getting harder to move due to dirt and sand. They had rigged some makeshift wheels but they were only temporary. Patches, being of carpentry bent, suggested perhaps they could retrofit the sleigh with larger wooden wheels that he could build or find along the way.

They started out immediately upon Patches and Lauren's arrival. They were grateful he was back alive and even gladder he had booty. They couldn't explain why their presence was unwanted, but it was. Aaron thought this cool reception might be because Patches was a stranger, but he was worried about other upcoming encounters including their final destination at Chapultepec

Park….*was his hard won information incorrect? Could they be going into a trap? Or was this all just a huge mistake?* They needed to know more before they committed themselves to any permanent settlement or solution.

Consulting the map, it looked to Aaron that they would have to travel west first to avoid mountains that stood in their way to Mexico City; they could then eventually turn back south again to travel towards Chapultepec Park. They really weren't equipped for mountain hiking nor were they in the state of mind to put forth the kind of effort that was needed to climb steep, tricky, rocky, slippery, and uncharted trails. Patches and Aaron had lingering leg injuries that slowed them down. So they followed the path of least resistance.

A penumbra of gloom had fallen upon them after this last encounter. All they could do, was what they always did, put one foot forward then again, then again and then again…moving one step closer to sanctuary if not redemption.

The day was getting late and they were on back roads which were not on their map. The vistas were getting quite beautiful, in the distance they could see the famed Cerro de la Silla, also known as Saddle Hill, with its unique topography resembling a horse's saddle, towering at 1575 meters. They soon found themselves in a wide valley without much cover and they started to see bollards again ringed by barb wired. They carefully avoided them because if they were to get caught in one of their snares, it would be very difficult to get out. It was still a mystery why there were so many of these placed throughout the countryside. *Was it meant to keep people out or to keep people in?*

Lauren was still upset by the loss of her sister and although she was a survivor by nature she was getting increasingly disconsolate. Patches came to her aide repeatedly and tried to console her, but it was difficult given the circumstances, they were almost on a forced march as they left Monterrey. His leg was still hurting and he was struggling to keep up the pace.

Serendipitously it was at this point that Lauren spied movement in the valley before them…it looked like a group of animals herded together, amazingly docile looking. As they got closer, the strays didn't run away, *possibly because they were domesticated?* Aaron and Adlartok cautiously approached what was a number of burros who were congregating together. They took rope that Oviak gave them and were able to tie three of the donkeys together. It was quite a find, especially considering they needed to make more speed and were mentally and physically exhausted. Patches hatched a plan to use them like pack horses to carry their loads. They soon learned that Lauren was an experienced animal handler; she had worked extensively at a ranch where they had horses, pigs, donkeys and other livestock. She knew how to properly tie up the animals and helped craft a backpack using the blankets and other materials they had. This would alleviate the great pain they were experiencing from dragging their provisions across the prairie. It was a real find—*Rara Avis*—just in the nick of time.

Starting to look like a motley crew, Aaron and his band had new-found enthusiasm for their expedition. Not having to trudge through snow and ice was comforting but the addition of a pack of burros to move their cargo brought them a reprieve they needed from the constant labor of moving the sleigh.

The next few days passed swiftly, for the first time in quite a while they made very good time, traveling a distance they reckoned of about 50 miles. If the burros were to survive, they had to keep them hydrated and find them abundant pastures with greens and hay along the way. The temperature was getting warmer and their thirst and water requirements were growing.

Patches was becoming more attached to Lauren and walked frequently alongside her. He learned that she was Mexican raised near the fishing village of Zihuatanejo made famous by Tom Hank's movie *Shawshank Redemption*. Aaron remembered a famous quote from that movie that applied to his present situation: "Get busy living or get busy dying." He thought about that often.

Lauren had moved to a ranch with her sister when the tourist industry died off. Ixtapa which was located nearby was once a thriving area of commerce due to tourism but there were no longer any tourists coming from the Northern Hemisphere. Its wind-swept pristine beaches were unkempt and full of sharp, tarred rocks and seaweed. Most beachside resorts had peeling paint and salt intruded decay. The famed Camino Real resort looked like a broken down piano without legs or keys—its outside walls fading full of termite rot.

Lauren and her sister Sarah had left this environment to go to a ranch where at least there was activity and a few square meals. They became trained ranch hands, starting their days very early, and going to bed at dusk. They were like two peas in a pod until they strayed from the ranch to see more of Northern Mexico where they were apprehended by the scurrilous lepers. It was a senseless crime which occurred too frequently.

That evening, they sat around their campfire in pairs-- Lauren and Patches together and Aaron and Adlartok. Sam was the odd dog out. When Aaron and Adlartok retired to their tent, Patches and Lauren remained outside sharing small talk. Eventually Patches moved in closer and he placed his arm around Lauren's waist. She pulled away slightly at first but then became more comfortable. Lauren had a long brown mane of flowing hair that wrapped around her hips. She was subtly attractive and full-bosomed with high cheekbones that gave her a noble look even though she was born poor on the coastline of Western Mexico.

He felt awkward, he estimated that Lauren was at least 20 years younger than him, but in this new climate changed world who was counting?

He touched her hair with the tips of his fingers, lightly at first, then deftly running the long tresses through the space between his thumb and forefinger.

She became aroused and turned to kiss Patches and they were locked in long embraces for several minutes before they undressed and consummated. Like Aaron, Patches felt revived and more alive since he could remember. For Lauren, she wasn't yet sure she really loved Patches, but she did respect him and felt a common bond. Her passion was more instinctual, borne out of base desire.

The next morning featured an unusually bright sun and high fecund clouds with the troop leaving early. Having their hands free of gloves, in Aaron's case one hand, they enjoyed the freedom of movement of their hands. They also had been dressing lighter and stowed the extra clothing in the burros' packs. They constructed a little carrier on one of the burros, so if

Sam got tired, they could situate him there. He did not like it at first due to the bumpiness of the ride, but eventually adjusted to it, and seemed to like it. It gave him an expanded view of the terrain.

As they moved closer to Mexico City, and closer to the equator, the sun would become less of a friend. The temperature could be expected to start creeping up and they would have to start worrying about heat stroke and exposure, but that was not a concern at the moment. More pressing would be their search for food as the Oviak and Monterrey food stores had run low. They had picked up some additional water that had melted into small pools at the edge of the Rio Grande, but that was running out too.

Adlartok was not used to the warmth and would be the one most likely to suffer. She had lived in a cold environment her entire life and was habituated to arctic living. But she had great reserves of strength, and Aaron thought she would adapt to the changing conditions.

The burros seemed happy to have human company. Aaron surmised they had been owned by somebody and then somehow lost--part of his reasoning was because of the branded letters he noticed behind the donkey's ears: "*WW*", it reminded him of something that made him feel uneasy, but he couldn't immediately put his finger on it. Then, as he thought about it some more, he remembered "Whitewater", but they were an airborne group, could they also have land-based units? Aaron didn't want to think about it.

They marched their way through many winding dingles and foothills while keeping well out of sight. Clouds of dust generated by the burros' hooves were becoming a concern—Patches rigged a pad that he tied to the bottom of their feet which provided some dust abatement—however this did not provide a total solution. Swirls of dust could be seen periodically meandering above their pack trail. It kept everyone on edge and alert to interlopers.

They were making good time, on the road for about a week, about 1/3$^{rd}$ the way to Mexico City, when disaster struck. Two of the burros got their legs entangled with each other, crashing to the ground, and one landed on Sam. Aaron, in a moment of supernormal strength, wrestled the burro off Sam's body, but he was too late. Sam was crushed and whimpering lightly. Adlartok came to the dog's side and inspected him; she began shaking her head from side to side at Aaron, as tears cascaded down both sides of her face.

Sam looked longingly at Aaron knowing his journey was over and he was not going to be with Aaron at Chapultepec Park. Aaron was crushed; his grief so deep that all time stood still, this last link with his past being released, like a burning candle being snuffed out.

Adlartok took Sam and carried him away from the others. She held him lovingly and stroked his fur, aware of the dog's deep pain. Without pause she very quickly snapped his neck like it was a chicken wishbone and the dog died instantly. She then cradled the dog and carried him back to Aaron and placed him on the ground. It was at this point that everyone recognized that Sam was truly dead.

A long silence fell over the group. The burros had righted themselves and were vaguely aware of the situation. Patches and Lauren were in disbelief and Aaron was heartbroken. Aaron and Patches decided that in the end the best thing to do was to cremate Sam. They dug a pit and placed wood in it and started a fire. Aaron gently placed Sam on the fire when it was roaring hot. They stayed until there were only simmering bones and then filled the hole with dirt. They camouflaged it with wads of fine debris so that no one or animal could find it. It was a grueling and heart-breaking exercise but one that had to be done. As they departed Aaron felt he left a part of himself with Sam — a part that could never be retrieved, Sam became a photograph in his mind that he could recollect and one that would never be forgotten.

The air was starting to get heavy with humidity while the sun was jettisoning high in the sky. The mid-afternoon heat was drifting across the valley and becoming stifling—even though they were down to one layer of clothing. Adlartok was comforting Aaron as best she could. Aaron was shocked by Sam's death. He just couldn't accept that one of the helpful burros killed his dog. He wanted to pull out his gun and shoot the burro; he never felt anger like this before. It was not like him that the only solace he could find was in thoughts of revenge. He knew it was self-defeating and unacceptable by his high moral standards. He strived to always be on spiritually higher ground rather than join the fray but in this case his anger was getting the best of him.

Aaron wandered back to when they first obtained Sam. He was a gift from one of his colleagues who worked at *Mycoflex Enterprises*, a cutting edge firm dedicated to the development of bioengineered animal breeds. Many Sam's' did not make it through the assembly lines to production; there were numerous deformed hybrids that were un-sanctimoniously disposed of away from PETA eyes and secretly buried in remote places in New Mexico. Sam was part of an exclusive club that was successfully bred according to a new and secret engineered code. They were trying to create dogs that could be used in the field of battle to gain advantage over the enemy. They had special characteristics like: expanded olfactory functions, oversized jaws with stone hard teeth that could be used like bolt cutters, multiple legs that could attain speeds up to 50 mph, dogs with advanced optics that could see forms clearly in the darkness and at great distances, and a whole host of other militarized capabilities. Sam, being a Maltese, was a "throw-away" dog, — they didn't really plan to use the Maltese breed in cold climate war tactics, that's why Aaron inherited him. Sam was essentially discarded from a litter of bioengineered dogs "gone awry".

Aaron came from a large litter too. He was the eldest of seven children, who lived with a mother who was verbally, but never physically abused by her alcoholic husband. His father left the family when Aaron was ten and his mother struggled to survive in Lancaster, NH. She worked nights cleaning patient rooms at a local hospital and waitressed during the day. Aaron remembered her as always being in white uniforms plastered with dirt stains from either the housekeeping job or with food stains on her uniform from the greasy spoon, Joe's Moose Diner, in town. She was a hard worker, a habit Aaron emulated when he went to secondary school, where he was studious to a point, this eventually driving him to a professorship at M.I.T. Unfortunately for the surviving siblings his mother died very young--one of Aaron's sisters found their mother on the couch one day, curled asleep, as if she had collapsed under the weight of all the hardship in her life--her last cries echoing into an empty room. This final stillness caused great pain for Aaron. Her joys and sorrows became his; he felt guilty about her death thinking he could have done more to prevent it while she was still living.

Though Aaron loved his mother dearly he still longed for a relationship with a father he never knew. One June evening this wish too was cut short. A policeman came to his doorstep and informed their family that his father died in a hunting accident in Bozeman, Montana. His father's shotgun misfired while on a grizzly bear hunt killing him instantly. He was cremated and his ashes scattered under a thorn bush near a local gin mill. A small sample of his ashes was shipped in a vial to Aaron's mother – she thought it was an illicit drug and threw it out only to learn later it was her husband's ashes. The rest of his belongings arrived later on a UPS truck. There was virtually nothing worth keeping. Aaron was given the only item with any value, a Bronze star. His father had earned it in Vietnam when he provided early warning of a Vietnamese patrol that was set to ambush his platoon. He was an advance scout and set off a flare to warn his comrades, risking his own life in the process.

Aaron felt like his father now as he strove to keep his party alive. Even though he was handicapped, he felt he needed to continue to be a strong leader for the sake of the group. He pushed thoughts of Sam into the back of his mind and groped forward knowing that each moment that passed was vital in their march towards Chapultepec Park.

From where they were, Chapultepec Park was straight south, Aaron reckoned about 400 miles away. Rte. 57 seemed to be a bit circuitous, but was a main road that skirted rougher terrain and one that they could easily shadow. In their current condition, they did not want to take the burros on any rougher trails that could cause another accident, potentially leaving one of the humans dead or losing a burro and their belongings in a slip or fall off a ridge.

They had to be very careful to avoid disclosure from above and worked to keep their movement inconspicuous. They made a group decision to travel at night now and hunker down during the day. This would be the last day they travelled so they wanted to make sure the burros were fed and watered so they could start traveling at night. Adlartok would attend to the burros and make sure they were in good shape to travel, Aaron was sure of that.

Occasionally the burros would pull on Adlartok's long braids of hair with their front teeth. She found it all very amusing until one of the braids got caught in the animal's mouth and the animal wrenched her to the ground. She had to slash off a 6 inch length of her beloved locks with her knife. It was the first time Aaron thought Adlartok was actually annoyed.

In retrospect, Aaron never really could understand how the U.S. populace, as well as other countries' citizenry never ascertained that their weather was being modified. All they had to do was look up into the sky on any given day to see the grid-like spawning of Chemtrails by high altitude aircraft. Did they think this a *Fata Morgana?*

What made these different were the deliberate pattern and overlapping that suggested intelligence behind their design. Aaron remembered testing one of his New Hampshire neighbors about it one day by asking him to observe the unusual expanding clouds in the sky. The neighbor looked up at the sky, darted her eyes across the horizon, and then started remarking about *The Housewives of Orange County* as if this anomaly was a normal state of affairs for the weather. It was at this point that Aaron realized that what governments were doing was going to be undetected. Later on, when the damage done was more recognizable, people ignored the truth, even though it was staring them in the face. Perhaps *Tolkien* was right in his allegory about hobbits; humans were most comfortable stuffed in their rabbit holes, preferring to live in the safety of darkness, not yearning for enlightenment.

Late afternoon they stopped to take a short rest before starting again. Everyone needed a break; they were unused to the warmer weather which was making them hot and sweaty and irritable. Patches seemed to be having the most problems with acclimatization. He had wet splotches all over his back from excessive sweating and he was straining to breathe. He had not been very athletic in his youth, reserving himself for polished discourse with those he considered his intellectual equals. This made him an out-of-shape middle aged man now struggling in the wilderness. He was lucky Lauren had taken to him; she repeatedly used a worn rag to wipe his forehead, keeping the salty sweat from running down and burning his eyes.

The landscape was changing. Thorny cacti sprouting flowery buds were becoming commonplace and the sides of ridges and mesas were showing their tanned hides free of the ice and snow that was prevalent before. Travelling in broad daylight had been risky business; a risk that Aaron later calculated was one they should have avoided. But all was well now except for the simmering memory of Sam which cast a palpable pall on the party.

They decided to set up their tents with the intent to doze off for a few hours before they started again. The burros were tied to a stand of stout sagebrush that they had found and left to graze on whatever they could reach. Patches and Lauren retreated to a tent together finding comfort from each other's presence. Patches was on the verge of heat stroke and needed some serious rest. Adlartok and Aaron took the first watch, watching the changing sky grow first a deep blue then a sullen black. They could observe many stars in the sky now as they were not shielded by towers of ice. Aaron wondered if one of those stars shone on a planet that also underwent severe climate change. It was believed that when the Earth's sun was warmer and Mars was habitable, perhaps civilizations had flourished there. By a few it was even thought that life on earth was originally seeded from Mars. Aaron was a bit of a skeptic on this subject but he became a believer of cryptic phenomenon when three years ago while hiking, he came across some large prints that ran across an abandoned covered bridge. He was hiking across the Ammonoosuc River near the town of Littleton in New Hampshire. He looked up and out of the corner of his eye he saw a huge man-like beast striding into the forest. Since that incident, and because of his top secret clearance, he knew there was more than what was being reported by the media. He also knew that there were many gag orders in place to hide much of what was happening and known behind the scenes.

This evening there seemed to be an abundance of shooting stars, many of them burning out very quickly as they dived through the atmosphere. Further south from them, they spied one shooting star that looked like it did not burn out, it seemed to land on the ground. That was curious and something that would warrant careful watching. While this was occurring the moon was slowly rising and it started to project a luminescent beam across the sagebrush so that their position was no longer invisible. This made Aaron nervous and uneasy. They no longer had Sam who had a knack for knowing when something was about to go wrong.

Things were going right in Patches and Lauren's tent. This was the first evening they were really together and Lauren was taking advantage of it. Once Patches was settled in, she slowly disrobed him and cleaned him up. He was in a bit of a fog but when Lauren undressed he perked up. They lay together for about an hour before they had intercourse. This was the most refreshing two hours Patches had in the past 5 years since his imprisonment. The sex renewed him and like Aaron he felt he had a new lease on life. He didn't know exactly what his true feelings for Lauren were but he had been starving for human companionship and for now that is all that mattered. He could sort things out later.

Before he could think any more about it, Lauren started fondling his saggy testicles in her hand and as he responded they were fully engaged again. When Patches was younger his quest for perfection had kept him out of many relationships – it was beginning to dawn on him that he should have more fully capitalized on his opportunities if only to make his life more pleasurable.

While Aaron was surveying the sky he was beginning to question again his decision to travel to Chapultepec Park. Really the only evidence he had heard of its existence was from the hearsay of people passing through the Japanese penal camp. Suppose it was not all true? He knew the park existed, he could point to it on a map, but he had no real proof that it was all that they thought it would be. They assumed the Mexican government was benevolent and would take Americans in – after all, that is what was humane. For years we had taken in the disenfranchised from Mexico, not always totally willingly, but we did provide a rich and safe environment for many of them to thrive in. They were also able to take advantage of, in most cases, our schools and social services.

What if the Park was another prison camp? Or a ruse to sell Americans abroad? Or perhaps it forced women into becoming sex slaves and the men were used as house servants? *Who really knew?* He couldn't presume anything, but he did. His head felt heavy with fatigue, his ears were ringing, and he felt like a large granite boulder had pinned him down to the bottom stairs of a large podium. Dare he speak to his comrades about his fears? He found himself in a state of indecision. He ultimately decided that disclosing his fears would just add to an already suffocating psychic load for his friends. This would be his Herculean labor, non-disclosure.

Patches and Lauren, after some more time, came out of their tent. Aaron and Adlartok did not take a turn in their tent, as the decision was made to move under the cover of darkness. Though hardly rested, Aaron urged the group to get ready to depart. The burros were still tired and it took some prodding to get them going again. Adlartok was a pro at this, if Aaron and Patches had to work with the burros, they would still be standing in the darkness not moving.

Although they would have the advantage of cover with the dark, there were other risks to be considered. Scorpions and venomous snakes were active at night as well as tarantulas that came out from beneath the dark damp crevices that they lived in during the balmy day. A strike by one of these could be lethal for one of the burros and extremely unpleasant for humans. They did not have antidotes available, especially in the case of an accidental poisonous snake bite. Rattlers were teeming in this part of Mexico.

They would also have to be on the look-out for human predators. Peripatetic gangs still roamed Mexico and they were opportunists. Their current location was uninhabited so their risk of being discovered would be low, but they did see something landing at the edge of horizon earlier and would have to remain vigilant.

Although Mexico was rich economically, much of the country was still barren and unoccupied with most of the population sequestered near or close to its major cities. Many of the villages and towns were functioning like remote outposts each sporting their own particular governance. In addition there were many "camps" in Mexico which were makeshift communes of people living together, stragglers, really, who lived off the land and who exploited passersby routinely. They did not have many possessions and were disenfranchised, comprised mostly of the poorer underclass of the country. Although unadvertised, Mexico was still a caste society like many other great powers. Its social structure was molded in the configuration of its great pyramids that had been built eons ago. A slim group of people at the top still controlled the nation's wealth. The poor were bottom dwellers and, as was usually the case, demographically they were the most populous.

The last days had drained their food supply and they needed to find more sustenance. As a last resort they could butcher one of the burros but they had become fond of their plodding, stubborn companions. There was a shared desire to survive that everyone in the group felt.

The trail that they were following meandered through a lightly populated area, part of a large wilderness area. Occasionally they saw some mud roofs of well-worn huts or a dilapidated shed but there was not much else in their path.

The sky was a glossy black except for the crescent moon that acted as a luminaire. Aaron reconnoitered they were several miles outside of Matehuala, one of the larger cities in the municipality of San Luis Potosi. It was an unremarkable hilly town that was known for one beautiful church that had a large clock face on it. Other than that, passing motorists would not even remark on it.

They were still a distance away however from that town. The burros were weighed down with the tents and supplies and walking gingerly, much to Aaron's surprise. The cool of the night must have provided them with added energy to walk.

In contrast Patches could barely keep pace with the burros and Lauren was falling steadily behind. They had to stop several times so that Lauren could regain her breath and Adlartok gave her a drink of water from their reserve. When Aaron took her pulse, he noticed that her eyes were widened and her heart was racing. He hoped she was not getting sick. Finding medical care was next to impossible and would be exceedingly dangerous. He didn't know where to find a doctor nor did he know if they would be welcome. His guess was that until they were safely at Chapultepec Park, they needed to keep their movements secret.

Adlartok came to the rescue again and helped support Lauren as she walked. Neither Patches nor Aaron were strong enough to offer more than moral support. Their passage during the night was uneventful and they made good time even with frequent rest stops. Patches commented on the ceaseless backdrop of glowing eyes watching them as they walked but none dared to challenge them. It was not a walk in the park.

Before the sun rose, they heard some strange sounds like a "woofing" call. Then there were some knocks. Aaron had heard something like this before when he was trekking in the White Mountains, this terrain was hilly but not as mountainous as it was in the deep forests of New Hampshire. It did have sufficient vegetation and small rivulets that could support larger wildlife. A second cry was deep and long and unsettling – it was inhuman but human at the same time. It did not sound like a bear which were not indigenous to this part of Mexico, although bears were now moving into this range, especially Grizzly and Brown bears, and there was talk of even Kodiak Bears. Adlartok seemed to understand the cry and knew what creature it was but she was unable to communicate her knowledge. She took her knife and began drawing large footprints in the dirt that were not decipherable. Adlartok was definitely spooked.

After a short romp they came upon a ravine that was shielded by a raggedy hill and a tall stand of trees. They decided to settle near there for the rest of the day, sunrise was in progress, and they needed rest. Lauren had taken a turn for the worse and was now feverish. Aaron was worried about her. She looked pale and drawn and the tips of her fingers were blue, signaling poor circulation. He had seen this before with frostbite and with family members who had lupus, but her condition appeared different.

She had a blotchy rash on her arms – they had not seen this the day before, it must have occurred overnight. They laid her down on a thick, cushiony blanket in the shade which shielded her from the increasingly hot sun. Adlartok found a cold water source nearby, a large pond that looked clean. They did not have time to boil the water and sanitize it as Lauren looked critically dehydrated.

Patches split the last of their rations, some tough, dried pulled rabbit and a chunky soup that Adlartok had prepared. They were all tired and hungry and ate up the last of the food like angry yard dogs fighting over kitchen scraps. They made sure Lauren ate more than her fair share.

They noticed Patches had beads of sweat on his forehead and wet stains lining his back and that he was in danger of dehydration also, so Adlartok and Aaron left him behind with Lauren when they went out in search of food. They were all still going through a period of acclimatization as their bodies were adjusting to a new normal. The increasingly humid atmosphere, sunbaked land, and other unseen dangers were also piling on stress that was taking its toll on their party. They needed rest and more nourishment to sustain them.

They searched the ground for signs of life. Even though foliage here was much lusher than that of the Cold Zone there wasn't exactly a bounty of choices to select from. Wildflowers like dahlias, cosmos, marigolds, zinnias, cacti, and palms were native to the area but they had no inkling of what could be consumed or what was poisonous. Adlartok found s large cactus she split in half, called Nopales. Its large oval stems called paddles were eaten as a vegetable. She must have known about the nutritious value of this edible cactus that contained minerals and was a rich source of vitamins and antioxidants. Its juice was a known immune booster. They bundled a bunch of them together with sinuous vine and carried them back to their camp. Adlartok strained about a pint of the cactus juice from the plant and slowly fed it to Lauren who now seemed weaker than before. She also roasted the cactus and made several shish kebobs for everyone to eat. Even though this food provided some calories they were still all operating at a deficit. It had been a long time since they had a full meal. Each day they were gradually losing weight and expending more energy than they were replacing calories. This further weakened them. They were entering into a dangerous catabolic state.

It was getting late in the morning and the sky was clouding up as Aaron and Adlartok retired to their tent. The burros were no longer braying and were asleep under a large cypress tree. The famed Montezuma Cypress, or Tule Tree, measures around 119 feet around, but is only 116 feet tall. It is believed that the tree is around 2000 thousand years old making it as old as the Roman occupancy of Jerusalem at the time of Christ. This particular tree was about 30 feet high and twenty feet wide, still making it an anomaly in the forest. Aaron dubbed the tree Sir Jingles in honor of his deceased companion. There were also some unusual rock formations in the area; boulders that were shiny of a grey and red tone. They seemed to mark the area off as something special, perhaps as a Mayan burial ground or cosmic landmark. Or perhaps this was just Aaron's wandering mind trying to fill in blanks to halt his creeping anxiety and stem his ongoing fatigue.

Adlartok seemed aware of the power of their setting. She was an expert in folklore and was trained in the use of medicinal plants and herbs by her elders. She had long taken advantage of herbals like Turmeric, Ginger, Aloe Vera, Ginseng, and Echinacea to promote healing. She was acquainted with some of the mystic traditions of her native tribe. The cypress tree and the strange rocks represented a religious marker for her that was not shared by the others. She knew they were in a place of power that guarded them and kept them safe from intruders.

The day passed peaceably enough, although the winds rustled the tents and the sun's heat scorched the parchment of their shelters. The burros stayed huddled in a small circle around the tree, panting where they lay.

Patches and Lauren slept dreamily as they tried to recover. The expedition was at a critical juncture where they needed rest and continued resourcefulness.

Adlartok awoke earlier than the others, late in the afternoon, before dusk. She was determined to find food as she knew their further survival depended upon this. She took her knife and bow and headed east through a thick glen of bramble. She figured small game was probably hiding in the brush and would soon be wandering out looking for food as the temperature fell. She came across some turkey eggs and stashed those in her haversack. She assumed where there were eggs there should also be meandering turkeys. She climbed a small ridge that was blanketed with startling purple flowers. She was not sure of their name but they gave off a poppy-like aroma. She noticed some honey bees swirling in the air doing a peculiar dance, apparently not affected by her presence. If Aaron was with her, it would have given him great satisfaction to see them, but she had left him safely asleep in the tent.

As she walked towards the edge of the ridge she saw some movement ahead of her. Hoping it was a turkey, she strung her bow and readied her aim. As she inched in closer, though, she saw that it was not a turkey ahead of her, but a group of grim looking men who had combat gear on. She also noticed they had parked four ATVs very close to a small pond and were discussing something. They were dressed in white uniforms that looked very light and flexible. Adlartok had no knowledge of the *Whitewater* organization, but if Aaron was there, he would think these men were an affiliate of the same operation, this time operating in Mexico. One of the men sounded louder and looked meaner than the others, he was gesticulating instructions with his hand making sure the others heard him and agreed with him.

If Adlartok knew more she would have realized they were talking about a sister group that had recently been decimated in the U.S. by a marauding bear. The same group Aaron had witnessed under attack.

The bears had just made it into Mexico and were a growing concern. Some people claimed that Grizzlies were migrating as well as black bears. The WW affiliate also found human tracks near the remains that indicated some people were there who witnessed the onslaught. They had followed the tracks south for a while until they lost their trail.

Even though Adlartok did not decipher all of this she could tell this was not good news. She stepped backwards, brushing a long cactus that grabbed part of her pants long enough to scrape her skin. This caused a small surface wound that was more of a nuisance than painful. However, unbeknown to Adlartok a few drops of her blood had fallen into a patchy area on the ground. It was barely visible, but there all the same.

When she returned to their camp she woke up the others and relayed her discovery. They hurried to pack up and left just as it was turning nightfall. They tried to cover up the tracks of the burros and lead them over areas where finding their presence would be more difficult, but this was also where the sagebrush and ground cover was more challenging to step through. But they knew it was a race against time. If they were being followed, it would not be too hard to pick up their trail.

The men at the other camp had decided to stay the night. They built a campfire and soon fell asleep. They did not share the same anxiety.

Central Mexico was strewn with twisting back roads, failing fences, clay-roofed huts and general poverty. The new affluence had not embraced this area. There was a fairly large population of diverse people, but much more in the way of aging infrastructure and unkempt plots. Haciendas were uncommon while windswept dust and intense dry heat were. The climate had finally changed for good and they could say goodbye to permafrost, which had been a constant hardship.

Aaron's group toiled through the night. They walked carefully, keeping alert for any unusual sounds of nocturnal predators and silently fearing footsteps of pursuers travelling behind them. They had walked so far to get to this point in their journey and did not want to see it jeopardized. The close calls and constant hardship had taken its toll. Fear of the unknown strips the consciousness of its vitality and being. It takes great spiritual fortitude to overcome this. Bright objects in the sky hovered across the horizon. Aaron wondered if they were close to an airport. These shapes were small and configured in a triangular shape, red and blue auras contrasted by a black night sky.

They could see that one of the objects was projecting an orange beam across the ground, though they were a few miles away. It appeared the vehicle was looking for something. They led the burros off-road and veered a safe direction away from the lights. They were heading south by southwest, still traveling mainly south towards Mexico City.

Lauren, though better, was still unsteady on her feet, and had Patches supporting her. The cool night air was invigorating and provided some comfort for all of them. Having lost track of time, Aaron thought it was July but it could have been September, no one kept track of time anymore. It was as if they had reverted to a primitive era when early man huddled in large groups in caves to stay warm and hide from the *terrors of the night*. They lived their lives tracking the movement of the sun, announcing sunrise and sunset until they died. There was no fanfare, no elaborate funerals; the bodies were buried a safe distance away from their camps, to keep the night visitors away, which could be saber-toothed tigers or inquisitive wooly mammoth. There could be whole other orders of creatures we have not discovered yet. Aaron thought that the diversity of life as it had existed before the Big Freeze was many times that of what we had unearthed from earlier epochs. There were still so many holes in our anthropological and archaeological history that needed to be solved. He wondered if we really even knew what may be beneath the surface of the earth. There had been rumors of underground cities that no one had ever bothered to explore on any serious level. We tended to listen to others and let them do their thinking for us. It was easier this way, with no need for any critical or expanded thoughts. People sleep walked through life, hardly wandering beyond the borders of what they could see and feel.

It was getting towards sunrise when the path took a hard right when a little village appeared ahead of them. It looked impoverished and perhaps inhabited by one of the native Mayan populations that had once flourished in earlier Mexico. They had to cross a shallow but fast-moving stream to get into the village; it was green with moss and full of floating pollen, so Aaron figured that it must be spring. Patches acquired a tick that attached itself to his leg's trouser; Lauren brushed it off with a flick of her forefinger. They would have to be wary if the area was infested with ticks, they could ill afford to get sick from Lyme disease. They did not have the antibiotics that would be needed to treat it. Aaron knew this was a grueling course of therapy that took several months of treatment where they placed a port in your chest; they would have to inspect each other periodically for red "bullet shaped" imprints on the skin, a sign of tick bites.

There was a market on the right side of the village, if one could call it that, it was a series of wooden milk crates piled up about four feet high and several feet long blanketed with various fruits and vegetables, many of them swollen and oozing and baking from the sun. Avocados, gnarly tomatillos, jicamas, which resembled giant turnips and chayote, were prominently featured. There was also an array of fish most notably large bass filleted and ready for the grill. Aaron remembered reading about mass fish die offs in Mexico before the Big Freeze, he had some concerns about eating them, knowing that Chemtrails fallout was probably responsible for the fish becoming toxic and dying.

It all looked good and nutritious to Aaron with the exception of the fish. They had been eating hard meal tack for a while and their bodies needed a different sort of nourishment. The only problem was that they had no currency. Apparently Adlartok understood the villagers' language enough to make a deal. They were given large canvas sacks of vegetables and food-stuffs, some ready-made, and they were loaded on one of the burros. It came at a cost however; they traded one of the burros for this large cache of food. Adlartok made sure it was the one who had tripped and landed on Sam.

All the transactions occurred before Aaron and Patches could protest, they were so hungry anyway, it probably it would not have amounted to much of a debate.

There was not much of a police presence in this part of Mexico but there were always roving eyes. They spent little time in the village, only long enough to draw some water from a deep and busy well. From some discussions with the local villagers, Adlartok had ascertained that other Americans had come this way on route to Chapultepec Park, so they were not without precedent. This probably contributed to the lack of curiosity about them. There was something nagging Aaron as they departed the area, it was a frustrating concern, but he could not pinpoint it. All seemed well on the outside but something was eating him up on the inside, a small swell now, but growing. He was missing something.

He remembered as a boy once running along a brook, trying to keep up with his friends, racing along the water. They were all going so fast that they lost track of time and distance and soon found themselves lost in the forest. They were looking for a favorite watering hole that they usually played in, but had missed the cutoff to the hole, which was a distance down to a small hill. It was only after the leader had stopped and the others caught up to him that they realized their mistake. They all felt mysteriously lost, out of place, unsure of themselves, because they missed the turnoff. That was how Aaron was feeling now--a sense of recurring dread of losing something that had no rational origin.

They walked several miles through a windy overgrown path that followed the road. As always, they kept a safe distance away trying to conceal their movements as much as possible. The sky was an overcast grey and pillows of clouds that looked like hoarfrost hovered above them. They stopped several times at watering spots as the burros thirst had increased with each passing day with the ever-increasing heat. Adlartok had stripped down to a tee shirt that was mottled with sweat and flattered her zaftig figure. Lauren was periodically panting and out of breath, asking for more breaks than they had planned to take. Even though night travel was cooler, it was exhausting.

So, they staggered forward, making haste but covering little distance in their ravaged state. They started their search for a day haven, where they could rest and get refreshed. The cool water they were able to obtain at the town's well was welcome, but the continued heat drained them of reserves and they were continually thirsty. It was looking more and more like Lauren had heat stroke and her pupils were bulging out. Patches was very concerned. A decision was made to stop near a murky, green creek that offered some shade as a ring of trees enveloped it. Aaron exclaimed: "The bottoms of my feet look like I have been stepping in lava." They were bright red and had dark circles of torn tissue dangling off of them. He stuck them into the creek and let the cool water embrace them. After several minutes he padded his boots with torn shreds of cloth he cut from one of his blankets. He felt confident this would help prevent further damage to his feet.

Adlartok busied herself searching for scraps of wood for a fire. Her leg was still oozing some blood where she had scraped it. She attended to this by applying direct pressure to the wound until she was sure it was sealed. While doing this, she spied a baby scorpion crawling under a rock near her feet. It took all her courage to steady herself while the little critter scurried back into its shady cove. She tiptoed away, all the time watching for any other disturbances on the ground that could indicate trouble. It was hard to see through the fine dust and silt that covered the ground; it was continually being buttressed by fine breezes that darted across the brush.

Adlartok's faced was smeared with mud; it somehow made her bushy eyebrows appear more beautiful, she looked like a Mongol princess on a Mexican safari. Her long legs and limber stride accentuated this effect.

Another thorny problem arose aside from the wound on her leg, she was menstruating. The accessibility to woman's hygiene products was very limited since the frost. Many women fended for themselves using home remedies to manage their cycles. This was also the case for Adlartok. Unfortunately she was now shedding blood in two spots which put her in greater danger of attracting wildlife and made her easier to be tracked. Luckily for her, cotton was abundant in Mexico and she did not have to go very far to find some wild cotton she could use to stanch the bleeding. Many early tribal people used to put females into isolation during their menstrual cycle, whether a pagan ritual or a superstitious practice, it is food for debate. The tribal customs of Adlartok's people would forbid that practice. They honored and recognized women as key leaders of the clan, Adlartok, as the chief's daughter, was especially esteemed.

While searching among some junipers and cacti she found a mother lode of wood. There were some branches of dried trees and some cut wood placed stowed away where someone trying to reach it would get cut in the process. This was disconcerting as it meant someone had been near this location recently. It was hard to tell how long ago as the neat pile of wood, although tidy, gave no indication of when the owner had cached it.

She hurried back to camp with the wood and warned the others. Lauren was now coughing up blood and her face was swelling. Perhaps she had picked up a parasite from the water they had been drinking, they could not be certain. Giardiasis was a common illness from untreated water and some people's immune systems were more prone to acquiring it than others. Aaron, although not trained in medicine, had a basic understanding of most ailments and was good at diagnosis. In this case, he was perplexed. Lauren's ill health would impede the progress of the group and Patches' attachment to her could be problematic if they were forced to leave her behind. Aside from the moral quandary this presented, if Lauren would be found, she would put them all at risk during an interrogation. With this in mind, Aaron was resolute in going forward, despite present difficulties.

They loaded Lauren onto the strongest remaining burro and tied her legs down to keep her from falling. She was very weak and it took the three of them to do this. Twice she nearly slipped off the burro but Adlartok caught her both times. Lauren's eyes were now oozing a purulent discharge that was discolored and noxious. Even though her legs were immobilized, Lauren was starting to flail around, as if she had some kind of seizure disorder. Patches walked alongside her helping to keep her positioned in her makeshift stirrups.

All this time Aaron remained steadfast and calm and urged the group onwards. Adlartok was limping slightly due to her leg wound but she did not complain.

"I don't understand why this is happening," Patches exclaimed, "she was fine before." "She is on such a downward spiral."

"We can try to find some medical help," Aaron said. "Maybe there is a shaman around who can offer some assistance. I'm not sure of the cause of her distress, could be physiological or psychological, hard to tell. I've witnessed rapid changes in children's health, but not so much in adults."

"I had hoped by now she would feel better. Let's not delay anymore. It is times like these I wish I went to Med School." This was far-fetched as Patches had an aversion to blood and would probably have fainted at the first sight of a human cadaver being dissected, all part of the Medical School experience.

So they trudged along through the rest of the evening and part of the next day trying to put great distance between themselves and their potential captors.

They finally stopped near a lip of land that had some strange geographical features. They found a huge colossal head that was part human and part animal sitting on a ridge. On closer inspection, Aaron noted it looked like a leopard or jaguar's head. He remembered that the Olmecs, an early Mexican civilization worshipped an entity that was part animal. Could this artifact be a vestige of this culture?

The huge head startled the burros and made them bray. They seemed uncomfortable in this setting. Aaron climbed up to the top of its edifice and poked around, to his dismay he saw a dimly painted "WW" that looked like graffiti on its base. For Aaron this represented another cause for concern. He did not tell the others. *Boy Whitewater does get around!*

They decided to walk another mile to a patch of land that was more inviting. There were actually flowering plants that they were seeing for the first time: Mist Flowers, Scarlet Trumpet Vine, and Night Scented Jasmine adorned the ground. Seeing these bright colors gave them hope and was a form of comfort.

They set up camp in this botanical garden. According to the map they were half a day hike from Guadalcazar, although they would not directly enter this town, they would be in the general vicinity. In 1620, it was founded by a well-known Spanish explorer, by the same name, Juan Cordoba de Guadalcazar. The area contained abandoned mining pits where coal, iron, and silver were extracted, but today the district was celebrated for the exquisite architecture of its churches.

Lauren seemed more comfortable laying in the tent where Patches could attend to her. The sky was streaked with red billowy clouds and by many birds that circled the horizon twittering out songs in an entrancing mix of melodies. Aaron could not remember hearing such beautiful sounds while in captivity in America. Even the cackling of crows contained intrinsic beauty. The juxtaposition of the sounds and their pleasant surroundings gave the place an eerie calm. Aaron was not fooled by this; he knew trouble was always a few steps ahead of them or behind them.

The last straw for Aaron was when he was directed to omit evidence about his findings on global climate change. Higher powers within the government were not that worried about the unintended consequence of depopulation. Some viewed it as part of an inexorable and natural cycle of extinction where the planet rids itself of predatory species like dinosaurs and humans that usurp the natural balance by consuming too many natural resources of the planet.

They knew their nanotechnology had gone astray and was out of control producing global food supply deficits as well as destabilizing the climate, but there was a "hush, hush" atmosphere in Washington. Aaron could not fully determine if it was because of their inability to do anything to solve the situation or if it was from some undisclosed evil intention to thin the population. In any case, he sensed the government was not acting on its own. Dubious banking syndicates and greedy global capitalists were at the controls. In Aaron's lifetime, 99.5% of the aggregated wealth of the global economic system was now owned by the top ½% of the people. Before the Big Freeze, the gap between the rich and poor had become a hot topic of discourse, and mass immigration was occurring planet-wide, where people of low means were gravitating to areas of higher wealth. This displacement also lead to further disregard to what was happening to the ecosystem as most people were attracted to accumulating more things without weighing the unintended effects on the ecology of the planet by doing so. We had oversaturated the planet with people and there was a need to find a happy balance.

They slept lightly, even though they were in beautiful surroundings. Lauren got progressively worse, and only known to Aaron, was exhibiting all the classical signs of chemtrails derived nanorobot poisoning…non-stop bleeding, puss-filled discharges, and severe headache. Although he put up a hearty front, he knew there was nothing they could really do, except wait for the inevitable. Patches would be crushed.

When they started up again the terrain became flat and it was deceptively quiet. Lauren was struggling to stay on a burro and Patches was holding her on for dear life. Adlartok was playing the role of advance guard as Aaron walked between her and the burros. The air was stifling, breezes almost nonexistent. They were impeding motion as if there was an invisible wall in place.

They were all tired. The kind of fatigue that comes with always having to be watchful, always fearing for your life, never being able to let your guard down, a type of weariness that men at arms could identify with, as they waited hours in the trenches for an enemy to advance.

In the heat of the day, the little critters that inhabited the floor of the valley were asleep. At night they were alive and moving. So besides the attacks that could come from the rear or from above, they had to constantly scan the ground in front of them for fire ants, scorpions, rattle snakes, tarantulas and numerous other dangerous creatures – Mexico had the highest number of venomous species on the planet – 80 in total with Brazil running close behind at 79. Aaron thought that many people probably died from accidental meetings with varmints along these paths. They were the "terrorists" of these backend hardscrabble roads, nature's true IEDs.

Aaron's world was going topsy-turvy. Arguably, he was doing the right thing by trying to find sanctuary for his friends. But even if he was successful in doing so, what would his personal endpoint be? Would he settle down with Adlartok eventually? Did he want to raise another family? Was he getting too old to nurture children? In Mexico, would he be able to establish himself as a scientist that was worthy of employment? After all, he was a part of the group that was involved in the climate study and geoengineering attempt that backfired. How would his role be received? Would it be better if he stayed undercover to avoid detection? After all, how could he expect anyone to understand the intricacies of his work and his exact contribution to it?

Aaron regarded himself as one of the protesters behind the scenes, not an enabler like numerous others who went ahead with an unproved scheme that eventually did more harm than good.

Would the Mexican government be able to discern that? There were few people in his study group left, they either died or were posthumously scattered across the globe. It was highly unlikely they would be able to corroborate his testimony. *They were more likely to convict him and send him back to one of the many penitentiaries.*

In the end, perhaps the best course of action would be to lead his friends to safety and then depart on his own before he was discovered. He reasoned that by the time they reached the destination he would be better, if not entirely healed. He then could make his way alone.

They had walked several miles and were going to march further into the night when they all stopped suddenly. A foul odor enveloped them, causing Lauren to cough and choke and the burros to bray incessantly. Aaron and Patches covered their noses. Adlartok ventured forward towards the origin of the smell.

They were in a marshy part of Mexico that was overgrown with bramble and honeyed flowers. They had seen several striped snakes during the night dart across the ground but had not seen any other signs of life.

Adlartok moved cautiously forward, first sliding down a small embankment, then past some misshapen rocks adjacent to a beaver's nest. There was a huge hole in the ground. She worked her way to the edge and peered in. Below her was a massive gravesite filled with the skeletal remains of hundreds of people. They looked like they had been there for a while. There was no evidence of clothes or personal belongings.

Aaron and Patches followed close behind her and were now surveying the pit. Patches was gagging and vomiting fluid as he approached. They both held rags over their noses, trying to stop the noxious odor from penetrating their lungs. Adlartok seemed immune to the smell, as if she had experienced this before.

Aaron went to take a closer look at the bodies. He started inspecting them with his one good arm. He asked Adlartok to help him turn over one of the grimmest, twisted corpses. What he saw alarmed him, it looked like some of the flesh was torn off, not by animals, but by excision from large carving knives. The grooves were too small for a scalpel and were not uneven and ragged like an animal's claw marks. It looked like the flesh was being purposefully removed from the carcasses.

They circled the site paying close attention not to slip or fall in.

He stopped at one point and gazed down. Thrown to one side near a smaller skeleton was a baseball card, of Derek Jeter, the famed Yankee shortstop. Oddly it was written in English and Aaron saw that it was a Topp's USA baseball card whose company was headquartered in NYC. Aaron wondered about this as well as the massive pile of bodies he saw before him. He kept the card and put it into his pocket. Written on the card in broken script was "help us please, we are locked up." It looked like a kid's handwriting.

He kept this information to himself. Patches saw the card but Aaron didn't think he recognized its origin. Aaron was an avid Yankees fan and knew about their colorful history even though he was a New Englander. They decided to walk back, refusing to talk about this unsettling discovery.

Upon returning, one of the last two remaining burros was down. Apparently the stench was too much for the poor donkey. He was barely breathing when Aaron arrived. Adlartok, as was her way, made short work of the burro. They carved the animal up in strips and stored the flesh on their one remaining pack burro. They buried the guts in the ground as best they could to hide their presence. This required Lauren to walk, which she did not complain about, but everyone realized she was barely up for the task. She looked increasingly pale and her constitution was at its weakest point since Aaron first met her. He noticed Adlartok was keeping a close eye on her and was incessantly working with Patches to keep her upright.

Aaron, while he was walking, surveyed his map again. Even though they had not lost their way, he knew they might not have seen some landmarks in the dark. He reckoned they were about 250 miles away from Chapultepec Park, somewhere in the vicinity of Santa Maria Del Rio, a small town. According to the map, the area was known for the Lourdes springs as well as an abandoned Franciscan monastery. The springs caught Aaron's attention; this might be a place for them to find fresh water. There also may be some haciendas around that they could potentially hold up in for a day or so, perhaps a summer retreat of a wealthy patron of Mexico that was unoccupied at this time of the year. It would offer some refuge and give Lauren a chance to recover.

"She's slip-ping," said Adlartok in her own unique brand of English. Patches had placed Lauren on a blanket and she was coughing up blood and phlegm staining the ground around her.

Her face was flushed and her hair matted with the journey's grime. Her fingers were involuntarily twitching and her gasps sounded very thin. They were losing her. Patches was holding her hand as Adlartok attempted to pump air into her lungs with her mouth. Aaron alternately pressed on her chest when he saw she was turning blue. She died a few minutes later, without notice or fanfare, such was her life.

When it was over, Aaron couldn't help but feel a twinge of guilt. He thought of his climate change colleagues and their unsuccessful experiments to control the climate. He felt Lauren's death may have been a by-product of that effort. She exhibited all the classic signs of the nanorobot syndrome they had documented before. In a corner of his mind, his failure to pre-empt climate change made him feel directly responsible.

They buried Lauren about a half mile away from where they were…off to the east in a peaceful enclave that she would have liked. They did not want her gravesite to be a marker for any unwelcome trackers. Adlartok and Aaron shared the grim task of burying her while Patches watched their belongings near the trail. His grief was clearly visible but he understood the necessity to contain it. Aaron was concerned that in a moment of weakness Patches might do something foolish. But he did not.

When they returned, they were all famished and heartily ate their dried meat rations. Patches barely touched his food but drank some water. The "pit" was still on Aaron's mind; he was unable to comprehend the "why" of it and did his best to imagine "where" all these people originated from. Were the victims lost refugees? Or casualties of a cold journey that were mass buried? Or were they purposely placed there for some other unnamed sinister motive? The flesh markings were what completely unraveled him and had sent his mind into overdrive. Usually these peak moments where the mind tried to make sense of otherwise unexpected discoveries were not fruitful, it was best to pause and consider the finding at a less stressful time. Oftentimes answers became visible when the body was calmed and the events could be recollected in quietude.

They were down to three again and one burro. Patches now became the weak link. He was emotionally distraught and showed signs of breaking down altogether although he was keeping a proud front. Adlartok had the strongest constitution and had been very dependable at critical moments. Aaron was the intellect behind the scenes, the driving force that made the most sensible decisions. The balance of power in the group had been shifting in recent days and was now fully settling on Adlartok. Her dogged determination and unmistakable prowess would be the determining factors if the group was going to physically survive.

Their immediate need now was for water. Aside from the Lourdes springs, the map showed a river flowing through the township of Santa Maria del Rio. The burro was becoming dehydrated and their water supply was dwindling. Mirages appeared in the distance appeared that gave the illusion that water was near, but they found this was only glassy reflections construed by the burning sun. The light breeze fluffed up Adlartok's hair and made her look larger than life, like an Amazonian defender of aboriginal rights. Her every action licked of purpose and she wasted no movement, a feline lioness where every second counted in the hunt. She was not hunting right now though; she was leading the group forward, forging the next chapter of their adventure.

After logging several miles, they came across a stream that looked like it became a tributary of a larger river, should they follow it upstream. Also, there were the outlines of a settlement beyond the river. Could this be Santa Maria del Rio? They would have to be careful as they got closer. The water looked clear and was running like bubbly champagne so they drank their full. The burro lapped up this crystalline liquid at the stream's edge for a long time replenishing her fluids. Aaron took time out to clean his wound; Adlartok helped him change the dressings and applied some of her medicinal poultice that accelerated the healing process. Patches sat off by himself, still grieving, and was reluctant to talk. He was dipping his head into the water and shaking his hair out like a wet bloodhound. His unshaven beard, unkempt hair, and slovenly appearance reflected his interior condition.

Unnoticed, heavy clouds had been slowly moving in and encircling the horizon with a long lasso. The rain started so suddenly that they had no time to find cover. The Mexican weather was not at all harsh compared to the *Cold Zone* but it did have its share of surprises.

They found relief from the onslaught of rain by situating themselves under a carousel of tall trees. It was poor cover but better than nothing, large drips of rain still seeped through the leafy umbrella. Numerous birds of prey that were perched on the canopy shared the cover with them, and occasionally bird droppings fell making the travelers' stay even more uncomfortable.

After about an hour, the rain subsided. Shimmering rays from the sun created a scarlet pillow of clouds in the sky. Animal sounds resumed and the parched game trails were now overrun with puddles of mud.

They moved on, not as cheerfully as before but with a kind of sullen desperation. They decided to follow a barely visible back trail that wound itself slowly towards the edge of town. Aaron was undecided about the level of risk he was willing to assume, as his chief concern, was for the safety of the group. There could be no turning back now, they were far away from the U.S. borders, and were really at the mercy of the Mexican government should they be apprehended. Their fate would be determined by the choices they made and the circumstances that befell them.

In his quest to save his family and the world, Aaron had failed. He was a pawn in a large global catastrophe he had no control over. In its efforts to save the planet, the rogue nanotechnology and chemical dispersal program had accelerated the vast cover of cold that now engulfed a large part of the planet. Aaron had tried his best to report on the scope of the planetary effects, but it fell ultimately on deaf ears. The wealthy elite had found cover underground and still controlled the majority of economic transactions aboveground, crime was now both privatized and publicized. While the rest of the displaced Americans were fighting for their lives, the political ruling and wealthy class slept comfortably and were secure in their luxurious bunkers.

To their relief, they did not have to enter the town. As luck would have it there was a roughly hewn farm with a stand situated along a shallow creek. It was located near a covered bridge that greeted them before they turned off the trail. The denizens of the farm were short on stature but long on compassion. They addressed them warmly and welcomed them. This sort of encounter left them reeling, after so many negative ones, they were not sure what to expect. The concatenation of prior bad experiences had left them inured to goodness. They wouldn't know pot luck if it landed right in front of them. Their wheel of fortune was consistently bankrupt.

"Have you travelled far?" a young woman with an orange beaded hat inquired. "You look famished."

"Yes, we have," Aaron replied. "We are looking for friends that we lost in America. They came here and found refuge in Chapultepec Park." He was gauging their reaction.

"Oh, yes" the man replied. He looked like her father. "Many people pass this way on that pilgrimage. It is a journey worth taking." He ended abruptly. "We can trade you some of our vegetables and a little meat for one of those blankets you have." He pointed towards the burro's pack. "They look hand sewn and strong, we have a market for such things."

Aaron was too tired to negotiate, without much of a fight he gave them the blanket they were using to cover Lauren when she fell ill. He hoped it wasn't contaminated. He didn't want to spread germs. He knew Lauren's sickness was probably due to poisoning from the Chemtrails, so he was not that concerned about it being contagious. He was hoping their overall exposure would be down in Mexico, it being part of the *Warm Zone. The program had really sprayed heavily in the Continental U.S. and Europe where it was easier to reach with commercial airliners and where those who could afford it resided.*

When Aaron was at M.I.T., part of his exasperation was with global economics. Capitalism and all its spin-offs predicated themselves on the assumption of growth ad infinitum. If the economy did not grow, the stock market would not prosper, the job situation would remain bleak, and there would be less actual money in people's pockets to spend. The problem with this, as he saw it, was that the planet had finite resources and a finite ability to support growth from an ecological standpoint. The *Big Freeze* was brought on by this greed for expansion where the planetary capacity to cradle growth was surpassed. This created an imbalance in the ecosystem which they were experiencing now. *Economic "growth"* indeed had limits and was intertwined with planetary survival. This equation defining the economics of survival had somehow been largely ignored if not berated by the leading bureaucrats of the day. They believed in endless aggrandizement and exploitation as a political and expedient economic strategy. It became the fabric of their being.

To think about these things was very painful to Aaron. What if they reacted earlier, before the tipping point? Could all of this have been averted? *Could he have played a larger role in convincing the powerful controlling interests of their mistakes?*

The dust cloud swirling towards them seemed surreal. It was coming off the side of a shorn hill that looked like it had been cut off by a large chisel from the sky. It looked alive, like a swarm of bees occupying a buzzing hive.

Then they heard sounds, not unlike night insect sounds, but sharper and louder like broken rotary fans. Above them, circling, about a half mile away, was a large white helicopter. They could not see it clearly in the distance, but alarm bells went off. *Whitewater? Whitewater? Could they be looking for Aaron and his friends?* Aaron's heart sank into his chest, his blood pounding in beat to the cacophony.

There was still time to run. But where to? They would have to leave the burro. There would be no place to hide it. Then Aaron remembered the "WW" brand on the burro and realized this would only make matters worse if this was indeed *Whitewater.* They would be accused of stealing property as well as investigated for their previous encounters with the group. They could also be returned or sold back to the camps for a sizeable bounty.

Their farmer friends, noticing their alarm, backed off quietly to the shelter of their stand. They had taken the blanket and were draping it over the side of a pockmarked and decrepit table when the burro brayed loudly, almost at the helicopter. It sounded like a call of distress, as if it remembered the sounds it was hearing. *Could that be possible? Like a homing signal?*

Aaron went over to the burro and sure enough he saw the "WW" blinking; he ran his good hand over the imprint and realized now it was actually an implant, with a RFID, not a brand. They were being followed.

This was no time to tarry; he motioned to Adlartok and Patches to follow him. They grabbed what they could carry and left the burro behind.

The helicopter was slowly working its way towards their direction. It was coming from the central part of town, hovering around some nondescript buildings that were partially blocking the view to where Aaron and his party were. They moved quickly as it passed over the town square, knowing they were too exposed not to be seen. *Aaron hoped that leaving the burro behind was not going to be their undoing, could he really trust that the farmers would not snitch on them?*

Aaron remembered seeing an old abandoned mine shaft before they came to the river. His plan was to work their way back there and hide inside the mine. Patches needed to pick up his pace as he was falling behind.

They heard shouting behind them and a ruckus. Perhaps the helicopter had found the burro or was calling down to the people there. Aaron did not know. He was pushing himself straight ahead over bramble and bushes, hurdling past a picket fence and then down a deep path that would bring them to the mine shaft.

When they finally arrived, the door was only slightly ajar, not enough to fit their bodies through. They seemed to be operated by automatic door closers that were jammed or rusted solid. Adlartok used the butt of her spear to jar the closer spring loose; this enabled them to create enough room to fit through sideways. Adlartok momentarily had the tresses of her hair wound in the push bar of the door; she had to use her knife to cut herself free. This occurred while they were hearing the drone of the copter racing through the field towards them.

It was bright outside, but dark in the shaft. It smelled of old vinegar and dried animal skins, and had the unpleasant feel of neglect.

"Let's not go too far, we might fall in," Aaron warned. There was just enough light to see the interior walls but barely enough to notice if there were drops on the side of their path. They walked slowly using their hands as guides along the left-hand wall which felt like crushed pumice and which left a chalky residue on their hands. Patches turned on a small flashlight they had acquired, so at least they could locate solid structures in their way.

They heard a flutter, probably from bats, that were located deeper within the shaft. They found a door along one side of the cavern; they went inside and saw some large inanimate objects in holding tanks that they thought were very unusual. Upon closer inspection Aaron noticed that they looked like people but altered in some significant ways. Their eyes were very wide and they had no eyelashes. They only had four fingers and were almost transparent. He could see into their bodies, where their circulatory system and other organs were highly articulated. Patches was scared. "Is this some type of scientific experiment that went bad?" he remarked.

There were long membranous tubes hooked to what looked like a perfusion machine, perhaps supplying the oxygen and nutrients that were needed while they were in either this embalmed or "hibernated" state. Aaron had heard of underground genetic experiments that were being conducted to create a hybrid human that could withstand the rigors of protracted space travel.

Perhaps they had unwittingly fallen upon one of the research centers. This one looked abandoned even though the creatures seemed markedly alive.

Adlartok was spooked by what she was seeing and took it as an ominous sign. Her people shied away from thinking about anything that conflicted with their life view which epitomized the goodness of nature and their linkage to the natural world. In her mind, this was voodoo or witchcraft, a place full of demons and evil spirits. She wanted to leave immediately.

Patches wanted to stay and study the problem a bit longer, but Aaron persuaded them to go back out to the main chamber and wait until they felt the copter was safely gone. In time, the rumbling subsided and the normal day sounds reappeared, birds were chirping and the wind rustled the worn hinges on the mining door. Aaron poked his face outside; all was clear as far as he could tell.

He slowly swung the door open and to his surprise two small men were standing there. They were about 3 feet tall and looked like dwarves. They had on what looked like one piece jump suits and looked amazingly alike. They spoke without moving their lips and asked Aaron what he was doing there. The sounds seemed to spring from Aaron's brain cells without him ever having to audibly translate them.

Aaron relayed back that they were lost and being chased and were in need of help. They had been travelling hundreds of miles in the intense cold and had barely survived. If they did not believe him, they could see how badly battered his other friends were. He projected an image in his mind of people that were ragged, worn out, and starving. It apparently invoked something as they gestured for Aaron to open the door to let Adlartok and Patches out.

Adlartok was confused; she looked genuinely frightened and hid behind Aaron. Patches was curious and started telepathically communicating with them, much the same way as Aaron had done. He explained their situation and the harrowing journey they had taken. He also conveyed that their destination was Chapultepec Park, a purported haven for Americans displaced by the climate change. The aliens seemed to understand and have compassion for their plight. They offered to take them to a place close to Mexico City so they could achieve their goal.

Aaron was not surprised by this encounter. He had known for a while there had been contact with extraterrestrials at high levels of government. His top secret clearance had exposed him to a variety of planetary issues that were hidden to the public both on earth and off planet. Indeed one of the solutions presented to combat climate change was to start colonizing other planets. To his knowledge, this was being done in secrecy.

Also, aside from the Chemtrails project, he knew the infamous Roswell, New Mexico UFO crash landings were real and that major aircraft companies in concert with the U.S. Military had been reverse engineering antigravity devices since the 1940's. He also knew that the military-industrial-government complex had technology that was fully 50 years ahead of what it was revealing to the public.

What he did not understand, is that if aliens were visiting the earth, why were they not helping humankind restore the ecological balance of the planet? Did it not also serve their interests to keep the planet intact? He had heard that EBEs (Extraterrestrial Biological Entities) were off-loading resources like Helium 3 from the moon and there persisted tales about the Anunnaki, a precursor to today's humans, who previously extracted gold from Earth to repair their damaged atmosphere on their home planet, Niburu, about 450,000 years ago.

When Aaron had explored some of these ideas further, he was surprised by how the rumors had a foundation in fact. During his time at M.I.T. he heard also through a space agency friend that the original colonization of earth had been conducted by colonists from Mars, as that planet's atmosphere was becoming degraded and unable to support life. At the time, he had nearly pushed it off, until he saw what was happening to earth's atmosphere. He had concluded that in some cases the only way for a planet's inhabitants to survive would be to colonize other planets.

If any of this was disclosed, the world's religions would be in question, so none of it was revealed. There were higher powers at work, of that Aaron was sure, but the configuration was much different than what most people believed. There certainly was more to it and individuals who died in the support of a particular religion did not have all the facts.

After further conversations, Aaron and Patches found out that these two beings were living underground in the mine shaft. They had hollowed out a small laboratory and were experimenting with genetic manipulation of the human species to create a hybrid that could withstand cold temperatures. They were inserting polar bear DNA into a humanoid body to create a creature that could stand upright and which had a cold tolerance of -40 to -90 degrees Fahrenheit. It all sounded fantastical, but that is all the aliens would reveal on this subject!

The aliens, who were called Siren Surani and Epiphaneyes, did discuss one other topic-- the perception most humans had of an illusory reality. They found it remarkable that after so many thousands of years the human mind was remarkably steadfast in a belief system that was grounded in 3 dimensional spaces. They were aware that some physicists like Stephen Hawking existed who were in touch with concepts like black holes and hyperspace, but for the most part the human race operated in a limited spatial platform. They communicated that reality was a tapestry of spaces layered in both space and time, with many dimensions in between. We were not able to access these levels but once the body ceased existing we could experience them. With the use of advanced meditation and hyperspace projection the aliens many centuries ago had found ways to work around this, but human nature was too bound to physical reality to enter any plane that was non-linear not connected to the Earth. Aaron's comprehension of this was much farther advanced than Patches and Adlartok, as he was exposed to theoretic physics during his tenure at M.I.T. For the others this type of dialogue was totally foreign. They said death for humans would be a liberating experience, freeing the spirit and promoting further development that would be beneficial. It would be like changing your clothes.

Aaron surveyed his map and he found a place that was 25 miles outside of Mexico City that looked like a good landing spot. The name of the city he was considering was Tepotzotlan. From this point, they could enter Mexico City from the West after about a day's hike, which would give them time to reconnoiter the area and figure out how they were going to announce their arrival.

Tepotzotlan means "among humpbacks" in Spanish, this was because the district was surrounded by a series of foot hills that looked like humpback whales. It was an area of Mexico that was home to larger trees like cedars, holm oaks and sweeping weeping willows. It also contained its fair share of rattlesnakes and other creatures that they would have to be wary of. Despite these dangers, they would be in a good position to make their final push to Mexico City.

Siren Surani gestured to them to follow him. Alongside the mine shaft entrance, behind a high palisade of rock, there was a concealed door. The height of the entrance was approximately ten feet high by ten feet wide sculpted right into the stone. He motioned with his small hand and it effortlessly opened. It was invisible to the naked eye.

In the back of the opening they could see a glowing object approximately 30 feet wide. It was emitting a blue light of varying intensities, almost like a solar flare. There was a long spindly catwalk that came down leading into the interior of the ship. Adlartok hesitated; Patches and Aaron had to all but drag her in. They put what was left of their dwindling supplies into what looked like cargo hammocks. Sensors recognized the baggage which they turned upside down and placed the objects into a transparent polycarbonate pod. The seating was also strange. They sat down on what looked like large reclined foam-filled seats that contoured automatically around their bodies holding them tightly in the space. Aaron never saw anything like this and was in a state of suspended disbelief, it was science fiction to him, but one which he was actually experiencing.

Epiphaneyes piloted the ship through the mine shaft's door, which closed quickly upon exiting. The ship noiselessly hovered off the ground several feet while moving sideways, showing no evidence of any pronounced thrusting. Aaron thought it was being propelled by an antigravity technology that was far superior to what the public had seen. The aliens explained that the ship also had a cloaking device, making it invisible to curious onlookers; it also could evade radar and any other sophisticated tracking device. The shimmering glow that emanated off of the ship was also transparent once outside in the open air.

With dust blowing underneath, the ship suddenly took off straight up at a high velocity passing through clouds and racing towards the heavens. Then, without any warning, stopped with hardly any force and careened towards Tepotzotlan. From what Aaron observed, the aliens never moved any levers nor did he view any source of instrumentation; the ship was tied into their neural frequency which supplied automatic piloting. At least that was what he assumed.

The trip took about 20 minutes; more time was spent finding a suitable landing spot, than the actual travel time suggested. In the end they decided to land in an abandoned military base in Sierra de Tepotzotlán state park. It was away from the heart of the town and it afforded much-needed privacy. They could follow the back roads and enter into a sleepier side of Mexico City, which was around 21 miles away. It was getting dark so they decided to find shelter for the night. They said their goodbyes to their alien friends, Adlartok still very bewildered by the whole encounter, Patches in a troubled state of denial, Aaron energized by the meeting.

They found out during their brief flight that the aliens had helped them further. They had lured the helicopter away from where they were hiding; more to protect their own secrecy, but it had the added benefit of helping Aaron and his friends. That helicopter was now chasing a phantom shadow across Northern Mexico.

Having left the eeriness behind, Adlartok took the lead in finding an overnight refuge. They were in a hilly area that was surrounded by a stand of large cottonwood trees. There looked to be a boggy area that was nearby, one they would want to avoid, probably teeming with venomous snakes and with slippery footing and muddy sand underneath.

Away from the trees stood an old mound, it looked like it had a door with a charred canopy, probably due to a camping fire that had previously sent heat rising scorching the roof in the process. Adlartok jarred the door open; it was rotting on its frame. She took a quick look inside and found a few small chairs, a block of stone that looked like it was used for butchery and some bedding that was rotting and full of dead insects and numerous bed bugs. Also, along the wall, there was a washed out picture of a woman and her child, Aaron looked back at her sadly. Their story would never be told.

The bedding had to be disposed of; bed bugs would make their stay very uncomfortable, as they were blood-thirsty creatures that fed on donors that could provide them with a continued supply of warm blood. Already anemic, living on a subsistence diet, the group could not afford to lose any more vital fluids.

There was some dry wood in one corner, which led Aaron to believe that this hut was recently occupied. It was placed in a neat bundle against one of the walls with an ample amount of kindling nearby. There was a long thick switch from a hardwood tree that looked like it was used as a poking stick to turn over embers.

The place had an aromatic smell, Aaron thought it may have been used as a smoking den or for some ritual in which various plants were smoked to induce altered states. There were still many shamans in Mexico who purportedly communed with higher spirits while in altered states.

Patches wasted no time nestling in a dark corner of the room, lying down on a worn, grungy looking mat. Aaron and Adlartok decided to take turns on guard duty. It was late in the afternoon and though fatigue was setting in they knew there was still work to be done. The synapses in Aaron's brain were exploding with psychic energy and the provocative series of events that just occurred were sending him into overdrive, so much so that he volunteered to take the first watch.

Adlartok retired to the makeshift shelter, resigned to the fact that she needed to sleep having been deprived of rest for so long. She found Patches slumped in the corner snoring. She thought she saw a fleeting shadow in the darkness, a vision of Sam, but it dematerialized quickly. She began to think her mind was playing tricks on her. She was tired beyond what she thought was imaginable, her devotion to Aaron though very bright and never failing.

Adlartok slipped out of her clothes and found a soft spot to rest her sore body. It was far away from the area where they had seen bed bugs. She wrapped herself tightly in a blanket with only her face showing – there were some locks of her hair wound around her head in a curious spiral. Her natural beauty could never be diminished by the environment; in fact her looks were enhanced by the push and pull of all the natural forces at play. She was not a person to carry her troubles around; she used them as motivation to succeed at whatever it was she was doing. She soon drifted into sleep thinking about Oviak and the village and what she thought she was missing.

Before she knew it, it was time for Adlartok's shift. Aaron surprised her though first, wrapping his naked body about her and coaxing her into some lovemaking. All this occurred while Patches slept soundly, snoring throughout their close encounter.

The next day brought in an unusually bright sun perhaps due to sunspot activity, Aaron would never know. There was light dew on the ground and everything seemed more alive than ever before on their trek. In Aaron's mind, he thought it might be that his relationship with Adlartok was taking off in so many different directions that he saw more possibilities in his future. Or it could be that they were at the end of their journey and the prospect of having closure was electrifying.

Patches eventually woke up and stoked the fire to restore it. They ate their last bit of rations, some dried gecko, with a few eggs they found near a large roost on a foundering tree. They dampened the campfire and set out, not before concealing as much of their presence as was possible. In the last day of forced march they did not want to have any encounters with *Whitewater,* they were just hours away from their destination.

From his map, Aaron was able to discern that road 57D wound its way into Mexico City. He reasoned that if they shadowed it, as they did before on the other roads, they could stay relatively safe. They were still unsure what their reception would be and he thought it best to keep their presence unknown as much as possible. The last two towns they would pass through, Cuautitlan and Buenavista could be possible rest-stops where they could refresh and gain more insight about the fate of American refugees in Mexico. Saint San Diego reportedly lived in Cuautitlan in the 1400's and pioneered a Franciscan settlement there according to the points of interest reference page on Aaron's map. It was hard to see the map clearly as it was now badly worn and smeared with ashes and wrinkled from being frozen then thawed so many times. Aaron and Patches' bodies were as grimy as the map, dirty, unkempt, and denuded of strength from weeks of exposure to the vacillating temperatures.

Patches, who was a bundle of nerves now that he saw the end was approaching, acted as rear guard. Adlartok swept out front. Aaron was in the middle as the navigator, with the specter of Chapultepec Park being at last in sight.

While Aaron was banished from the scientific community because of his findings and his failure to suppress his version of the truth, the American government did finally stop the dispersion of nanorobots in the Chemical cloud shield program. Although they kept on spraying to conduct deflection of sunlight they used a reengineered formula that included less volatile compounds that posed a lower threat to the environment and water & food supply. Aaron was not aware of this, but his activism had served its purpose by playing a small role in the decision-making processes that guided these changes. However, it was too little too late, so many of the weather changes were irreversible and already in progress. The public never became fully aware of the problems; they were never able to tie the trails in the sky to the events happening to the earth's climate. Eventually the scientific community was disbanded in the United States and either took refuge underground or they went abroad to find a safer haven to live. This migration of intellects was akin to the diaspora of science talent that took place after WWII from Europe when the brightest European minds fled to the Northern Hemisphere.

It was a short walk from Cuautitlan to Buenavista. Buenavista was the larger town of the two and was more of a population hub, replete with commerce. They hoped to get refreshed here and find some fresh water to cool off and to rehydrate.

They detoured off the side road seeing the specter of the town rising in the distance. They could hardly conceal themselves anyway as the flat land of the town was part of a larger valley that extended for some miles. There was a large drainage ditch they crossed over that had brown scaly residue on the side of a culvert. They noticed some dead rats and fecal matter in the water. Aaron was hoping that this was not part of the potable water system.

Patches remarked: "This looks like either poor engineering or a back-wash system; I wonder where its source is." They could see a long dark tunnel underneath the structure. They were no longer adventurous and passed through the area quickly.

There were actual billboards in the town, something they had not seen in a long time. Advertisements for Ivory Soap, 24-hr. deodorants, and visits to the U.S. with cruises down the Mississippi River were featured. The Mississippi River cruise would never happen as it was entirely frozen except for the portion that emptied into the Gulf of Mexico. And much of the Gulf of Mexico was a vast graveyard of entwined human bodies that had come from Florida and floated into the sea.

In the center of the village there was an open market where fresh fruits and vegetables were clearly visible – avocados, mangos, corn, guanabana, mushrooms, and zucchini were all for sale. Aaron traded some of the provisions they would no longer need – fire starter, axe, and some spare woolen blankets for some of the fruit. When they ate the fruit, it was like a million different tastes exploding in their mouths—it was that good. Some people were staring at them with snooping eyes and they started to feel unsafe as a general feeling of malaise swept through them.

One small Mexican boy began shouting: "Americanos'," which signaled their need to retreat. Other people began looking at them, in turn leading to additional looks and glares, enough to hasten their exit further.

Aaron, aside from becoming perturbed, was starting to have second doubts. His trepidation was becoming more palpable. What was waiting for them at Chapultepec Park? He half-wanted to walk back and retrace his passage into the valley and mountains from whence they came. But that would never do. They had advanced this far and had met each obstacle head on and fought through. He was not a coward but he was not a fool. What really waited for them in Mexico City? He wished he had Sam now; the dog had the gift of prognostication.

They found another trail that wound around 57D. It did not shadow it like the other, but it remained close enough for them to follow. There was more dust in the air in this part of the country because there were more farming plows in operation and motor vehicles blowing grime over the rural roads. Patches had developed a chronic cough and he was now in total misery with the additional smog in the air. It would get worse when they got to Mexico City, it was streaming with cars and the air was unable to move out of the valley as it was cordoned by high mountains. The heat was oppressive during the day, the nights cool and breezy. Aaron also remembered that the famed Pyramids of the Sun and Moon were located about 30 miles northeast from the city; they would be coming from the northwest, so they would not see them. These were the 3rd largest pyramids on the planet and a possible source of interest to the aliens who dropped them off. Some people believed pyramids were ancient homing beacons used by EBES to navigate the stars. The aliens who were captured in Roswell, NM had said so.

Adlartok was starting to pick up the pace. Patches and Aaron could hardly keep up with her. It was as if she knew they were on the verge of finding peace or at least answers to the questions that had been nagging them.

# CHAPTER 3

# CHAPULTEPEC PARK

Nearing collapse and living in a nether borderland, Aaron mustered all his energy for the final push. Patches was in the back of Aaron and Adlartok but was falling steadily behind. His life, at this point, was never more a patchwork of pains and emotions like the whitewater of a coursing river. He was on all fours, scrambling to climb up from the swollen river of his life. He joined Aaron and Adlartok on an unwavering course to redemption, an opportunity to extricate themselves from the suffering of their plight.

Untamed deer and prancing indigo rabbits could be seen darting along many bridle paths. High in the sky, birds of prey circled around, keeping a sharp eye out for humans that might lose their way or who stumbled. In all niches of the animal world, there was appointed work for each creature that kept the larger tapestry alive and healthy. Travelers who fell ill or who starved on the road served a purpose too.

Ahead of them, Aaron noticed some muddy tracks that ran past a fast-moving stream. They were grouped together and looked like a stampede of buffalo, but this was not the range of buffalo, they preferred colder climes. Aaron did not recognize the imprints. Patches also could not decipher them. Adlartok looked closely and narrowed her eyes but did not disclose anything. Whatever it was, it seemed to be going in the general direction of Mexico City, although taking more of a circuitous route.

They started to slow down when they saw Patches was gasping for breath. His heart rate was high and he looked faint. He had been miserable ever since they lost Lauren and his fatigue was increasingly noticeable. He needed a rest. They found a spot near an interesting knoll; it looked like a large honeycomb of a deserted bee colony. Aaron knew of Africanized Mexican honey bees that were very aggressive but this hillock seemed tame. They laid down some blankets near the foot of the hill so Patches could rest comfortably. Adlartok left to look for some medicinal herbs while Aaron kept a close watch on his friend. His left arm was almost totally healed, but he had phantom limb syndrome where he would feel tingly, burning pain and sensations of hot and cold in the area where he was missing his hand. It was a strange phenomenon he was not able to explain. He had read about it, but experiencing it first-hand was another story.

While Adlartok was gone Patches got gradually worse. He started to moan in pain and talk gibberish calling out long forgotten names from Civil War history. His legs started to shake and a few minutes later he died, for no better reason than he had lived this far through this long trial. When Adlartok came back, she just shook her head and they buried him inside the small hill that now acted as a gravesite. Aaron was too numb to grieve long. They left a few minutes after they hollowed out Patches' eternal resting place.

It was the two of them now, like it was meant to be in the beginning. Both suited for and deserving each other. They were the strongest in their group and they would face their futures together.

Later that same day, they came upon Mexico City. They felt resting the night would be the wiser course of action and they would try to find and descend upon the park in the first morning light. They did not expect a welcome party, but they did expect to be treated civilly and regain some of their dignity, which they had all but lost on their odyssey.

The morning light was subdued by grey shafts of sunlight. It was colder than normal and the night animal sounds had given way to a sudden stillness. Adlartok woke up first and drew some water from a cask and boiled it to ready it for cooking. Aaron awoke slowly, barely remembering where he was, he would have remained firmly in the tent if Adlartok did not rouse him.

His hair was curled up into a flip as if half his body was electrified. He patted down his hair with the edge of his walking stick and went into the brush to relieve himself.

*"Rara Avis" he thought to himself.* He was still a free bird but one that was rare and refined. He had hurdled over the challenges set before him and was now moving towards his final goal with clarity. He thought of the others they lost and pallor came over him that almost made him retch. But seeing the strength and beauty of Adlartok gave him cause for hope and a new beginning. His body electric was prepared for epiphany.

Startled by the hordes of people they saw before them, Adlartok and Aaron stole behind some copper-colored buildings. There was a huge caravan of people coming towards them. They were dressed in bright colors and wore bold Baja jackets, sombreros, serapes and custom-made huaraches. It seemed like they were fleeing something, perhaps local magistrates or a political protest. Aaron had no conception of time.

They seemed hurried, as if they were bothered by something. But rather than risk being seen prematurely, Aaron and Adlartok stayed in the shadows, now having more questions than answers about what was their fate.

Based upon Aaron's map, they were following the boulevard Anillo Perif Adolfo Ruiz Cortines which would bring them into a central portion of the vast 2000 acres of Chapultepec Park. He calculated they were 3 – 4 miles away. Before long they could see massive wall towering ahead of them, something on the scale of the Wall of China. It was green in appearance, encased by old ivy with a horde of birds clinging to it. When they got closer they could see flower pots on the ledges with seating areas that looked casual and friendly. Large lounge chairs sprinkled the top of the wall, more like viewing areas than guard posts.

Around the perimeter of the wall there was not much activity. All of the noise they heard before ceased about 100 yards from the wall. The sky above the complex was imbued with wispy clouds that looked more artificial than naturally formed. Aaron thought he saw what looked like Chemtrails floating above the park. This sent a shudder through him.

They walked slowly towards the wall, convinced there would be freedom on the other side, too tired to resist the pull of sanctuary.

Aaron's arm throbbed with every step forward as his heart pulsated to the beat of his every step.

There before them, stood a large monument. Aaron tried to convince himself it was a mirage. A large "WW" situated in granite marked the side entrance of the park. Aaron kept looking at it, at first he thought it was an "R" for refuge as his sight was faltering through tears, but then it dawned on him that their long trip had meant nothing. It was a path to damnation and further imprisonment.

A few moments passed before they heard the roars, many loud and defiant, come bellowing from over the wall. They did not sound human. They certainly did not sound inviting. Whatever they were did not matter to Aaron as he walked slowly towards a large gate encased in the wall. It was not open but it looked like he could peer through one of the oval-sized panels to see into the belly of the park.

He saw a large lake towards the back of the property and some stone paths. There was no sign of humans. They had either all run away or were perhaps in hiding in another part of the park?

Then, about 50 feet away, he saw a large brown-grey grizzly bear feeding on something. It did not look like a fish from the lake. In fact he was holding a human arm in his jaws. Farther away, there were maybe 100 grizzly bears playing in the shallows of the lake, who now called Chapultepec Park their home. It looked like they were tossing parts of torsos, arms and legs around playing catch.

Unknown to Aaron, the day before the park had been overrun by a raiding party of grizzly bears from the panhandle of the U.S. They had been traveling for weeks pillaging the countryside. They had made a raid during the night on the inhabitants of the park, catching them totally by surprise. They had bulled over a gate on the other side of the park and forced entry.

The Americans that were imprisoned there and were not eaten were now in hiding all over Mexico City. The Whitewater guards were massacred and now resided in the bellies of the Grizzly bears in the lake. They were able to fire a few shots which did more to enrage the grizzlies than stop them. They had fled with many of the prisoners. Human parts were scattered throughout the compound.

Aaron swung his pack over his shoulder and waved to Adlartok. He turned his back away from the wall, feeling at once bewildered and in shock at what he saw.

As he reached Adlartok, he was surprised to see in the sky the Chemtrail he had previously seen was transformed into an image of Jingles fondly holding Sam. He grasped then that their trials and the expedition were less about reaching a destination and more about enduring relationships. He knew there were more adventures awaiting them, but for now, the love bond between them would be their Chapultepec Park. He held Adlartok firmly in his arms, realizing their personal journey was just beginning.

Tomorrow they would think about what to do next.

It would depend upon the weather.

Jingle Bells.

Made in United States
North Haven, CT
05 August 2022

22283334R00104